Someone
Just Like You

Other books by Sol Yurick

THE WARRIORS

FERTIG

THE BAG

Someone
Just Like You

SOL YURICK

Harper & Row, Publishers
New York   Evanston   San Francisco   London

The stories in this book first appeared in the magazines listed below:

The Noble Savage: "The Annealing"
Story: "The Child-God Dance"
Transatlantic Review: "The Siege," "The Passage," "The Bird-Whistle Man" under the title "Bird Whistle," "Tarantella," "Not With a Whimper, But . . ." "The Age of Gold," and "And Not in Utter Nakedness . . ."
Quarterly Review of Literature: "The Before and After of Hymie Farbotnik, or, The Sticking Point"
Award Avant Garde Reader: "Someone Just Like Me . . ."
Confrontation: "Do They Talk About Genêt in Larchmont?"
The Bennington Review: ". . . And a Friend to Sit by Your Side"

FIRST EDITION

STANDARD BOOK NUMBER: 06–014783–0

LIBRARY OF CONGRESS CATALOG CARD NUMBER: 75-156569

To Francine.
In times of success and arrogance
you laughed and reminded me of my mortality
but when I was depressed
you stood by me without reservation.
That's a real Comrade.

CONTENTS

THE ANNEALING
1

THE CHILD-GOD DANCE
26

THE SIEGE
46

THE BEFORE AND AFTER
OF HYMIE FARBOTNIK, OR,
THE STICKING POINT
67

THE PASSAGE
83

THE BIRD-WHISTLE MAN
95

TARANTELLA
103

SOMEONE JUST LIKE ME . . .
112

NOT WITH A WHIMPER, BUT . . .
133

DO THEY TALK ABOUT GENÊT IN LARCHMONT?
177

THE AGE OF GOLD
195

. . . AND A FRIEND TO SIT BY YOUR SIDE
209

"AND NOT IN UTTER NAKEDNESS . . .
230

Someone
Just Like You

THE ANNEALING

SHE lived from day to day and didn't much care which day it was. If she laughed once or twice, laughed big that day, she had it made. If she cried more than she laughed, she knew it wasn't her day. Sometimes it wasn't her day, not really, for weeks on end. Sometimes, with that liquor sloshing around in her, it was her day, her night, her everytime.

One day Minnie D. and Olivia Santiago had a fight. Minnie was big, plump, easygoing, and golden brown. Olivia was black with purple shades and hated niggers anyway, scorning them with a proud look on her black Castilian face. She pushed all the time. Minnie D. was easygoing, a soft-laughing girl with seven children out of five fathers, and a dead or deserted husband posed stylishly in a Woolworth's gaudy frame. She had a lover, Leroy, who never laughed, and beat her for her relief money twice a month. Olivia had six children. That morning she discovered she was pregnant again and would have to get the supplementary relief, and that entered her in that slut Minnie's class. She had a hard-working husband and she still couldn't make it and so she started the fight. She passed Minnie's free-and-easy kind of door with the two, three, malodorous garbage bags which Minnie planned to bring down if she ever got to leave sweet Leroy lying all manlike in the bed, not caring that it was all adding to the three or so generations of stench accreting in the hallway. Olivia yelled at Minnie through the door, telling her, "No-good nigger get that garbage out of the hall," and tiraded her about how that was what the niggers were doing to honest, good people. And her Nelson, he worked hard at the job and made the money, and people like that, like that Minnie, they loused it up for everyone. Minnie, screaming "You no-good spic bitch," came piling out of the door, wearing only a white half-slip, her plump, round good nature gone, her teeth bared, and her eyeballs all yellow with blood and hate. Olivia was thin, but she was full of the great hate too.

They fought all the way down from the third floor to the ground floor and boiled out into the street. They pulled hair, twisted breasts; they bit, scratched, screamed, drooled; they kicked; they gouged. The neighbors came to the doors and stood, laughing and shouting encouragement, picking sides. The kids screamed with delight. One of Minnie's sons came tearing up the street, leaving the little card game he was playing in, to kick Olivia's oldest daughter in the slats. Ramon, Olivia's oldest boy, had to be held back from putting a flick-knife into this cool card-player, Alonso.

They fought their way out to the middle of the street where, half naked, they tried to push one another into a greasy pool of oily water, pulling, snarling, while everyone stood around and said things like, "I put five to four on that fine fat girl. Man, look at her." Minnie, not laughing at all now, her great

2

breasts shining with sweat, her slip almost gone, a few festive shreds holding on to the elastic cutting into her soft brown middle, kept swatting mightily. Olivia dodged, ducked, and kept trying to close in so she could sink her bright white teeth into Minnie's throat, or better, her breast. A joker, wearing a motorcycle fly-boy cap with a white visor, stood behind the crowd and stopped traffic like a policeman, or a general. All the windows were opened and everybody was having a ball, looking out. Leroy, the lover, hung out, yelling, "Give her one, Minnie, give her one good, you hear?" laughing to beat everything, and that was the first time he had laughed in three weeks, not since he had scored in a poker game, scored in a craps game, scored with a little light-skin girl way up in Harlem, scored. Hinton, Minnie's middle boy, whereabouts of the father unknown, not since he was conceived, stood in the kitchen and contemplated knifing Leroy. He didn't have the nerve. He was nine years old.

Some do-gooder called the fuzzy bulls, and they came tearing around the corner, sounding the siren loud so everyone would know they were coming and could compose their little stories about they didn't know who, or what, or when. In that sunken Sump of Brooklyn by the Canal, everyone minds their business, Officer. The crowd scattered to the stoops and stood there like good little stupids, only seeing, peaceful, grinning because it was such a good fight. But Olivia and Minnie were in earnest and didn't hear a thing. Minnie, looking like a fat, good-natured hula dancer, swatted Olivia finally, catching her low and bringing on the miscarriage Olivia wanted so badly. If she hadn't felt so bad later, and her pride hadn't been hurt, she wouldn't have done a thing. The policemen stepped out of the car with that slow dignity they had, squaring their chests, hunching their shoulders, fingering their guns, swaggering as if to say, it will be your arse if anyone starts anything at all. The crowd fell silent, watching. Hard boys, cool boys, from the territory for miles around, had materialized on the rooftops and stood around, looking down into the streets innocently. The cops, they missed nothing at all.

"Who started it?" the cops asked. Minnie, panting and triumphant, shrugged her shoulders and said they were having a discussion that had gotten out of hand. Seeing that she had won and Olivia was smeared, her clothes torn, her face bleeding, filthy with oil and water, Minnie was inclined to laugh about the whole thing. Olivia hated Minnie more, but there were codes you never violated. Not there in the Sump. "Come on, come on," one of the cops said impatiently. The street became very still and the cops knew what that meant. They were hated for breaking up a very prime battle. It was like taking away red meat, chitterlings, a little cheap whiskey, or the TV when everything else was gone. Minnie shrugged and smiled an innocent smile, folding her arms, and tried, with some degree of dignity, to cover her vast breasts, which were exciting the men and boys in the crowd, not to speak of the cops. No one said anything, not even Olivia, and the cops told Minnie D. they could run her in for indecent exposure, for disturbing the peace, for any number of things. Minnie whined she wasn't doing nothing, Officer, and someone shouted, "Aw, let them alone," and Olivia stated it was just a friendly, if somewhat athletic, discussion between two friends. The cops, not caring if the bastards killed one another, muttered threats, told them all to go home, clear the streets before I run you in, but knew that in the middle of such a mob, running anyone in might be more trouble than it was worth, considering no one was hurt. Minnie, clapped on the back by a few of her kind of women, who knotted around her to hide her gleaming nakedness, left the field of honor, beginning to forget because it was past. Olivia, comforted by a few of her friends, was bleeding from scratches, from the nose, from her vagina. Her miscarriage had started.

Leroy, feeling full of fun, having enjoyed himself thoroughly at the fight, gave Hinton the last of Minnie D.'s relief money, and told him to go and bring a bottle of something good to drink, and not to forget, or run off, or do anything wrong, you hear, boy? And before Hinton had even gone out the door, he took Minnie and laid her on the bed to reward her bitter, bitter life with a little something sweet for victory's sake. Hinton lingered at the door, watching, till the unbearable groans and moans and screams started, and wished he had had the courage to stab Leroy when he had the chance.

Olivia, being bathed by her neighbors, chattered bitterly. When everyone had left, she sat down and wrote a revealing letter to the relief people. She named names and stated facts, and even, in the heat of her burning, scorched pride, she overstated things. She wrote that Minnie beat her children and this was untrue. In fact, Minnie frequently interposed herself between Leroy's fists and the kids because she loved them. That kind of pain she could take, and did.

Mr. Jones, the relief investigator, came, responding to the complaint. Since it was not his normal time to visit, he came when Leroy was at home, lying half naked on the bed. Minnie D. told Mr. Jones that Leroy was a distant cousin and a good friend who sometimes stayed over. And when he stayed, he gave money for his food and brought little presents for the kids. Mr. Jones shook his head. Minnie was an old-time sore point with him. The kids stood around as they always did, not looking directly at the investigator, but somehow managing to radiate hostility. It never even occurred to Hinton, wearing a torn shirt, and stinking, to see irony in what Minnie said about the presents Leroy brought for the kids. As for the oldest, Alonso, he was too concerned about a rep with the boys, the clothes he bought out of stolen money, and his straightened, exquisitely marceled hair. Alonso and Leroy had a healthy contempt for one another. But no one was betraying, saying anything more to the investigator other than that they needed money. The money grant wasn't enough. The complaint was a tissue of lies. Mr. Jones sighed. He had worked hard with Minnie, through "cousins" like Leroy. He had tried everything, all the proper social-work techniques and a few improper ones. Mr. Jones had threatened. He had pleaded. He had appealed to Minnie D. as one Negro to another. He resented that she lived a life apart, wild, bounded by *now*, sloppy, meaningless. He pointed to himself. His wife teaching. His two affordable and neat children. His little house in Queens. His sense of tomorrow. All that, all of it, could be Minnie's too. She just told him her troubles.

Over the years, it had been a case of not knowing or caring that there was tomorrow. Mr. Jones knew the tomorrows and the promise in store for the world of man when all the inequities would be righted. It was a matter of managing, cleaning, meeting deadlines, marrying, saving, keeping appointments, and bringing up the children with a sense of the future. He couldn't understand Minnie D.'s recurring fall from grace. She drank. She had lovers and had children. She spent her money on the wrong things. Bright, impermanent things interested

6

her. If Leroy didn't get the relief money first, it was fried chicken for a few days and little food thereafter, unless she didn't pay the rent or the utilities. Once, they cut off the lights, but she cheerfully tapped the meters. They had fought it down the years, irresponsibility and procedure, Mr. Jones and Minnie D. But this time, Mr. Jones knew they had come to the end of it. It had been arrests, Children's Court, Domestic Relations Court, Child Placement, foster homes, private agencies, the truant officer, the Bureau of Child Guidance, the Mayor's Committee on Multi-Problem Cases, the Society for the Prevention of Cruelty to Children, the Department of Health, the Department of Buildings, the Office of Rent Control, Visiting Nurses, Homemakers, memos, endless memos. But misspending Minnie D. was always getting a little drunk here and there, getting hurt, going to clinics, to this doctor, that chiropractor, and the other faith-healer, or spending it on one bright blue silk dress she wore on Saturdays for the big nights when she left the children in charge of Alonso, who tied them up, and went uptown with Leroy. Well, she needed to laugh, didn't she? Mr. Jones, he wouldn't understand.

Minnie wondered who had done this to her. Somehow she couldn't connect Olivia Santiago with something like that. It was a simple fight and everyone forgot, now that it was over. Mr. Jones was hurt, annoyed at the presence of Leroy, who looked sullen. His look seemed to say, don't ask me no questions, boy. Mr. Jones, perspiring in his Ivy League suit, his striped rep tie a little askew, asked as few questions as possible and made notes in his little book.

When he returned to the office, Mr. Jones worried about finding a way out. "Close the case," the supervisor glibly said. He couldn't bring himself to do that. She would be back, getting relief, in no time flat. He had an idea. He would frighten her with the insane asylum. A new discussion with his supervisor seemed to indicate, as they say, a psychiatric interview. Yes, perhaps, Mr. Jones thought, it would scare her. Very little else did. In order to get approval for a psychiatric interview, Mr. Jones had to state the reason a little strongly. But after all, he reasoned, wasn't chronic irresponsibility a form of psychosis?

He wrote a letter to Minnie D., telling her to be home on a certain day, or he would surely close her case and cease relief. And to make it certain, he scheduled the interview for check day. Minnie D. didn't mind and told Leroy he would have to be out of the house then. Leroy, who had come back after three days gone, was willing to be gone for three days more. He had the need of a fix and wanted money since there were no relief funds left. Of course, Minnie D. wasn't going to tell that snotty Mr. Jones she had spent the money on Leroy, gambled just a little, gotten drunk and laughed a lot, bought Hinton a red tie, and herself a foundation and baby-blue suede pumps, and it would be another month at least till the electric company bothered her.

The psychiatrist was a woman named Ostreicher. She was a German refugee of the thirties who had kept on cultivating her accent, but to no avail. She had never been able to get an expensive clientele. She was unable to write any books. Every time she came up with a new theory that would perhaps revolutionize psychoanalysis, Karen Horney, Erich Fromm, or Wilhelm Reich wrote a book about it first. She was bitter. She had to work for the city in order to make a good living.

She was perfectly on time at nine in the morning, and stood in the quiet sunlit street, littered from one end to the other, watching all the little children playing. She stood, waiting for Mr. Jones, a stolid, squat monolith in expensive tweeds. Her sturdy legs were stuck like the feet of conquerors into sensible English walking-shoes. Mr. Jones was ten minutes late and she was filled with hatred and loathing for the imperfect and incorrect Relief Department. When Mr. Jones appeared, she looked at him with contempt, feeling that somehow he didn't belong in those Ivy League clothes. One button of his button-down collar was undone. It seemed to her that Mr. Jones belonged with the clients. Because he was late, her day had already started badly.

Mr. Jones excused himself politely for being late. Dr. O. could not really accept it at all. She adjusted healthily to these things, of course, but she knew, being of the old Freudian school, that there were always the unconscious impulses. She asked Mr. Jones to fill her in on Minnie D. It seemed to her that Mr. Jones's memo was just a little too sparse. Neglect, irresponsibility, repetition of patterns—they were common things that were, true, neurotic, but not in and of themselves psychotic, you understand. Mr. Jones understood that. Of course, she, Dr. O., was glad to examine the woman. But then, wasn't it a waste of taxpayers' money if there were no basis of commitment? Mr. Jones hemmed a little, and hawed, and became committed under the stern, disapproving stare of the doctor. He had another thing to blame Minnie for. He tried to meet the doctor halfway. He had had courses in psychology. He talked in very learned terms about the refusal to ventilate problems, hostility patterns, destructive patterns, recurrence of the death wish in the shape of the dead, the deserted husband, the five putative fathers, the Leroy-figure, long, black, lean and saturnine, who was capable, in equal parts on equal days, of largess or destruction. He beat the children. All the casuals who tramped in and out of Minnie's life beat the children. They were a noisome, smelly lot. And then, didn't it follow, because Minnie placed herself in those situations where she was permissive of the beatings, the neglect, the hunger, that she accepted, condoned, approved in effect? So he told Dr. O. that she did beat the children. Dr. O. nodded her head approvingly, noted everything Mr. Jones had to say. When he had finished, Mr. Jones was sweating a little.

He led the doctor up the stairs, past all the paint-cracked doors, past and up the stairs through wells tilted crazily, ready to collapse everything to the bottom, past the numberless doors where the mad mambo music poured out, the sullen-sad jazz singers sung their blues of living, and through the great banal beat of the morning soap operas coming in on the TV. They passed the little stenchy cubicles shared by two families to a floor, and the graffiti gratuitously graven onto the walls, obscening the world and telling it, them, those, the fuzz, and everyone to go and . . . Outside Minnie's door, the light bulb had burned out, and the hallway was a pool of black limned with little lights where the cracks under the doors showed. Mr. Jones lit a match for Dr. O. to find her stolid way, stepping over the shards of lives, the dust, the dirt, the grainy grease, and avoiding the garbage bags Minnie hadn't gotten around to bringing down. In the sputter of the going-out match, they saw, emblazoned in unseen red, Minnie D.'s lipstick, Hinton's little rebellion. "Fuck Leroy," it said, and if ever the landlord got around to putting a bulb in the hallways, Hinton or some other one of Minnie D.'s kids was going to be whopped. They could hear the big booming sound of a radio coming out of Minnie D.'s door and her contralto singing a swinging song, full of life, full of today's happiness. It was Friday, the check was coming, and she had a little something out of the left-over bottle Leroy thought he had hidden. They were going to go out that night and none of the children was sick for once. Only the minor little cloud of Mr. Jones, looming no larger than a punitive fist on the horizon, was coming that morning. Today she had a little future and that was tonight. She didn't much care what followed tonight, only that she drank, she danced, she got loved by Leroy, and slept very soundly indeed.

She was wearing only a pure-white slip when she answered the door, and her skin glowed dark and rich brown. Plump against it they could see the counterpoint of brown skin, the breast and belly lines, the emphasis of the large, lazy, child-caring nipples, and the black pubic triangle. She had been seen by Mr. Jones, to his great discomfort, like this before. Minnie D. let them in. Dr. O. followed steadily, smelling every-thing out. When they saw the doctor's face, they all stiffened because the inaudible alarm note went out. The children stood around, clean as Minnie felt she ought to get them, sullen and resentful, not looking at the newcomers, staring everywhere else, or at one another, or reading torn comic books. Only Hinton looked at them, wishing he had stabbed Leroy, won-dering if he could take a knife and stab everyone in sight, especially now his mother-slut, Minnie D., dressed in her pure-white slip and naked underneath. Alonso, the oldest, the cool poker player, sat, impeccably wearing his gang uniform: white shoes, white pants, a blue Ivy League Paisley-print shirt, a stocking on his head to keep his marcel in perfect wavy form. Sitting aloofly, Alonso, on a three-legged kitchen chair with a bongo between his legs, kept up a constant little subliminal mutter like distant, dangerous drums. The youngest cater-wauled in his crib and the radio boomed the bouncy, swinging accompaniment to what Minnie had been singing when they knocked.

Mr. Jones did the honors, telling Minnie D. that Dr. Ostreicher was really Miss Ostreicher, a social worker wishing to ask a few questions for a survey. Minnie D. regretted that she had only bothered to clean the kitchen, where Mr. Jones usually did the interviewing. Dr. O., standing there, looked them all over and knew immediately that it was a family beyond hope, beyond redemption. She looked at the soft brown skin of Minnie glowing delectably around and under the pure-white slip. "Put on your clothes," she snapped. Minnie D., trying to be pleasant because she was still on tonight's dust of having a ball, smiled at the hard, square-faced lady and said, "Won't you sit down?" Mr. Jones skittered a little over the floor, trying to adjust the kitchen chairs for everyone, and caught the hard, look-at-you-there-man contempt look of Alonso, who muttered the drums derisively. A roach scuttled across the floor, banana-peel bound. Miss O. said that she was Dr. O., not a social worker at all, and that she had come to examine Minnie D., and to put on some clothes. She cracked it out in her hard, let's-get-things-clear voice so that everyone shut up, even Alonso. He stopped the drum mutter against this hard, hard authority and tried to look cool and insolent, and make me, man; but she had. Minnie, not understanding what it was all about, smiled painfully, starting to come down out of her dream, and went into the other room to find something she could put on over the pure-white silk slip. "What I need a doctor for, Mr. Jones?" she called in her whiny voice from the other room. "Nothing wrong with me at all. I have my health, praise the Lord." Mr. Jones looked at Dr. O. as if to say, was that necessary? But, taking in the implacable, methodical face, the hard, square shoulders bunched up in the rough and ready cloth, the thick thighs curving through the rough skirt, the gray stockings—he knew it was necessary. He was a little ashamed to have been bested in front of the children, especially Hinton, whose disturbed confidence he had succeeded in winning with bright bribes of candy.

Dr. O. took out a notebook and put it on the table. She tapped a little silver pencil and waited, uncaring in the ring of hostile dark faces. She appeared to listen to the sounds of morning coming in through the alleyway windows. She watched a hard bar of untrammeled sunlight blasting onto the floor, shining on the caked cracks between the boards. She picked up a little silver vase on the table, containing dusty, artificial flowers, looked casually underneath, and saw Hotel Something-or-Other written on it. She put it down and gave a look of triumph to Mr. Jones, which was understood by everybody but Mr. Jones. "Get these children out of here," she told Minnie D. when she came in, compromising with propriety by wearing a tan, stained skirt, leaving her breasts unbound, and bouncing softly, rustling in white silk under Dr. O.'s avid, hating stare. Minnie D., trying to hold on to the remnants of a smile, shooed them all out, even Hinton, who never went outside at all. Alonso took off his stocking with careful insolence and slouched out, every line of his body, his neat clothes, saying, do me something, man, do me something. "Whew," Minnie D. said when they had all trooped outside, "raising a family is sure hard work," and smiled a propitiatory smile.

"No one told you to have so many children," Dr. O. said. "Could you turn off the radio and get the infant quiet?"

Minnie D. could feel something unreasonable forming inside her. Her cunning mind was good enough to tell her that there was something more to this whole bit. Mr. Jones had always been friendly, making his fusses about keeping clean and getting rid of Leroy. But the hard-faced lady with the icy eyes that kept looking at her in some certain way—she meant a little more. And when Minnie felt that way, she began to close herself up, get the look on her face that said nothing at all, answered sassy because they wanted something from her she didn't understand. She tried to get Leroy out of her mind.

"Put something on," Dr. O. told her. "You are indecent."

Minnie D. shuffled to turn off the radio, to find a blouse, to come back slowly to the metronomic ticking Dr. O. made with her little silver pencil to mark Minnie's movements.

"What you have a doctor here for?" she asked Mr. Jones.

"It's Central Office's idea," Mr. Jones told her, somehow caught and unable to say too much, ashamed because no one was acting very nice and he didn't know what to do about it. Two buttons of her blouse remained open, for spite.

"What day is it?" Dr. O. asked Minnie D., snapping out her question as if to say, why are you so evil, why are you so resistant? Minnie D. just looked at her as if to ask, what is your bit, why come on so salty? She didn't know. They bugged her more. She didn't bother to answer this silly, silly question at all. It was check day. Who need know any more? She looked coolly at the doctor. The doctor nodded. The interview was going along satisfactorily. "You don't know what day it is?" she asked Minnie D., looking at the deep cleft where the spiteful buttons didn't button, and at the way her haunches strained against the tan skirt.

"I know what day it is," Minnie D. told the doctor.

"You do?" the doctor said with benign hatefulness, nodding with the proper degree of meaningful gesture, and wrote this

14

in the book too. Mr. Jones, writhing inside to see it happen this way, poured his calm oil on the water. "Mrs. D., tell the lady what she asks for. She is on your side."

Minnie D., seeing the hard eyes take her apart and leave her nothing at all, knew this witch was never on anyone's side. "April eighteenth," she said, packing contempt into those little words. The doctor was a little ahead of her and finessed Minnie D. by interpreting attitude. Then they relaxed for a little silence while the doctor looked around the room with hate, with loathing, with don't touch me. Those sensible shoes under the heavy feet moved swiftly and crushed a roach making advances. "Where did you get this?" she asked with a policeman's triumph, holding up the little silver vase and spilling one red cardboard rose onto the greasy checked linoleum. Minnie looked sullen and shrugged it off.

"Why are you asking me these questions?" she asked.

"Where did you get this?" the doctor asked and made minute notes on minute reactions. Minnie D. feared what the doctor wrote in her little notebook. She could almost feel the happiness slip away completely, almost irretrievably, and feel the blackness come down on her, down like depression, down like candy and sweets and liquor taken away. She thought she could hear the rattle of the letter boxes being opened up and everyone crowing with satisfaction. They had made it for another two weeks without discovery, pulling out the window envelopes, hearing the satisfying rustle of cellophane ripping, holding their checks. It came drifting up the stairs. It was a feeling like dancing in the streets. All that laughing. And the shopkeepers rubbed hands because it was payday, and eager liquor-store people looked out, welcoming from behind their just-ordered cartons of whiskey. And she felt a little sad, left out. She had to go down and get her check too. But she didn't hear what the doctor said, only coming back to the little scene to see the doctor writing it all down, whatever was asked and not answered. Client, having obviously stolen the vase, avoids all mention of it. Blocks out, blanks out, mild catatonic state, stares into space, has difficulty focusing attention. "What did you say?" she asked. Mr. Jones, the spirit of help, wondering how they had gotten this psychiatrist, started to ask the question again. Dr. O. stopped him with a gesture. "How much is five and six?" she asked Minnie D., sounding like talking-down-to, and treating Minnie D. like a child. Minnie D. was stung a little this time. "I'm no child," she said.

"And that depends on how you answer the questions," Dr. O. said with galling sweetness. They sat for a while, quiet. Minnie D. struggled with it. It was all different from dealing with Mr. Jones. When Mr. Jones tried to come on hard and asked his penetrating questions, she whined a little and cunningly, shrewdly avoided all pitfalls because she had been playing this game for so long a time. But she could sense that she had gotten off on the wrong foot with this hard lady and this lady was going to put her down hard or break a gut trying. She wondered what she had done to antagonize this lady. Here was a menace. The worst kind. She could see it. She could hear it. She could smell it. She knew it. She should play the good client and answer the questions, whine where she should whine about how hard times were and how hard it was to manage and how hard it was to bring up children, and know nothing else about anything. She knew what the doctor was doing with her, but she couldn't help herself. She was beginning to play it as the doctor wanted, play it to lose her head, play it with a little dignity, and the dignity of it was going to cost her the check and the night with Leroy. "I'm no child," she told the doctor again.

Dr. O., with infinite and cunning patience, asked how much nine and five were, what day it was, did she hear strange voices? Was it winter, was it summer, what season of the year was it anyway, and how did she care for her children? Minnie D. drove herself out of her dream of tonight, her sleepwalk of now, and weighing all the factors, answered the doctor. But she couldn't fight the black tide of anger that welled up inside her the way it had with Olivia Santiago. She answered the questions sullenly, so sullenly, and the doctor wrote not only what she said, but how she said it. Mr. Jones began to feel it building up like angry crowds gathered in the dusty streets staring down the cops, or like the boys, leaning in their white, white pants on the corner and waiting for the action. Who knew? The action might be you any time. He knew. He saw what Dr. O. apparently didn't see. But that Dr. O., it didn't matter to her one way or another. She had looked upon the soft brown Minnie-flesh and she was disturbed. She had seen the sullen faces of Minnie D.'s children, the rotting building, the shouting and singing in the halls, the littered streets, the pervading smell of the nearby canal choked with garbage and dead flesh, the little silver vase with the artificial flowers marked Hotel Something-or-Other, and the helpless face of Mr. Jones, quick to jump to conclusions of neurosis and psychosis. She wasn't going to be stopped. Not Dr. O.

Minnie D. sat there, not looking at Dr. O., not even facing her, but looking away, yet sort of toward, out of her shrewd peripheral vision, seeing it all and knowing it all. But that basic wisdom of hers was robbed by so many hungers and by the dream of tonight and Leroy. The timelessness of life, the

17

ball tonight with this half-month's stipend, the thought of that check sitting there in the mailbox itched her as if she were tickled, or fingered. And what if that sweet rat, Leroy, sneaked back, took the check as he had before, forged it, and went out and had himself a ball, leaving Minnie with her squalling brood? Surely one of the neighbors would come in and give her a drink out of pity and good spirits, but what was that compared to a ball anyway? She sat there in her tweed, Dr. O. did, and was unrelenting and harsh and every time she spoke, she got Minnie D.'s back up so she could feel hair pricklings at the base of her spine, and all the way up to the nape of her neck.

She kept muttering, "Talking to me that way, like I was my bitty child, Hinton. I ain't no child," while Dr. O. kept obligingly putting it down, and she said challengingly to the doctor, "Put that down in your little book. I ain't no child."

"Now, Mrs. D.," Mr. Jones said. But she kept up with her dangerous mutter.

"Is that the way the children are always dressed?" Dr. O. asked.

"What's the matter with the way my children are dressed?" Minnie asked, stung again. "What do you expect me to do with the little money the relief gives me?"

"Now, Mrs. D.," Mr. Jones said, "you know that this is all I'm entitled to give you." She kept up the muttering. "And anyway, you have misspent the money so many times," he reminded her. "And what about Leroy?"

"Where did you steal this?" Dr. O. asked.

Minnie D. rose, angered almost beyond endurance, and screamed, "I didn't steal this." Leroy had given her this little present, together with the little clutch of paper flowers so cunningly and artfully painted like the real thing. Well, she thought, maybe Leroy had not gotten it the right way. But her man was a little like a child, meaning no harm, like her sulky Hinton, perhaps, or like her Alonso. And if the truth were known, there were more roaming the street who were worse, much worse. She didn't say this. She said, "If you keep on talking that way, I'll throw you out." But she saw that if she went after Dr. O., she would get her hide whipped. Dr. O. was no Olivia Santiago, but she had shoulders like a man, legs like a man, and big hands that could handle her easily. She was a little afraid.

Minnie D. started for the door. "Where are you going, Mrs. D.?" Mr. Jones asked.

"I'm going to get my check," she said because she couldn't control herself, thinking about it down there in the rusted mailbox, tortured for it. "Sit down, Mrs. D.," Mr. Jones said. She started to explain the possibility of the check being stolen.

"Sit down," Dr. O. told her. "I am not finished with you." She opened her little black doctor's bag and took out a stethoscope. "Strip to the waist," she told Minnie D. Mr. Jones stood up to go into the next room. "You don't have to go," Dr. O. told Mr. Jones.

"I'm not taking off my clothes while there's a man here," said Minnie D. to the doctor.

"Do as I tell you."

"Look, I'll go into the other room," Mr. Jones said. The doctor shrugged her shoulders as if to say, what did it matter, and smiled her contempt for Mr. Jones, who kept hopping from one leg to the other. He went into the doorless other room and stood by the window, looking out, studying the depressing back alleys, seeing white rags fluttering on the clotheslines, pigeon flocks, kids climbing up and down the fences, a scene of domestic tragedy taking place in another window. A man was beating his wife silently and she got beaten without screaming.

With insolent grace, Minnie D. took off her blouse, slipped the shoulder straps off, and stood, half naked, in front of Dr. O. She was a splendid savage, warm and defiant brown, big-breasted, full-breasted, her face frozen with black, sullen dignity. Dr. O. jabbed the silver weapon of her icy stethoscope between her breasts, making Minnie's skin goosepimple. Minnie jumped a little and lost that splendid, defiant look. Wielding the forever icy tip of the stethoscope, unconcerned, Dr. O. pushed, jabbed, probed, listened, and felt Minnie here and there, her hateful white hands prying over Minnie's body till she was ready to scream. Does this bother you and does that bother you and if Minnie answered with her voice full of obvious hate, the silver tip flickered out to touch her and make her shiver in punishment. Then Minnie sat while the doctor whaled her with a rubber mallet to test her reflexes, hurting her a little, the way she used it. "Do you drink? Take drugs? Given to sleeping too much? Have sleepless nights? Special troubles when you menstruate? How often do you masturbate? Dream? Don't dream? And how many times a week do you have sex with men? With women?" the doctor asked, seeming not to care about the answers while she listened, tapping, toying with the silver vase, making Minnie jumpy, so that sometimes she answered without thinking and had to retract what she said. The doctor took it all down, sitting there, pin-neat and mechanical, clean and well dressed, untouched by the stink of cooking greens and baby piss and deodorant. Minnie, who had never worried about it too much, sat there, half nude, finding that her uncontrollable hands and arms tended to cover herself up in the face of that long long stare the doctor stared at her. "Come back, Mr. Jones," the doctor called. Minnie struggled to raise her slip, put on her blouse, was fumbling around, clumsy, entangled in straps, cloth, and her own flesh. Mr. Jones saw and turned away as if he had overlooked something new in the fascinating true-life scene being played out across the alleyway. Seeing how Minnie struggled with the blouse, Dr. O. wrote down that she had poor motor responses.

And before Minnie finished buttoning up, the doctor asked again where she was, what city, what borough, what district, what planet, lashing her with questions, and did she beat her children? She played with the silver vase and let another flower fall to the floor, and Minnie kept getting more nervous. She tried a digression. "Why are you picking on me?" she asked the doctor. "Why are you white folks against me?"

"But I'm not white," Mr. Jones said.

The doctor didn't bother to answer, it being obvious to everyone, even to Mr. Jones, abstracted in his backyard, that being picked on was a delusion of Minnie's. She put it down. Paranoid delusion. Thinks she is not being helped by the relief people and is being picked on by the doctor who is, if anything, benign beyond belief. Ascribes it to racial prejudice. Accuses dark Mr. Jones of this too. Mr. Jones, feeling that everything was all right now, came back into the room and stood behind Minnie, leaning against the soiled stove.

And the doctor started it again, asking questions sweetly this time, asking them with a let's-humor-her kind of patience that no one missed, not Minnie, not Mr. Jones. Minnie, she couldn't play it anyway because she knew that final flood of anger was going to come up, up, up in her and she was going to have to try and hit, kill that woman.

"It has come to our attention that you beat the children,"

Dr. O. said. Minnie said it was untrue. Minnie said she might hit them to keep them in line. Every mother did that. She never beat them. The doctor looked at her for a second, and almost abstracted, hefted the silver vase a little bit with a questioning look on her face. Minnie, unable to take it anymore, knocked it out of her hand. It fell, silver, to the floor, scattering the paper flowers and a little water one of the children had put into it to make them grow. "Don't go bugging me," she screamed. "What you trying to do to me?"

"Nothing at all. Nothing at all," the doctor said softly, looking like hit me, try and hit me. They sat there, silent, Mr. Jones horrified, not knowing what to do. "Did you think," the doctor asked, "that those flowers would grow in that water?" Minnie couldn't even laugh at such a stupid question anymore because the doctor had wound her up too much. "If you don't get her out of here, something bad is going to happen," she told Mr. Jones. "Why don't you answer me?" the doctor asked, softening the harshness of her low, hoarse voice. Minnie got up, went to the kitchen drawer, and pulled out one long bread knife and appealed to Mr. Jones: "Get her out of here." The doctor sighed slowly, stood up, put everything into the little black medical bag, snapped it neatly to, buttoned the top button of her jacket, and said, "Let us go, Mr. Jones," and walked out.

Mr. Jones smiled weakly at Minnie D. and followed Dr. O. out into the hallway. He followed her down the stairs and to the front door. She turned and blocked him from the street, holding him there in the rancid hallway. "You were right, Mr. Jones." He couldn't seem to understand her. "She is obviously paranoid. We will have to commit her," Dr. O. told Mr. Jones.

"But . . ."

"I will write out the commitment papers for you. You will go back. I will send for an ambulance. And, oh, yes, the police."

"But . . ."

She took out a pad of commitment forms and began to write: "Potentially dangerous . . ." Mr. Jones saw. "You drove her to it," he told Dr. O. Dr. O. looked at him. Under her pale eyes, he could only perspire and hate Minnie for what she had made him do. Dr. O. reached out suddenly and her thick hand quickly buttoned his undone collar. He felt the tip of her pencil touch his chin. Dr. O. kept looking at him and continuing to write a breviary of disturbances. Feeble hatred shook him. Dr. O. was beyond hatred. She tore, with a neat, ripping sound, three copies. One for him. One for the ambulance attendant. One she kept for herself. "Go up and wait for them to come." He turned and went back up the stairs. The wood creaked, ripping slowly loose from the walls.

They sent two policemen as a precaution till the ambulance came. The policemen stood around and looked at the patient suspiciously, fingering their nightsticks. They were ready to move fast because you never know how strong these looneys get when they blow their corks. Minnie D., bewildered, sat between them, not knowing what was wrong. The policemen noticed the fallen vase, the spilled water, an overturned chair, the implied violence, and watched her, making pleasant conversation with Mr. Jones. Minnie D. kept muttering over and over again, "What did I do?" When the boys in white came, dragging, as a matter of course, a straitjacket, she blew her top completely and jumped Mr. Jones, who was trying to tell her that everything would be all right if she kept calm. His tie was torn loose, his Ivy League suit was ripped, and she made a deep, bloody scratch up the side of his face. Like two accomplished pikemen lazily practicing their art, the police, dispassionately, almost sorrowfully, hit Minnie D. right and left, knocking her one way, catching her with the other nightstick to bounce her back, so that she bled bloody sideburns down both sides of her face. As she dropped, the attendants dressed her like a bad little child in a long, confining straitjacket. They mealsacked her down the stairs, her head drooping and bouncing on each tread, blood coming down on the steps. She screamed again and again and again. Leroy, who saw it all, wisely waited until they were gone and went to collect the relief check to ball it up that night. He accepted. Mr. Jones went around to collect the children to place them in institutions and foster homes.

Minnie D., she lived it from day to day and almost cared what day it was because they were going to observe her for ten days and if she was good, they would have to say she is sane and let her go. But she looked around at the looneys, whom she was not like, remembered Dr. O. and Mr. Jones, and the way the policemen clobbered her right and left, and wondered about the children and Leroy, who had certainly taken all the money and spent it on drinks and some slut up in Harlem. Had a ball on her money while her children were there, everywhere, and she was here without reason, falsely accused. So she kept blowing her top whenever they talked to her. She couldn't feel it ahead for ten days to play it cool, because there is only *now*.

And in ten days, it was still now, and they put her away in the state bin for another six months, away from all the goodies, except for a little smuggled-in liquor she worked off in one way or another. And in time, how bad can it be? The anger died slowly and she whined to the doctor that she was all right again, she will be good, she had done wrong, which is most of

24

all what they wanted to hear. They let her out in six months; they gave her back her children; they found her an apartment in another part of the Sump district. Leroy heard she was out, found her, and they set up housekeeping again. He beat her at checktime and gave her the kind of loving she needed, and in nine months, she had another Hinton-baby.

THE CHILD-GOD
DANCE

THEY would end it here, Bascom thought. Coolly clad in a loose, blue and green tropical shirt, he sat on the lip of a shallow arena. He watched the outlines of a lacy fringe of luxuriant ferns, reaching high into the air around the bowl, fade with the sunlight. Beyond, there were cycads and ginkgoes; farther down the hill, grass-palms grew. He could feel the hot dampness rising, bringing out the first sweet smell of moist leaves. MacTavish, wearing white, sat next to Bascom and looked anxiously at him.

MacTavish had told Bascom that afternoon, "You must see our dances. It will be a little change in the midst of all this business. Our people would insist on it."

Bascom hadn't been enthusiastic; he had seen "native entertainment" all over the Caribbean.

"But this is one thing you haven't seen anywhere else, I'm sure," MacTavish said. "It's really different, really authentic."

Weren't they always "really different; *really* authentic"? Bascom wondered. However, it had been a duty he owed to

American Estates development; the rites might be used to entertain tourists, if they were any good; if they weren't, they might be made better. So Bascom had let himself be blindfolded and led up here, before sunset, to a secret grove high on the island's mountainous spine; it was when they took the blindfold off that the mutter of tom-toms encompassed him.

"They invoke at night," MacTavish whispered. "Then the God comes."

Of course, Bascom thought. Wasn't it always at night? Would the rites stand the light of day? He waited patiently.

The drums stopped. Two natives came out into the clearing. They set up skulls on poles and walked to the center of the arena. One, a mulatto, wore a blue and green shirt. The other was a woman. Bascom thought it would be the usual nonsense —sexual rites, he was cold to it.

The drums began a pattern. The two natives moved. They danced. Someone was making a sound like an airplane motor.

"The price is too high," Bascom whispered. "Ever since I stepped out of that plane, I've seen nothing but decay. Hardly developmental material . . ."

When he had arrived he had seen St. Cunegonde, set in the sea, flicker green underneath the wide turn of the twice-a-week plane. The island looked suspended in a hot mist floating, not so much on the sea, as a part of it; a bluer and greener fusion into solidity of weed-covered sea.

Bascom had been rowed from the plane in a red boat decorated with lidless eyes. A purple-skinned native poled the boat. The haze that held the sun stank of rotting fish and decayed weeds. Fish fragments floated in the stagnant bay waters. Bascom had stepped onto the crusted quay, walked a few steps, looked around, and planted his attaché case in a clear space. In spite of the importance of the occasion, there were no bands, no fanfares, no native songs. The boatman tied his boat, walked to the nearest shade, sat down against a crumbling wall, and fell asleep at once. Bascom walked in widening spirals around his attaché case, looking around him.

Two had come to meet him; Mr. MacTavish—with whom he had communicated—and a mulatto. Mr. MacTavish, who represented the island planters, looked old and tired. His hair seemed to blend into his fading grass hat; his seersucker suit drooped, limp and shoulderless, and there were widening sweat stains under his arms. MacTavish looked unused to wearing jackets.

Bascom smiled his trim smile; the heat had not yet begun to dull the knife-edge creases of his corded trousers. He shook the enervated hand of MacTavish, imparting his own vigor. The mulatto had not come out into the sunlight, but stood in the nearest shade, looking at Bascom. They started to walk into town. Bascom turned and looked at the attaché case on the ground in the sun. The mulatto didn't move. Bascom looked at MacTavish, who smiled back as if he had difficulty in focusing. MacTavish turned and stared for a second at the mulatto, shrugged his shoulders, and got the attaché case himself. The mulatto hadn't stopped looking at him, Bascom saw, as they continued to walk. As they passed the mulatto, MacTavish handed the case into the shadow; the mulatto almost dropped it: he hesitated and then followed, holding the attaché case clumsily.

They walked from the wharf into town. Cobblestones, littered with fruit husks, goat dung, and fish heads, led from the wharf to the town. Though he talked constantly, Bascom stared into the glare and through the bars of opaque shadow, seeing, more and more, the hopelessness of the place. He couldn't begin to impose a vision of the future over the noonday dullness yet: everything was steamed and stifling. They passed still pools covered with green scum; flies buzzed over bones and dung; natives slept in the shadows; everything was heat-wavered. St. Cunegonde was a distillation of all the dreary, hot, Caribbean ports festering on the sea; it was all the places Bascom had known before American Estates had come in and made them fit.

He watched MacTavish as they exchanged amenities, and as they passed through a wall of shadow, he was surprised to see that MacTavish was really young. What must the other planters be like, Bascom wondered, if they sent MacTavish. Presumably they had sent their shrewdest, their most energetic man, but when Bascom took MacTavish's arm, it felt soft through the cloth. It might be possible, he thought, to get the island cheaply enough. He stared through it all till the island itself became like a painting on a scrim, wavering in the illumination of the future. Bascom realized that he had even gotten used to the stench.

MacTavish was explaining that they didn't want to carry on the routine of planting, of striving, any longer. It was a matter of getting enough to be comfortable, to have enough for themselves, for their immediate descendants, to make provision for everyone. "Were the natives a consideration?" Bascom asked. Apparently they were. But not in the way MacTavish meant it. To get it as cheaply as possible must exclude the natives. The joy of coming battle excited Bascom, made him feel alive and vital in spite of the heat; but he had kept his voice neat, level, even a little chilly. . . .

Bascom looked at the dancers. They were dancing out some story. The other dancer, the woman, flitted ahead of the mulatto; she wore white. It was probably to be a defloration rite, Bascom thought. White shoes arced on the dirt floor. The mulatto rubbed his hands as though he was about to do a conjuring trick while MacTavish whispered his price again. He had been sticking to that figure for three days; it showed that he had reached the bottom, or thought he had.

"Be realistic," Bascom said. "Considering what we've seen . . ."

Bascom had become a burst of cold energy slicing through the hot days. He had moved swiftly through soft, rank sea-winds and the reek of lush vegetation.

"Our price is . . ." MacTavish had named a figure the first day. That he had named it too soon was a sign of weakness.

"But I haven't seen it yet," Bascom had said. "I can't buy without looking." Now he had come to know the island completely. He learned about its years of vital promise and its hundred-year senescence. Every night he sat in his room in the crumbling Victorian House, ignoring the mosquitoes, collating his notes into a report, figuring out on his slide-rule the cost of converting decay into building, the price of making inertia into energy. He never heard the singing and the shouting of the natives or the sounds of the drums simmering down from the hills: he had heard these things too many times all over the Caribbean. He never noticed the new moon, embedded in the air, being moved across the sky as if the island were forever caught in a stasis and the sky itself moved. He never saw the golden quarters accrete into orange halves and tumesce, finally, to a red globe. He thought ahead and couldn't hear the slow, unoiled creak of the fan-blade orbiting a lazy shadow around him: rather, he heard the endless hum of a phantom air-conditioner.

Every day that month, MacTavish was dragged after Bascom. Bascom chose his times well. He made his expeditions in the heat of the day when MacTavish's energy ebbed. Progressively weakened, blinded by the sun, suppressed by the stickiness of the jungle, choked by the road-dust, MacTavish became more and more at the service of the untiring Bascom: trying to lead, MacTavish was led.

MacTavish would pause in the sun, reeling a little, smelling of whiskey, and wiping his face, catching his breath, patting with trembling fingers the straws of his disintegrating hat. Bascom would smile, give a fastidious glance at the decay, and shrug. Bascom's fingers drummed on his attaché case, and they would move on. Bascom never lingered long. If he missed something, he preferred to come back; he always moved and made sure MacTavish moved. MacTavish stumbled after; he had discarded the seersucker jacket. Bascom made sure that his chill cord clothes were always pressed and neat; he wore a tie. He saw that even the natives, usually the most vital people wherever he went, had lost all drive. They were like glistening black, brown, or purple shells gleaming in the sunlight. Watching the two white men driving or walking fast, they sat timelessly. Bascom noticed and thought he would introduce the clock; it was the business of American Estates to breathe life and regularity into this amiable decay.

But by the end of the month it had become such torture for MacTavish that he kept rubbing his fingers to his temple as if he had a perpetual headache. It had been a relief to both of them to consummate the final signing of the papers on the veranda of Victorian House as they sipped at the inevitable Caribbean rum drink. They were both exhausted after a final forced march along the spinal ridge of the island. Everything was ready except for the figure, to be inked in before signing.

But Bascom paused. "I don't know," he said. "It's still too much." And he named a much lower figure.

"But I thought we were ready."

"It's not as easy as that."

They argued it again. They stopped. They parted. They slept on it. In the morning, Bascom sent for MacTavish and said that there were things he had to see again. MacTavish asked if they couldn't decide it right here. He explained that some of the money was for the natives. Bascom thought that was disastrous, but he said nothing. After all, American Estates would need the natives. Then he said he thought the idea commendable, but it was a question of business, not charity. Then he asked MacTavish why he had never left the island. MacTavish, tired, smiled and said that it was too much trouble. There wasn't enough money. There was much that bound a man to this place, and yet . . . MacTavish had been to Europe once: he remembered. Bascom implied that MacTavish might be able to leave, and quickly, if he sold out at a reasonable price. Unable to bear another day in the heat, MacTavish proposed the native rites instead.

Before setting out, Bascom had taken off his cord suit, his tight-collared shirt, his tie, and put on the native cloth shirt and soft, thin slacks. As they had a few drinks, they decided not to talk about business at all that night: they would simply enjoy the show.

Now the drums were rising to a crescendo. It was almost dark. The two natives lifted their rum glasses high. Then the woman was thrown down and mounted by the mulatto, who grinned as he raped her. A great scream went up from the bushes, a wailing scream. When the mulatto had finished, he reached and ripped a piece of paper from her loins, stood, and held it high over his head, kicked her aside, and danced, shaking the paper and laughing. The woman writhed, and her heels drummed on the floor. Her face was contorted, but enjoying; her eyes glared; her hand still held the glass; the liquor had been spilled before she had tasted it. There hadn't been much imagination to it, Bascom thought when everything became still, and the last orange glow sifted through the bushes where the sun had set.

MacTavish stared at the two figures. The last dust of the dirt floor settled, flickering like clouds of mist in the torchlight. "Still, a *whole* island . . ." MacTavish said.

"You know, this might have a tourist appeal," Bascom whispered. "It should be . . . toned up." He grinned.

MacTavish didn't answer; he was thinking about business.

"What happened to the sugar trade?" Bascom asked, keeping him off balance.

"It could be revived without too much effort. We make a little rum . . ."

"And exports?"

"None."

Bascom turned away. "Aren't they going to do anything? What can they possibly do for an *encore*?" he said and laughed.

There was a shout somewhere in the jungle. A homemade cymbal beat a clash that didn't ring true, somewhat cracked and flat. The torches flashed out and Bascom saw the ancient fretwork of fronds and creepers, limned for the last time in orange sky before that too disappeared; then the night air closed in, muggy, full of insects, almost palpable. Bascom smelled wood-smoke and something wild and fusty: sweat, as if many natives were very close to him.

The torches guttered and burst into flame again, spotlighting the mulatto, MacTavish's man, in the center of the arena. He wore nothing but the trappings of his role as Master of the Revel: feathers, a piece of fur, a skull rattle hung on a string tied around his waist. The usual things, Bascom thought. The Master bowed. It was as graceful and practiced a bow as any maître d'hotel might make, an exquisite mock of a bow, trained by centuries of very correct breeding. For a second his action turned the jungle into a civilized place, as if the bare ground were an intricate parquet. Bascom was surprised they could evoke such subtlety.

"Who is he? Does he play a part in all the rites?" Bascom asked.

"I saw it once. I was younger," MacTavish mumbled. "We all see it at one time or another. It's one of the Child-God rituals. I never knew he was part of it. I suppose they all are, aren't they?" he asked Bascom.

Bascom shrugged. How would he know? He had never heard of the Child-God. Probably, he thought, the usual voodoo under a local name. He looked at MacTavish's staring, half-drunken eyes.

"I should think the land alone would be worth . . ."

"There are no minerals, nothing at all. You people support yourself, no more. It's beautiful, I'll admit. But ask yourself: how much is that worth? How beautiful!" Bascom said of the dancers. Six dancers had come out of the forest, advanced, and danced as the drums throbbed, weaving a pattern. The steps began with the usual intricate stylized agitation that had taken centuries to evolve, and fell away to something slower, almost purposeless, timeless. The dancers moved with lazy, waving motions, dancing the hot, lazy island, immutable, rocking in the impossible green of the sea, like an old ship forever caught in the fabled sargasso, an old mystery drifting, undulating on an older mystery.

The rhythm changed and quickened. Metal tinkled a time-beat for the History Dance. The first people came. The French came and conquered the Indians. The French soon died out, and there was no one left. Negroes and Indians lived a new life. For fifty years the ancient ways merged. They lived here as they lived in Africa; lived as they had before they had been enslaved. Old Gods were forgotten, all but the oldest, the newest, born of Negro and Indian: the Child-God. Bascom wasn't sure what had happened to the French; they had just stopped being; he couldn't understand why. He wondered if the Gods had cast them out, and thought he was silly for thinking it. Probably plague or some such rational explanation. The British had come and taken over. They had enslaved the soft natives again and abolished the cult of the Child-God. The natives worshipped in secret; there was a long struggle and some sort of revenge. Bascom couldn't be sure what the gestures indicated here. Yet Bascom was startled that he understood the meaning of almost every movement, as though he himself had suddenly become initiated into its mysteries.

He was also surprised at the vitality of the dances, for he was a connoisseur and had seen native rituals again and again. These movements were fresh, neither tired nor stale, not the mere orgiastic swayings the natives put on for tourists all over the Caribbean. That was the trouble, Bascom thought; the natives saved their energy for dances, not for the world where it was needed. That would be changed when American Estates moved in, he thought. The cracked iron note beat insistently, coming through the involved throbbing.

"What kind of cult is this? I've never seen anything like it," Bascom said.

"You don't offer enough. You know it's not enough," complained MacTavish.

"But I'm not a free agent," Bascom said, watching the dancers. "Personally, I've grown to like St. Cunegonde very much, but . . ." He shrugged.

The drums fell to a quivering whispering as time held still for more than a hundred years. For the Child-God there was no time; it was always now. They danced a dance of sweet equilibrium. The planter lived his life side by side with the native in peaceful brotherhood. Planting, civilization, the island, all slowly decayed, but the living was good. The food was on the tree for the taking; how could they want? Bascom began to understand what had happened, and he thought, seeing it pranced there, he would make them want. But something lingered, something alien to Bascom's way, something he could feel, smell, something at first fetid, then sweet, that gave the natives their soft zest for living. Bascom couldn't understand what it was, this something that took hold and, somehow, seemed attractive, curiously dignified: to live this way and strive no more. It made life a thing of wonder and chance and it slowly began to take hold of Bascom, but then he moved violently and blew on his hands and rubbed them and tapped his fingers rapidly on his shoes. They had surrendered to the sweet slime of decay, become drugged in slow, delicious corruption, and Bascom, shuddering, looked at MacTavish; MacTavish was weeping.

"You see, we buy and sell islands. The place is no good unless we can do something with it," Bascom said, trying to shake off the spell.

They were dancing the future now, the dance of what would be, as the natives saw it.

"First, we'll make St. Cunegonde an attraction for Bohemians, the intellectual drifters. It will be very cheap, advanced, unspoiled, primitive; all that nonsense. After a few years, the rich will discover it, take over, and make it expensive and exclusive, forcing the avant garde out."

They danced the building of the new hotels. The natives became hungry, they found jobs, they became greedy; slowly their ways changed. The last of the planters died, melted into nothingness in the face of the terrific American energy; their money would not save them.

"Finally, we'll permit it to deteriorate, and then the tourists will take over."

The visitors arrived, strutting. They moved without grace, in swift jerks, jingling and clicking, staring, touching, laughing, allowing themselves to be cheated. But they were fat and got fatter; they laughed on the beaches; they laughed in the hills; they laughed in the tame jungles.

"Hordes of nouveaux riches, the vacationing secretaries, schoolteachers on their ten-day, pay-later plans, will come in. It will take about ten years. There'll be money in it for everyone. Everyone."

Bascom watched the waddle of a plump tourist, bathing in the sea; the dancer waded down into the rippling earth, disappearing, laughing. They did it with mirrors, he thought.

A native woman danced with pride, needing no other ornament than her nakedness. She was beautiful. She moved, not with the false, mincing show of the corrupt native, but simply. She heard the tinkling. She held her hands over her ears. She fled from corner to corner, darting among the uncaring tourists. The noise followed her everywhere. The tinkling gathered into a great, rhythmic jingle, growing louder and louder, permeating the jungle. She was bathed in a shower of silver; the glittering dust mixed with sweat and she gleamed as if she was plated. She walked around the arena, holding her breasts high, squeezing them, jiggling them in her hands, laughing. The tourists, not caring, took what she gave and passed on. She became wilder; she danced the Money Dance too.

Bascom painted a glowing picture for MacTavish: a hotel on the mountain ridge, towering over a white, coral-cement town, perhaps on this very spot: the vista on the misty, green spine of the island that jutted like a wave thrown up high by the ocean. But it would cost money. They couldn't spend everything on the land alone. "Take it or leave it," he said.

They danced the Survival. Not accepting the new ways, too aloof to give in, some natives starved. The last few impotent men held on to their customs, until finally, toothless, holding limp palm-leaves, they flailed the air feebly, unable to conjure up the Child-God. They no longer had the strength or the courage. They showed their rituals to the tourists for money. The last Master died. The last cave of the Child-God was bulldozed flat. The Child-God died. The tourists came and went, never fearing the first, the last, the most terrible of the Gods, the Child-God, walking over where he had once existed, vibrant with life.

Bascom had to admit now that the rites were unusual, powerful, and evocative. He saw the island as he had always seen it, and it was familiar, sterile. He shrugged. A little chill wind curled leaves and grasses. "Take it or leave it," he said again, feeling unnaturally depressed.

Then everything was silent, frozen and waiting.

MacTavish shrugged his shoulders and said he would sign.

They began dancing the Now, which they symbolized a postured, frozen second; the mulatto who danced Bascom was triumphant; the woman who danced MacTavish was supine. They had their celebratory drink, united by what they had done to the island. Bascom wondered if agitators had gotten them from the other islands.

The Master danced in again. He carried a polished rod ending where the bloody feather was tacked on; he waved the piece of paper he had seized from the loins of the woman, and Bascom stared; it was a copy of the contract. The Master touched his stick to the contract. MacTavish's name blazed out on it, written in blood. MacTavish looked down at the ground.

The drums crashed. The dancers stamped their right feet. The drums stopped. The dancers waited in the stillness, looking over their shoulders into the black silence. Everything faded. Bascom felt the great watching multitude in the jungle. Bascom glanced at MacTavish, who sat there, looking up now, staring at the fading stick and his disappearing name written on the contract. MacTavish had been insulted; but he looked only terrified.

Stones pounded, drums throbbed. The torches flickered once and burst into terrible brilliance, turning the arena floor bright as white sea-sand. A head, bloody at the neck, rolled slowly across the floor toward them. Sand stuck to the blood. Bascom stood up. Dead eyes glared up at him; it was MacTavish's head covered with blood. It was so real that Bascom had to turn to his companion, while MacTavish, trembling, sat and stared into Bascom's eyes. Bascom looked down. The head was made of straw. Bascom shook his head at the marvel of it. Mirrors, he thought, all done with mirrors, but the thought didn't amuse him. The Master came farther into the arena.

"My God," MacTavish moaned. He made the sign of the cross in the air. Someone laughed in the jungle. A great shadow fell across the torchlight. The Master waved his wand. The shadow disappeared. MacTavish stared at the lights in the arena and muttered.

"Pull yourself together," Bascom whispered sternly. "Have a little dignity. What do you think they're going to do to us, sacrifice us?" He smiled, and sat down.

The Master had begun a long speech telling them what they'd done to the island.

"You don't know," MacTavish mumbled. "Jesus Christ, save us!"

It is not the time for that, Bascom thought.

"This is no place for Jesus Christ. Here is before that one," the Master said.

"What do you think they'll do?" Bascom asked.

MacTavish's words tumbled out. "The Child-God—something sprung wild and fresh out of the teeming fecundity of the jungle; a terrible force that killed friend and enemy; a primal power; an enormous black baby twice a man's height that ate the vegetation, tore meat, gibbered, squeezed life out of its victims so that the mouth bubbled blood, and the guts dribbled out, the body crushed—a creature taking joy in screams, tearing off limbs, smothering with love, devouring with want, petulant, irrational, primeval . . ."

"Is it money they want?" Bascom asked.

"No. It's nothing like that."

Bascom interrupted the Master's chant. "The law . . ." There was loud laughter in the jungle. "And if not this law, the people I represent will get you sooner or later."

"Your law is not this island," the Master told them. "He knows," he said, pointing to MacTavish. "He knows. There is no law here but the Child-God's. This is his world. He takes his own."

"It won't help you," Bascom said.

"He is the youngest and first of all Gods. He has no law. He is before all other Gods. No one who comes here can circumvent him."

"Nonsense," Bascom said, but he was afraid. He knew what the natives, inflamed by their rites, were capable of doing. He perspired; the night air chilled him. It was MacTavish's fear that made him more afraid. He wondered how terrible their tortures could be; terrible indeed if MacTavish, who knew about these things, quivered at clever straw images.

The Master began to sing softly. At first, his head was bowed. His shadowed face looked down gently, tenderly, as though he were crooning to a sleeping child. His hands made caressing gestures. Slowly, his head raised. His face began to lose whatever tenderness it had when he looked at Bascom and Mac-Tavish. A new note crept into the crooning voice, something harsh and strident. "O Child," he called. Bascom heard a bird shriek in the jungle. "O Child, come out."

The drums sounded, rising and falling, beginning to quicken. Something was wakening. The forest throbbed with the beat. The refrain was answered from another part of the jungle. Stones pounded, drums throbbed, iron clanged, wood clicked.

"O Child, come out of your cave."

The beat fell apart and became annoying, nagging. The ragged noise offended Bascom's sense of order. He could make nothing of the drums or the singing now. The Master began to dance the Evocation. MacTavish shook, communicating his terror through the hot air, and Bascom grabbed his arm to give him a sense of strength, a sense of dignity.

The Master invoked. "O Child, dwell in the hurricane." A

wild reed flute played conjure music. Babbling, MacTavish told Bascom that something was foaming in the jungle, forming in the thick humidity, bubbling out of the loam, coming out of the quick warmth of earthen loins, a something these people had held onto all these centuries and knew how to conjure up.

"O Child, dwell in the waters. Spout to heaven. Hurricane and mow the lives."

Bascom wondered how they would kill him. He wondered if there was any sense in running away into the jungle, but knew, somehow, that that was what they wanted.

The Master moved this way and that, hopping in wide, crippled circles, feet beating on the floor, uncoordinated, shaking the earth. His arms waved, hung limp, jerked, the fingers clutched. The Master drooled. The Master then was the Child-God, simulating early movements after birth, moving without meaning, a great, terrible infant in whom the nerves were not properly connected.

The uncoupled eyes focused in different directions. The Child grew. The hands of the Master reached out and there was a great green and blue butterfly fluttering helplessly in them. He squealed with a child's sudden shout of delight, hopping up and down as he held it high. Then he tore off the wings, the legs, the feelers, cramming the body clumsily with both fists into his mouth. MacTavish moaned again. The Master shrieked and laughed. Then something in the jungle gurgled back from a rustling of leaves.

Something was dancing up and down in the jungle, although Bascom could see only the random gleam of highlighted skin, leaf sickles shining in sine curves, a dust of spore pods dancing, all disembodied. The Master minced forward and picked up the straw head and held it aloft, the blood dripping down on his hands; then he bent low, straightened up violently, and flung the head far into the darkness. MacTavish looked past the Master to where the head had been thrown; he fell over and lay on the ground face down.

"O Child," the Master sang, "are you satisfied?"

"No!" a choir of hidden voices wailed. And Bascom knew they had worked themselves up too far to go back now. They were going to kill him too. He almost wished he could die by suggestion like MacTavish so they wouldn't torture him. His shirt fluttered on his cold body.

The Master stood in front of Bascom. "O Child! Roll the stone aside and come out of your cave!" Stones pounded.

The wailing sound of the Master's voice chilled Bascom: did he hear something in the darkness?

"The Child-God is coming."

Bascom heard the drums pound and iron clang. He waited. He wouldn't move.

The Master held a knife. Bascom watched the knife. The drums were silent. Bascom heard petulant, impatient screaming coming from the jungle. He saw little lights flickering on the black obsidian. The Master came very slowly toward him, striding stiff-legged, as in a trance. Bascom was being given some kind of a chance. He was terrified, afraid of the knife cutting into him. "The Child-God is coming," the Master screamed. Wood clicked. Rattles shook. Bascom stood up and waited for the Master.

And the Master came at him, holding the knife in front of him, pointing the black stone point first, moving it toward Bascom's throat.

Bascom couldn't think. Tiny insects bit at his face. Little

fears formed and froze in his mind as he heard the great stirring in the darkness. He knew he mustn't move, he mustn't believe; for to move was to panic and to panic was to run into the jungle. . . . He felt the point press into the rigid flesh of his throat as the Master chanted, "O Child, come! O Child, come!"

The pain made Bascom turn cold as the knife broke the skin, and he felt the coldness come out of him, crystalline, clear, logical . . . icy blood flowed down his neck. He felt it hesitate, tickling at his collarbone, and go over, flow irrationally down his chest and belly. The sensation almost made him want to squirm and scratch, but he stood stiffly. He looked at the Master's eyes and saw them, not as eyes, but as things to focus on, to hypnotize himself, to keep from running away, to keep from feeling the pain the knife would make. The noise in the jungle had risen to a great, thrashing stomp that came closer and closer. Soon, Bascom thought, they would break through and come into the clearing.

"He comes," the Master chanted.

Bascom waited. They waited a long time. The Master's eyes began to roll. "He comes," the Master pleaded. It was a cry of hope. Bascom waited.

The knife was taken away. A great moan sounded from the edge of the clearing. The Master jumped back, screamed, and threw the knife, like an arrow, into the man-high fronds. A scream from the shadows answered, and the Master plunged into the darkness beyond the clearing.

The fires died out. Bascom waited. But nothing happened to him. He felt colder in the morning chill. The sky was now a pastel gray. Insects slept. The last drumbeat stopped.

Bascom was alone. He sat down and looked around in the

gray dawn light. At the edge of the clearing he could see now the violently crushed and sprawled body of the Master. The Child-God had come. . . . And MacTavish he saw, too, closer, still face up on the ground. But he was stirring now and making a sound like a moan. Then his heels drummed on the ground, he gibbered idiotically, and suddenly he turned and lay face down, sobbing.

Bascom continued to sit, a little foolish in his tropical, butterfly shirt, shivering in the cold breeze coming up the hillside from the sea. Then slowly, almost sadly, he got to his feet and started down the wet, fern-bordered path to town. Where the fires made the lights earlier in the evening, the trees seemed to be dying, cycads had crashed to the ground, and leaves from the ginkgoes had fallen. MacTavish would follow later, Bascom knew. They would sign the contract in town.

Bascom, drained and empty for the time being, was borne away from the island in the regular, twice-a-week plane. Above the island once more, he looked down on the hills and forests of St. Cunegonde. There it lay, a steadfast and everlasting green, its clear white beach against the smooth blue of the sea: now, he reflected a little sadly, it was quite like any other Caribbean island.

THE SIEGE

AFTER twenty-seven years and two hours of departmental contact, it came down to just this moment . . . the three of them, Kalisher, the social worker from Friends of the Community, Miller, the relief investigator, and Mrs. Diamond, the client, were immured in a stasis. She refused to show them the fourth room.

They had contended with her for two hours. Her head was kept turning from Kalisher to Miller; they pressed, wanting to know; they ranged from kindness to brutality. Now they sat resting in the cluttered kitchen. They could hear the constant gurgling of water in the decayed pipes. They inhaled the thick smell of chicken or fish. Miller kept cataloguing. For the third time he made a neatly printed list: piled food cans; boxes of dry cereal on the washtub cover; two kinds of Kosher soap; grease-spattered pictures of her long-deserted husband and her runaway son hung over the stained sink; a pot of soup—enough for two—was being heated over a low flame. Mrs. D.'s wary little eyes watched him out of a mask of wrinkles. Miller held his pen poised above his case-book. He sat stiffly.

Mrs. D. sighed again; Miller knew what he had known before: they were never going to get into the room beyond the bedroom. How had it escaped notice so long? Neglect. Past investigators had come in, questioned briefly . . . she met the bare essentials of eligibility: her case was hopeless. She was alone: deserted: too old and sick to work now. They had made their inspections quickly, noted nothing except her statement that it was a closet, perhaps wanting to get away from the stench and from having to listen to a long, old lady's complaint. Or if they suspected, did they really want to fight this old woman? Leave well enough alone. That was the trouble, Miller thought: everyone left well enough alone.

Mr. Miller had gone to see Mr. K., her social worker at Friends of the Community: did he know about the room? After all, Mr. K. had worked with her for three years. Mr. K. knew nothing . . . he had been concerned with her psychic welfare, helping her, an old, disturbed woman, adjust. Miller had expected Mr. K. to be angry at the deception, but Mr. K. had broken into a wide smile and said that it explained so many things. "She gave me a weekly cup of tea, Mr. Miller, but that was all. I begin to see it, how much she hasn't ventilated. I thought we were relating well. . . . My God, Mr. Miller, aren't people wonderful?"

"Wonderful?" Mr. Miller had asked. "But didn't you investigate?"

"It isn't the business of Friends of the Community to investigate in the same sense the Relief Department investigates, Mr. Miller," Mr. K. had said.

"All right, I'll close the case."

"But you can't do that. She'll starve. She has no resources . . ."

"She probably has a boarder."

"It isn't as simple as that. Have you . . ."

"She has a boarder and therefore, extra income."

"But Mr. Miller; please. It might be more than a boarder," Mr. K. had said. "Why don't we go over her case completely?"

Now Miller didn't care anymore. After two hours of questioning, the required veneer of polite, investigative procedure they had agreed on was about to peel away. He had spoiled six sheets of his case-book with elaborate doodles. Mr. K. was more patient, Miller saw, but that was because Mr. K. accepted. Miller thought Mr. K. was ridiculous; he simply didn't know. Sly Mrs. D., in spite of her years, poverty, swollen ankles, pipette legs, was faster on her feet than Mr. K. Her hands were crumpled into grasping roots by arthritis. Miller looked away from those gnarled, calcified bones. He wanted to go. She made him feel uncomfortable. He was afraid she might reach out, touch, and infect him. She sighed. Her lips wrinkled into fleshy rays and her righteous mouth pressed tightly against the three or four teeth she had left. Miller knew they were beaten unless one of them—and it would have to be him—was direct about it. Miller's leg shook up and down on the ball of his foot; he lost count of the shakes. He had no patience for the long, unprofitable silence necessary to proper social-work atmospheres.

Kalisher pointed to a picture. "Your husband?"

"Don't touch," she told him.

"Mrs. Diamond, we're only trying to help you," Kalisher told her while his eyes tried to look past her.

She sniffed. She had learned. In the past she had been betrayed. "To the grave you'd help," she said. She was sharpened by those tricky years of contact with investigators sent to deprive her; her cunning must beat them. Kalisher, dripping honey, talking "adjustment" and "rehabilitation," soft words, had come before. The Millers too; without pretense, hard, un-caring: their looks said "You're cheating." Did they know or care how it was to live like she lived? She fought them all. She held on. "How much longer am I going to be able to stand it?" she asked matter-of-factly. Torture and martyrdom were some-thing she imbibed with the thin, white farina she ate every morning. To remind them they had done this to her, her hands picked and clutched at the frayed rope that pulled her brightly flowered housecoat together.

Kalisher saw a soft, gray wisp of frail hair float out against the loud colors of the detergent boxes. His heart went out to her. He knew what psychic martyrdom moved mothers. He was reminded of those art-photographs of old people's hands; wonderful, abiding roots. He heeded the plea of those hands. If poor Mrs. Diamond could only know his feeling . . . warm, empathetic community flooding through his veins. His face shone. He could barely see through his glasses. He knew and understood the pain and anguish of withstanding them, the providers, the father-figures. She wanted freedom and resented needing them. It was why she fought. It was why she rejected. He smiled.

Miller was afraid her housecoat was going to fall open. He saw that K. was about to tell Mrs. D. again how long she would be able to stand it. But Miller was tired after the two-hour siege. He was tired of sitting in the kitchen in his coat; he was sweating in the steamy atmosphere. He was tired of having to divide his time between Mrs. D. and Mr. K. A splotch of grease seemed to expand, slowly seeping up through the checkered tablecloth; he moved his sleeve away. He was sitting on crumbs. Mrs. D.'s clock said three: he didn't trust it. He was hungry. He was tired of making lists and neatly narrowing spirals in his case-book. It was the grabbing motion of her hand that decided him.

"Mrs. D., we've been here for two hours. You realize that. We haven't got all day. You're not our only case. Are you going to show us that room?"

Kalisher shook his head imperceptibly, disapproving. Smiling apologetically, he hastened to undo the harm. He talked Yiddish to Mrs. Diamond to show her he was really on her side. The long discussion hadn't begun to faze him; does one unravel a complex or pierce through to a pre-psychotic personality in a mere two hours? Kalisher interpreted departmental policy. His voice droned soothingly through the kitchen as he tried to reestablish contact with her. He asked her to help *them* . . . as people. He thrust blame on a vast impersonal machine that ground down the lives of clients, investigators, and social workers impartially: the three of them were pawns; really allies. *He* was here to protect her interests. He hinted they could make some kind of arrangement. "It isn't him," he told her, "it's the department. Mr. Miller doesn't like prying. But he has to see every room in the apartment. It's his job. You understand."

"If he doesn't want to do it, then why do it? I never heard of such a thing," she sniffed.

Twenty-seven years of getting relief and she never heard of such a thing, Miller thought. He saw a sly roach follow a cupboard crack. She could quote the manual, chapter and verse; she knew her rights better than the both of them. He couldn't see signs of a boarder: no man's shoe, no sock, no half-smoked cigarette or cigar was left; she was careful.

"The *department,* Mrs. Diamond, the *department* wants him to look around. It's the law. But . . ."

"So why are *you* here?" she asked.

She saw Kalisher's greedy look. She had been fooled by sneaks before. They had worked it out together. They were the enemy. They came around saying, "Listen to us; we're on your side; tell us everything; we can do something for you." Once she had a little job, a few extra pennies; how else could you live? She had listened to them. They had closed her case. She now knew better. Back to the relief office she had gone and made a scene, screaming for two hours till, to get rid of her, they gave her help. For them it was some kind of game; to see if they could deprive her. She knew. If she passed their tests, she was safe for another few months. But this time . . . two of them . . . they knew . . . she was choking . . . circles in Miller's notebook . . . what did those mean? Tight strings quivered under the flesh of her neck. Why did they sit there, playing, laughing at her? Her hands felt weak. Did she have much left? She was worn down. Her hands held tightly to the rope around her waist.

Miller saw she didn't have anything on underneath the housecoat. He watched her spit into the sink and wash it down. His pen tore a little hole through his case-book. She was old, diseased, dirty, possibly senile. If they could put her in a home . . .

"The way to stop it," he had told Mr. K., "is to take her and put her in a home."

"She wouldn't go. After all, she's lived there for thirty years."

"It's the answer."

"You can't do that. She wants to be independent."

"Don't they all?" Miller asked sarcastically. "Who's stopping her, Kalisher?" and they had sat down and read the two-inch-thick case record . . . twenty-seven years of contact.

"This is a waste of time," Miller said.

"You wouldn't think everything had been covered. But yet . . ." Mr. K. said.

"Look at that." Miller had held up some sheets. "That's three times she's cheated the department. Why do we bother? We'll ask to see the room. If she refuses, we close the case."

"You can't do that. She's an old woman. She's disturbed. You can't treat a human being like that."

"She's got a boarder there. She's probably got more than enough money saved by now."

"It's not the material things; it's that she gets support from the welfare situation."

"Support is right," Miller said.

"I don't mean it in that sense," Mr. K. had said, being obviously patient with Miller. "And I don't think she has a boarder there. I think . . . it's pretty clear, isn't it? Don't you see it? Look at all these social-work contacts."

"I see that she's a miser."

"That's a sickness too."

"She's got mattresses stuffed with money . . ."

"Miller, everyone has a treasure house . . . but it's a hiding place, of psychic possibility.

"For God's sake, what . . ."

"That room is an extension of her . . . a part of her psyche." Mr. K. had smiled at him.

"She's laughing at you, Kalisher. She's a miser."

"She's a miser, but not in the sense you mean it."

"I won't argue the point," Miller said; "but departmental rulings on added income are clear."

"Listen, she's a sweet old woman, a free soul. She needs to bring forth her problem. She wants love and understanding.

52

She's been left by her husband, deserted. She's been brutalized. She's been kept on a substandard existence."

"The budget allows . . ."

"Mr. Miller, you can't break psychic needs into grams, calories, municipal food reports, or monetary allotments. Such treatment demeans . . ."

Miller thought that Mr. K. could never admit she might be intrinsically brutal, only that she was sick.

". . . and she blocks, represses, she can't relate, she's compulsive, antisocial, she conceals. It's a form of hoarding, yes, but why, Mr. Miller; why?"

"Mr. Kalisher, who cares?" Miller had said.

Life would be more organized for her in a home, Miller thought, and this couldn't have happened. Going by the psychological book was well and good, but could you rehabilitate those arthritic, withered hands? Could she be sent to work? Years of support had made her parasitic. Don't starve her, but let her at least follow the rules. She was doomed. If she didn't show him the fourth room very soon, he would cut her off. She knew her duty. His pen jabbed through the sheet again. He saw her cunning eyes dance mockingly in her decayed face. A little smile showed the tip of one black tooth. He tried to breathe calmly: the reek, like fish, of the bubbling pot was too much for him. He began another careful curve on a fresh sheet of paper. Of course Mr. K. would fight a case-closing; not until he tried every trick of pleading with her; whining, ingratiating himself, all of it. Miller slid his chair back a little. He saw Mr. K.'s soft, loose-lipped look, his indefatigable smile. Mr. K. missed the point, Miller thought. Mr. K. was trying to get into the fourth room with Mrs. D.'s goodwill, as if he owed something to her. She owed *them*—if she got ten dollars a week rent, the usual rate—and it had been going on for—he would be liberal—only ten years, then . . . No, her goodwill didn't matter; it was an unnecessary handicap. If they simply went away, left her alone, didn't bother her, sent her checks twice a month, *then* they would have her goodwill. If they left her the hidden resources of that room, *then* they would have Mrs. D.'s endless goodwill. He started to loosen his tie and stopped.

"You just want to take away, out of spite. I never heard such a thing. To come in, to tear me apart," she was muttering, convincing herself that they didn't have the right. They were playing with her. They were going to take everything away from her.

But Kalisher was lovingly patient; it didn't bother him that his undershirt, and now his shirt, was drenched. He permitted her to act out her aggressions. He talked to her as he might to his own mother, striving to rest those neurotic terrors. "Of course he doesn't mean *you*, Mrs. Diamond, but some clients are cheats. Some clients have television sets, washing-machines, telephones, cars, all sorts of things they try to hide. You understand."

"So what has this to do with me? What could I have to hide? On relief for twenty-seven years; what could I buy? A twenty-seven-inch television set on what they give me? I can hardly afford what to eat."

"No. No, Mrs. Diamond. I don't mean *you*. Heaven forbid," Kalisher told her; "but that means that Mr. Miller will be able to record in the case that he saw and checked everything. You see?"

"So? Let him put it down."

"But that wouldn't be honest; just to put it down, I mean . . . Now what could be in that room?"

"Nothing. Before, I told you; nothing."

"Then what do you have to be afraid of?"

Miller saw that Mr. K. would have gone through it all a fourth time; a fifth time; a sixth time if necessary, probing, using that soft, that silly, that sympathetic approach. Miller moved violently; the table jarred. A cup clattered. He looked up. Her hands clutched at her chest. He saw that she had never stopped looking at him. "So we have to look into the fourth room and see what's there. Who knows," Miller forced his lips to grin, "maybe you have diamonds there, Mrs. D."

But Kalisher laughed quickly to show her the idea was beyond the realm of the conceivable. He saw Miller's twisted lips tensed over his teeth. He had worked so hard to win her, and every time he almost had her on his side, Miller compulsively spoiled it.

"Now supposing," Kalisher had said, "we work it out that you play the villain and I her hero. You attack; she comes to me, you see. My relation with her is a little different, warmer than . . ."

"Why bother?" Miller had asked again. "I ask. She shows. Why cater to her whims?"

And Kalisher wondered why Miller was blinding himself. He was rationalizing his hostility to Mrs. D. into a fetish for carrying out rules. Didn't he see what was perfectly clear in the case record? Kalisher had almost been tempted to see how long Miller might go on without seeing it . . . what . . . who was in the fourth room. "Because she's a human being."

"She's almost a cheat. The boarder . . ."

"Does that make her less a human being?"

Mrs. Diamond didn't think Mr. Miller's quip was funny. "Drain my blood," she told them. "Make me suffer. Go ahead. What does a human being mean to you? Do you know pity?

Take everything from an old woman. Are you human beings?"

Being human had nothing to do with it, Miller thought. Pity? he had none left. He had seen too many clients. He knew them. Animals, he thought, just animals. No amount of readings in social casework would give them dignity. Leave "humanity" to the K.s. She was alien; a constant drain on public funds; she could bring no returns. What would happen later? She would die alone, like an animal. Her body would lie there for days in the gloom. Someone would smell rotting flesh and call the police. They would exhume her. Her burial would cost the city. Unless, of course—and he could sense it—the secret boarder found her. Miller intersected circles with squares, enclosing equal areas.

Watching her, Kalisher felt something inside of him wrench to see her suffering. He felt sure that she was appealing to him to save her; to save her secret. For he had said to Miller, in the office, "The husband deserted; the son, Paul, sixteen at the time, ran away from home twenty-one years ago."

"What has that to do with it?"

"There it is." And Kalisher had felt the glee again.

"What? I don't understand."

"The missing son. He disappeared without much explanation. She never complained. She never called the Missing Persons Bureau," Kalisher told Mr. Miller. "Isn't it obvious?" and left it unsaid.

"Don't be silly; things like that don't happen. She has a paying boarder. Don't be romantic. My God, what wishful thinking." Miller had almost shouted.

"Wishful?" Mr. Kalisher had said and wondered why Mr. Miller fought it so hard. "I know of cases like that; they're not as rare as you think. It's what any mother really wants to do."

"It's all stupid nonsense."

"He'd be thirty-seven now."

Mr. Miller had refused to credit it.

But suppose, Mr. Kalisher had insisted, the missing son had been living in the little room for the last twenty-one years? He felt it. It was right. He knew it. He had the insight. "Think of that kid in the warm room, like a womb, really, secured to her forever. Think of her feeding two people on the allowance for one."

"Or think of her as getting extra funds," Mr. Miller had said. They had argued it out. In the end Mr. Kalisher had agreed reluctantly to go along with it. What she hid in the fourth room represented the core of her existence. He nodded knowingly at Mr. Miller. But Mr. Miller was looking into his case-book, rejecting the situation. Her face's old nobility, the wrinkles that time, privation, yet dignity had engraved there, was spoiled only by the fearing eyes and the neurotic denying quiver of the lips; she couldn't bring it out; she wouldn't deliver herself of the guilt. "You have no idea, Mrs. Diamond," he told her, his voice trembling in a rich, inaccurate Yiddish, "how much it hurts me to have to do this. Believe me. I'm on your side. I understand." His smile should have told her he had seen deeply.

"I know you. I know you all. Watching me all the time for something. You want me to starve. Look at me. Look at the way I live." Her twisted arm, waving, took in, for Kalisher, all of the suffering, the poor, the sick, all the lonely, old, and deserted in the slums.

Miller noted; the tablecloth was fairly new; the kitchen chairs were not too old; the dish towels were serviceable; and through the cupboard glass he saw that she had two sets of dishes, one light blue, the other white. She burned two candles in glasses; she was rich enough to afford that nonsense, Miller thought. She wasn't starving. It was a question of what the boarder earned and contributed. The signs were hidden, but he knew. "Lady, you've managed to live, somehow or other, for twenty-seven years and never once did you admit you had an extra room. If I hadn't happened to recheck the registration of this apartment, I wouldn't have known either. *You* wouldn't have told me, would you? What about that, Mrs. D.? What about that?"

"No one asked me . . ."

"I'm asking now . . ."

She stood, hunched over a little, pulled in on herself, waiting for them to make their move. "There's nothing in there; I told you."

"Why haven't you ever shown that fourth room to any investigator, Mrs. D.?" Miller asked, pointing his pen at her.

She sniffed. There was nothing Kalisher could do for her either. He sat there, smiled, and felt his hands strain and tremble.

"No one asked. There's nothing there. It's none of your business," she told them.

"I've been reasonable for two hours; it *is* our business. *Everything* about you is our business. We give you money. *We keep you alive*. It has to be our business." And Miller saw she understood now. She had him alone to contend with. Kalisher was out of it; *his* agency didn't dispense funds; Miller's did. He sat before her, fuming because of her stubbornness. He crossed out a figure; he could compute it when he returned to the office. He made it very clear to her, stressing it, lingering on it. "Sooner or later we find out, lady. If you have nothing to hide

. . . You know, you wouldn't be the first person to cheat the department. You won't be the first to be caught either."

Kalisher's wounded sigh sounded helplessly in the room; and then he realized . . . Miller was jealous of his relationship with Mrs. Diamond . . .

Miller couldn't wait anymore. "We know you have someone in that room."

They were caught in the thick smoke of Miller's cigarette: it hung in soft eddies. A thin plume of steam spurted from the pot. Did he detect a gleam under the tears, Miller wondered. He began to boil. "Who's in that room?"

"I can't show it to you."

"You won't . . ."

"Let me starve. Tear me apart. Kill me. Take everything away. Throw me into the streets. My life . . ."

"Don't be foolish. Who's . . . "

"Don't talk like that."

"A boarder?"

"Twenty men in a closet. A dormitory," she said. Their voices were growing louder.

"Or . . ." Miller smiled at Mr. K. ". . . your son?"

She screamed. Kalisher leaned forward, looking at her face; his mouth was open and moist. "My son! My son should only be there." Her face was twisted. The black teeth showed. Her hand clawed toward Miller. He slid back; the chair feet screeched on the floor. "Who ever heard of such a thing? Where do they dream up such things to torture me? You got nothing better to do with your time than to torture an old, sick woman? It gives you fun?"

Kalisher's mouth kept opening and closing. After that in-human violation of casework principles, that sadistic wrench-ing-out, what could he possibly have said? A little while longer, another ten minutes, and it would have come out easily; she would have shown them the room. Each sob that shook Mrs. Diamond's body shook him too.

"What have you got to hide then? What are you making such a fuss about?" Miller asked loudly.

"I'm not making a fuss. There's nothing there. Dirt. I'm ashamed. The door has things laying in front of it."

"You're trying to make me look a fool. You're not ashamed!"

Miller looked at her and shrugged his shoulders.

"An old woman . . . I'm so tired . . . Only rags. Why don't you just kill me?"

Miller nodded.

Kalisher was horrified at both of them . . . hating. He was appalled to find that reason had failed in the face of primitive emotion. Mrs. Diamond and Miller's hostility was steaming and overpowering in the small kitchen. "Kill you? Kill you? What kind of nonsense are you talking, Mrs. Diamond? Who talks of killing you? Kill my own mother, you should say."

She knit together, for the last time, a fragility of bone and a meagerness of flesh. She clutched at the flowers on her breast. She clenched her toothless mouth and shook her head. She wouldn't listen. She would starve first. She fought her own weariness. She fought them. She had outwitted them, out-fought them, outscreamed them in the past. It would pass. She gathered herself to start screaming.

Miller looked at her and rose. He capped his pen. It was pointless, undignified, to have to fight her. Calming himself, Miller thought it wasn't a matter of anger; could the depart-ment be angry? It was a matter of balances and perspectives. They had given too much to this old woman. That was it.

"Mrs. D., there's nothing more I can do for you. We've been patient," Miller told her. "Let's go, Kalisher."

"Now wait a minute, Mr. Miller; surely . . ." Pale, anxious, Kalisher pleaded.

"No."

"But look . . ."

"Look, nothing. There's nothing to look at. Two hours . . . She won't cooperate. She won't show us the room. She's simply not eligible. Let *your* agency give her funds."

"Don't be hostile."

"Don't give me that jargon."

"For God's sake, be a little objective."

"Not eligible; simply; he says," she said bitterly.

Kalisher tried . . . "You have no idea, Mrs. Diamond, how all this pains me. You have disappointed me. You have hurt me."

She looked at plump Kalisher's face and saw all that professional social-worker's pain, that charitable sorrow. His breathless eagerness she also saw. She didn't believe his sorrow or his hurt; she believed his greed. There was nothing left. She would starve to death. They stood up, towering over her. She was between them and the kitchen door, standing in their way. "What are you going to do?" her dead voice asked them.

"Close your case, Mrs. D.," Miller told her.

"I'll die," she said.

Kalisher's lips were round and he shook his head. Miller looked over her head.

She had fought too long; she understood; it was final. "Don't go."

Kalisher tried to look out the window into the gray, drab yard, but had to look into the living room. He felt a soft tic in his mouth muscles. Miller uncapped his pen. They waited.

"All right," she screamed; "all right. Look. Do what you want with me. Make a fool of me. Look." The last wailing shriek, the sum, that final sum of the years of humiliation and deprivation came pouring out of her. "Look!" The word hung, wailing in the stillness. Her hands hung by her sides. She turned and went out. They followed her.

They went through the living room. The room was spotless, clean and unused. On the floor, flowers faded into an old Persian rug. Stained-wood shelves nailed to the walls held cheap little porcelains. The rose-colored wallpaint had long yellowed into sallow orange. A bronzed chandelier holding fake, pasteboard candles with flame-colored bulbs canted a little loose from the cracked, white ceiling. The flowered brocade covering the couch was unworn at the hand-rests. Old group-photographs hung on the walls in black frames; stiff, family figures, long lost, stood still, paled, as if the sunlight's fading fused figure and background into one. There was no dust anywhere; Miller tallied the hundred gimcrack vases, the glazed figurines, and saw that she had been able to afford these. Kalisher noted her compulsive neatness and knew she entombed some dead, traumatic moment here too.

The bedroom was dirtier; she lived here. A cheap chest of drawers stood against the wall. She showed them a closet holding a few frayed dresses. A gold-faced clock ticked. Another row of pictures, faded relatives, were lined up in front of the mirror on the chest. Kalisher picked up one of the pictures showing a young Mrs. Diamond standing next to a boy who towered over her. "Is this your son?" Kalisher asked. "My, how big . . ."

She snatched the picture out of his hand, wiped its glass on her housecoat, and put it into a pocket. "Torturing me isn't enough?" she screamed at him.

A double bed was against the door which, she had always maintained, led to a closet. A blue chenille spread covered the bed. A pair of cracked shoes stood underneath. Miller pushed the bed aside. It rolled, bumping on the uneven floor. The shoes were turned over and swept aside. He looked at the floor, trying to detect permanent scrape-marks which indicated Mrs. D. moved the bed back and forth frequently. There were no scrape-marks, but Miller couldn't be sure. They listened carefully, but only heard Mrs. D.'s sobbing. Kalisher could feel a little tightening of his throat. Miller thought of the computation . . .

She looked at them, standing, waiting for her. "So? Go ahead. Go," she told them. "Tear away my skin. Open my body." Kalisher watched Mrs. Diamond carefully to see how she was taking it. Politely, Miller stepped back, seemed to bow a little, and waved his hand, arcing his pen, almost courtly in his concern now, giving her a victor's magnanimous courtesy, restraining himself. Kalisher's rimless glasses were misted, hiding his eyes. But she folded her arms over her stomach. One hand was forever crooked into a clutch that plucked spastically at her elbow. She looked away, petulant, stubborn; her lower lip overlapped the unsupported upper lip.

"Go ahead, Mrs. D.," Miller told her.

She refused to answer. They could see a tear roll, break apart, and proliferate in the seams and wrinkles of her cheek, making one side of her face gleam. "Maybe we should come back tomorrow? I mean maybe you want time to think about it?" Kalisher stumbled. "I mean, she should have time," he almost shouted at Miller. "Well, I mean somehow it isn't right!" Miller pushed the door in. He looked. Kalisher's breath was at his ear.

"See," said she. "Treasures," she said.

The endless maw of her existence she filled by grasping. Against the day when she would be deprived, utterly, she collected. The little departmental pittance was on loan to her by a capricious God. She knew; because here they were, two messengers of that vengeful God, ready to snatch back everything from her. She delivered up the pains of accumulation: threads; scraps; ribbons. The room had never been lived in; it was reduced to a passageway between two banks. Old, frayed chinos, now washed and shining; damasks, double and single, she had piled to one side of the room and the other. Faded pants and chintzes, all neatly scrubbed and of rare value, were carefully folded. A bright swatch of flowered cloth, picked out in pinks, blues, and reds, was spread next to a meandering green nylon ribbon bubbling cool, like a tongue of liquid, shining brighter than the light that filtered in. Strips of material, carefully ripped from brocaded chairs and couches, she saved from rot. Cloths of gold, she had, and secret bolts of Eastern silks. No. There had never been any point to anything any of them had told her. They didn't understand. She knew better.

Miller recoiled and turned his back on the tumbled mess of cloths, cartons, the thick, choking welter of rags, the old smell of must and entombment, the fast dust-motes that danced in the heat-wavering sunlight, streaky from crusted windows half blocked. He wrinkled his nose at the fetid stench that fumed up from the shards of her diseased mind. He shuddered, smelling it, hearing the thick stillness; he tried to turn away from it quickly before he was contaminated. But he felt the perspiration break loose again and pour down his chest. He looked

64

away from that sickening sight of her soul, looked away from the pulsing festoons of dust hanging in the gloom. No welfare manual could account for it, no amount of planning and regimentation could straighten it out. The dust-rats stirred and came for him, and his skin itched unbearably. He felt, for one second, as though something had been opened inside of him; warped fingers warped his mind; her sickness, for one terrible second, was his sickness. He tried to make a notation in his notebook, but closed it.

Looking past him eagerly, Kalisher's face clouded over as he craned to see; stretching till he almost fell into the room. He tried to see if there could have been a burrow under the piles. He saw dirt; he had labored in vain. "Is that what you've been fighting us for for two hours? Really, Mrs. D." She had merely acquired. She had saved. Where he had expected warmth, he felt the chill from all the little items that, no doubt, she translated into funds. All the hours he had spent with her were meaningless. She had made him look stupid in Miller's eyes. She had fought for the leavings of strangers. He added two more hours to the debris. He turned and glared at the cold tear that silvered Mrs. D.'s avaricious cheek; she was laughing at him. He scolded, "You should clean up this mess. What if a fire breaks out?" Kalisher saw that her eyes were hard, bright, glittering dryly.

Past them she scrambled and closed the door. "You satisfied?" she asked them. "You satisfied you made a fool out of an old woman?"

"Just our duty, Mrs. Diamond," Miller tried to answer coolly. He made a notation in his case-book; a drop of sweat blotted the entry. Her distorted and demented face leered at him.

"Some duty, to torture a dying woman."

"We weren't torturing you, Mrs. Diamond," Miller sighed, "don't be dramatic."

"That stuff is a fire hazard. Get rid of it, Mrs. D.," Kalisher told her again.

She made a gnarled club out of her hands and waved them at Kalisher and Miller, laying blame on their heads. Her house-coat flapped open. "So who cares? I'm alone. There's nothing for me. There never was. What do you care? Let me burn." Her hard shrill voice rang out and she began to weep tears of joy and deliverance.

Kalisher and Miller looked at one another, embarrassed. "Mrs. D. . . ." Kalisher began.

"Oh, come on," Miller said, plucking Kalisher by the sleeve and leading him out.

On the stairs, Kalisher told Miller, "She's probably got money hidden there."

"You want to look for it?" Miller asked, walking down. "You still want to pick through that sickness? Go ahead," he said. He was half a flight ahead of Kalisher.

THE BEFORE AND AFTER OF
HYMIE FARBOTNIK, OR,
THE STICKING POINT

HYMIE Hero, the weight-lifter, had a bad dream. It was a hot August night. He dreamed he was assailed by forces of evil and sickness. They were making a ninety-seven-pound weakling out of him; they sweated him down. The light sheet over his body was unbearable; each fiber was woven out of steel and he could barely move under it. "Be a man," he said to himself; "be a hero in the privacy of your own home." He arrested the dissolution by falling into the pose that had won him Mr. Cropsey Avenue.

But then he ballooned. He thrashed under the cover as his three years of magic training and abstinence flowed out of him. He was lost. In monstrous pulsations he went from fat to thin, unable to stop at any point of bodily perfection until, a pasty thing, potbellied, pin-necked, his shameful body stopped changing.

But Hymie heard the clarion call of rescue. The bugle voice of his teacher, Artie Kleinsinger ("Reducing our specialty") sang, "All the great strength stars have known what it is to face discouragement when their muscles will not bulk-up any-more and their poses will not jell; when it seems as though they will never break through to the pure empyrean of muscle stardom. Everyone reaches their sticking point; all the greats have known despair, Hymie. It is then, when facing the mirror and the tapemeasure's truth, that the men are separated from the boys. There must be, within you, the will to be dedicated, to break through that sticking point, through the muscle-barrier of despair. *They* have persevered and won through. Why not *you?* Yours in health." It gave him hope. He woke.

It was still dark. The luminous hands of his bedside clock pointed to four-fifteen. His body was tense. He was covered with sweat, but he had been saved. The feeling that his body had been destroyed persisted. He got up. He turned on a little night light and looked in the mirror. He saw, dimly reflected there, that he had lost nothing after all; his whipcord biceps peaked to almost-championship size, his triceps were limned splendidly, his pectorals compressed magnificently, and he felt the blood flushing through his body again. He went back to sleep.

Hymie had to make his own breakfast every morning. "It's enough I have to look at you eating that. Should I feed you? I wash my hands of you, monster," his mother said and no longer cooked for him. His father sat at the table, drank poisonous coffee, smoked a lung-destroying cigarette and sweated in the heat, old before his time. Hymie heard his mother shuffling around in her bedroom. Godfood, Hymie ate: the juice of four oranges he hand-squeezed ("One of the best wrist exercises going, if you do it in strict form"); Neptunic protein-pills ("Like an invalid," his sarcastic father sneered) filled with seaweed and kelp essences; six eggs, soft-boiled, liberally sprinkled with wheat germ; and giant-forming fare ("What do you call that?" "Tiger's milk, Pa." "What goes into it?" the father asked. Hymie chanted a liturgy of tasty nutriments: "Whole milk, dried milk, yeast, blackstrap molasses, vitamin pills, high-protein pills, liquefied bananas, malted." "Wonderful," his father said. "And you mean to say that tigers drink this?"). Where is the hero honored? Hymie thought. Far from the home he must fare. Far from the father for love. His father looked into his cup; unable to take the strain of so much purity, he blew devastating clouds of cancer-causing smoke at Hymie.

The hero's mother wheezed in. She was fat, shapeless, waddling through the heat out of her bedroom's gloom. She poured herself a cup of coffee. She drooled condensed milk into it, put three spoonfuls of tooth-rotting sugar in. She sat down and folded her shapeless arms on the table in front of the cup, cradling it as though protecting it from the contamination of what Hymie consumed. Her beady eyes stabbed him. He couldn't bear to look at her decayed figure. "Should I ask where you're going today, monster?" She was using it like a name; it was a terrible thing to call your son, he thought; what did she want of him? His mind prepared a diatribe for her. "Mother, leave me alone," he said.

His father got up and went into the other room. "Where are you going?" she called after him. "That's right, run away."

"If I didn't run away and earn money, I wouldn't be able to afford your son's nectar."

"Awww . . . Father . . ." he called.

"That's right. Laugh," she said.

His father, buttoning his shirt with thin fingers, looked in for a second. "If I don't laugh, I have to cry. When has God seen such a reversal? This gem, this pride of Jewish Intellectual culture, a village strongman."

The thought of what they wanted of him, some skinny, cave-chested bookworm with eyes bent only on books, appalled him. Didn't they see what splendor they had before them? he wondered. He tried to see himself in the shine of the stove-gloss; the warped tin thinned his image. He didn't want what they wanted, he thought; was he really their son?

"Do something, you're his father."

Do something, Hymie thought, do something, Hymie hoped. He felt the hair prickling on the back of his thick neck and his shoulders bunched. He moved suddenly and almost spilled his precious glass of brown fluid.

"What can I do? He'll beat me up," he told his wife. "Doesn't strength give you any grace?" he asked his son.

Hymie couldn't understand why the sarcasm hurt him. Look at *him*, Hymie thought; a wide-behinded man knotting a tie. Hymie could knock him over in a second; one blow and . . .

"Laugh, always laugh."

His father shrugged his shoulders and went to work. Hymie went back to his room and put on his V-form T-shirt. It bore the imprimatur of the Hercules Health Club (Artie Kleinsinger, Chirop., Prop.; "Bring in the body, we'll do the rest"), a weight-lifter atlasing the world triumphantly aloft in a military press. He wore tight chino pants and walked with a stately step. Destiny was written on his body. He saw himself pass in all the reflecting surfaces. His arms were held rigidly, bringing out the muscles. Proud and strong, he proceeded; nobly was his waist sucked in, a demigod faring forth. His mother conjured into her cup, telling it, "Look at him, look what I have to endure." She seemed to listen to what the cup's muddy mouth told her. "Freak," she said. "Circus man. Baby's mind in a man's body!" She said it every day. Away from this witch's wailing, moving from his mother's madness, Hymie went. "An arm as thick as a leg. Freak!" came muffling through the door.

Alone in the hall, he straightened up and started to pose. The act shook off the pain of their ignorant insults. He thought he heard spy-holes in the doors click open and he stopped. He heard the iron clang of number nine's door. He jumped and hoped he hadn't been seen. A raveled nymph in a pink house-coat, the neighbor (he sometimes helped with packages and fled) smiled. Her hands held garbage. She had morning-white skin and hair too red to be real. Her pasty hands were rough but, beringed, glinted against the brown, grease-stained paper like icing on flaky pastry. Through the soft material of her housecoat, Hymie could see the sad droop of her unfettered breasts flanking the crackling bag; he looked away. Hymie couldn't help remembering his mother's insinuations and his father's: "You should learn a little from her. After all, she's your age."

"Hymie darling," she said. "How wonderful you look. So pure." The blood surged through his body and came to the surface suffusing his whole skin. Her smile was slightly gapped; he thought she mocked. "My goodness, Hymie, you're becoming like an Adonis, aren't you?" she cooed. "Hold open the incinerator door for me." Her eye held him; he thought that perhaps she might admire him. He looked at her and held the door open. She pushed the garbage bag in, brushing past him. Clearly, his keen eye saw her neck; it was wrinkled and its skin a little freckled. Her red hair was speckled with touches of paler red at the roots; there were gray flecks tangled there. But the shaming young flash of her white teeth and the painted red rim of her glistening lip made his chest swell up to its full forty-eight inches. The world-lifter was stretched and became a squatty lump holding a marble. The odor of her hung there: cigarette smoke, ashes, orange-rinds, sweat, stale perfume, impure but disturbing. He blushed again and his chest deflated to forty-four; the globe-grasper became reedy, too thin for the world he hefted.

Hymie left, feeling her amused eyes on his back where a stain of sweat revealed that his dedication had not yet burned away his unnecessary humanity. "Are you going to the beach on such a hot day?" her hoarse voice questioned him. "No," he told the hot stairwell, "I'm going to the gym." "My, what dedication. A regular Adonis," her voice whispered. Through the walls he could hear the flames roaring up and consuming the garbage. He left her and thought he glimpsed, over his shoulder, that imperfect smile hover—mocking or approving, he didn't know which—far above him in the hall's gloom.

Through the heat he wandered, far from home he roamed. To Artie Kleinsinger's Hercules Health Club he came. He eschewed the chain gyms; they had girls and distracting chromed weights and were for dilettantes. "LOSE WEIGHT!" a sign admonished over the door. Artie Kleinsinger, shaper of heroes, maker of men, purveyor of the Mr. American Dream, told him, "It's good to see you working out today, Hymie. It shows real devotion." Hymie felt proud. Most of the regulars had held on till the first heat wave: Mingo (who once did a six-thousand-sit-up penance), and Pulver (who worked for the time—he already tore apart a telephone book every day—when he could pound nails and bend dimes with his bare hands), and he had worked through the worst of it. But he had been alone for two days now. He felt lonely. He hoped they came.

The first clink of the weight sliding onto the bar soothed Hymie. In the dusty stillness, poising before the mirror, he was free to daydream, to see himself clearly at last. Squatting, back bent over the bar, brooding, almost eyeless like Greek statues, he concentrated. He heard the stillness, and then nothing at all. He felt the skin on his body twitch; he inhaled deeply with short, sharp inspirations; he felt, first the lungs, then the body, then the arms, then the fingers, then the skin filling and flushing with blood. The mirrored body tensed. Arms that hauled rails, back that knotted and bent in the pulling, shoulders that swung the sledgehammers onto spikes, heroes that made America, all, heaved the weight onto his chest. A grunt of stale air exploded out of his mouth. In the mirror, muscles stood out, massive arms that had squeezed opponents to death, arms that clutched the whole world, heaved aloft the simple enemy: the weight. And yet those vein-vined arms were graceful enough to be donatello-ed onto any statue, he thought. Hymie felt full satisfaction in the dusty quiet as strength resolved all problems now.

Artie Kleinsinger, eater of fish, watercress, sunflower and psyllium seeds, the quaffer of raw honey and rose-hip tea ("Never never never meat!"), bustled through from the massage room to the steam room bearing towels and sheets over his still-massive arm. He told Hymie, in a voice full of nasal wisdom, "You've made genuine progress, Hymie, in these past four weeks. Keep this up and, God willing, who knows?" Hymie felt the full satisfaction of deeds done and deeds appreciated. And after all, Artie Kleinsinger had himself developed from a despised, asthmatic weakling into this muscular mentor who had held the American bent-press record for four consecutive days of unparalleled heroism. Who else could understand? Hymie wondered. He thought of a witch's face, red hair, a soft body, far gone in decay beneath the housecoat, the smile that may have mocked, may have pitied . . . could she understand? He dismissed her eyes and looked at himself in the mirror over which was tacked the exhortation to "GAIN WEIGHT!" He appraised carefully, expertly, each minute part of his body to see what effort had wrought, what minuscule progresses he had made pumping his muscles up to glory.

He worked for two hours. No one else came. He had been deserted by his fellow heroes. He felt betrayed. They were at the beach—he knew it—glorying it. Willing to dispense with discipline, they would be stuck into immortal poses, tanned and oiled, bronzed on the white sands, burned against the blue sea, luring on, in spite of their professions of scorn, all the high-school naiads. It was the third day now that they pursued their false vision. It was hard working alone in the dusty heat, urged on only by the beckoning vision in the mirror. He heard his heart pump revivifying blood around his system. He heard the clink of the irons on the mats, the slap of his wet palms on the steel bars, and watched his figure, slick with sweat, ripple through the stillness.

At twelve the flabby men who paid service to the steam room came in. They permitted their aged flesh to be pounded, kneaded, and adjusted by Artie Kleinsinger. Hymie, with his buddies, cross-eyed Mingo and Pulver, could withstand the covetous glares of the old ones. Like statues washed in sweat, but cool, aloof, as made of bronze or gold or copper, they barred old men from their companionship forever. But alone, unprotected, Hymie felt clumsy and awkward. Artie Klein-singer's clients ("Prominent civic leaders; leading businessmen in the community") were men with illusions of youth. They skipped rope a few times on their spindly legs, or did ten minutes of wheezing calisthenics, or punched feebly at the light bag and, unable to maintain rhythm, gave it up to vindictively maul the heavy bag. They groaned in travail on the medicine ball or took an aching ride to nowhere on the stationary bicycle. A paltry old man, seeing Hymie unpro-tected, told him that when he was young, he had been strong too; natural strength, none of your artificial stuff, of course. Had he been young, Hymie wondered; did they all come to that? The mirror told him that he must work harder to im-mortalize himself. He felt the old man looking greedily at him. He dreamed of shapes not dreamed of by the makers of old statues. After all, he thought, now science served to make men of grosser blood. He saw, like a ghost of promise, the real self behind the streaky illusion; it had thick, gladiatorial pecs, life-guard wide shoulders, coconut delts, elephantine traps, barn-door lats, chiseled abs, tree-trunk thighs, and melony calves. It would be a final apotheosis. But he couldn't concentrate; wheezes drove everything out of his head, stares made him feel silly, and he couldn't get the full benefit of his workout. When he found he couldn't even handle his usual weights, he quit.

In the steam room they sat like Roman senators. White sheets were tucked under their flabby armpits and held against their bodies by flaccid arms. They were bent over, cackling with mysterious laughter, dim oracles who talked in whispers of women and money. Why did they make him feel inferior? he wondered. He was stronger. It wasn't because they were older. Artie was older. Artie didn't make him feel inferior. In an effort to escape air thick with steam and cigar smoke, he rushed his shower, going from lukewarm to icy too fast. He was not refreshed and began to sweat while he dressed because he had too much energy left over. When Hymie was dressed, he tried to talk to Artie about some special exercises calculated to make massive forearms. But Artie was servilely "sirring" some old man in a shiny black suit; Artie brushed Hymie brusquely off.

The western sky was piled with thunderhead clouds held away by an invisible rampart of air. Lost, Hymie wandered in the hot streets, not knowing what to do. He met the maenad of number nine. She wore a white, sleeveless, low-necked dress and looked cool. She struggled with a shopping bag but did not perspire. Under the white, her breasts were lifted now; she wore dark stockings and white spike-heeled shoes. Her hair was bright and unremitting red now, bound with a blue bandanna knotted on the nape of her neck. The limp blue ends lay against the red of her hair and on the white skin of her shoulder. "Hymie, help me," her hoarse voice implored. Sweating, he wondered by what magic she managed to stay so cool, how she managed to seem younger in the blazing light which should have exposed her corruption. She talked about the great louts who would no longer help a lady and what a gentleman, what a special gentleman Hymie was . . . did he know that? she asked.

She walked up the stairs ahead of him; her ankles were thin and taut; her calves were still surprisingly good. As she climbed her monologue became softly punctuated by pantings.

She said, at the top of the stairs, "I used to be able to run up without stopping. What happens to us, Hymie?" On the landing she moved ahead of him in the dimness, somehow mysteriously and vaguely seen in the hall's twilight. Hymie followed after, walking past his own door, past the incinerator, as if he didn't know his own floor. If his mother caught him carrying groceries for her, she wouldn't stop giving him hell for months. She stopped suddenly and fiddled for her key. He came up behind her and bumped into her. The bag nudged her. She giggled. She smelled only of perfume now.

Her apartment was cool and dim. The hot outdoor light beat against, but was stopped by, bars of shadow. He heard the perpetual whirr of a fan going and there was something comforting about the sound of it. The television lit up the darkened living room. "What do you know," her hoarse voice said, "I forgot to shut it off. Bring the bag into the kitchen. That's a darling, Hymie." The television was showing some interminable ladies' program that ran from morning to afternoon. The women were giggling; a soft-faced man was laughing, cooing questions and awarding prizes.

Her throaty murmur filled the little kitchen and drowned the squealing sound of the television and the tap of the faucets dripping. The kitchen was laid out like his mother's, but somehow her voice made it all seem different. He became unsure of distances and was clumsy. She confronted him with a cigarette. He shook his head and told her, smugly, that he never smoked.

"On account of training, you mean, Hymie?" She smiled at him. "I wish my husband Sam were like that. He used to be a fine, strong boy, but he let himself go all to pot. Cigars. Could I offer you a drink, maybe?" He had visions of gin and tonic. He imagined it cool to taste, sophisticated to hold; he

77

could almost hear the clink of ice and the fizz of soda water, the way he had seen it on television. Nevertheless, he told her that he never drank. She smiled and said, "Not even water?" He tried to laugh easily and blushed; his voice was high and tinkly. She said, "A little ice cream? There's some in the freezer. I'm always prepared for the heat with a little ice cream." She brushed past him. Her body pinned him. He felt soft surfaces beneath the hard cool white of her dress envelop him and hold him as she reached past him into the refrigerator. He said, "No. No thanks. Ice cream is fattening." She said, "Then maybe milk? A drop milk?" "Milk I might," he said and sat down suddenly at her table. A burst of laughter came in, shrilling high and clear from the television in the other room; a cowbell clattered and a buzzer razzed. A clean glass passed over his shoulder. Her arm flickered past his eye. The inside flesh was soft, milky, out of condition; it almost touched his cheek. He reared back a little and felt stabbed in the back by softness; he leaned away and the table stopped him. She came around and sat down opposite him. Her burning lips circled the cool spoon and sucked strawberry ice cream. As she leaned forward, he could see the flesh of her bosom underneath the loose skin of her dress, white as vanilla, round as dumbbells.

He spilled a little milk; he felt a rim of milk around his upper lip. She said, "My, you look so fine and muscular, like a regular statue, Hymie. I bet the girls are all crazy for you. I remember you were a skinny, snotty kid and now, practically overnight . . ." And now he was a weight-trained, vitamin-filled, power-packed man, Hymie thought. "What happens to us?" she asked. Hymie didn't know what she meant. "More milk?" she asked. He shook his head but she got up anyway

78

and poured for him. She leaned against his back. "Don't be bash-ful. Drink. Drink," she breathed in his ear. The milk churned inside of him and chilled him. "Seriously, Hymie," she sighed, "we get old and our bodies go to pot. We get our little pots," she giggled and patted her round little pot. It was terrible, Hymie thought, the way her stomach jiggled, the way she had no muscle-tone at all, the way she had let herself go to . . . Her red tongue was paled to strawberry.

They went into the living room and sat on the couch. Halt-ingly, he started to expound the Message to her. He forgot his embarrassment as he talked. He explained the muscles and their functions; she nodded wisely. Her eyes were gray and young, her hands pale against the maroon brocade of the couch, and her dress rustled on the smooth cloth. The television set was bright in the darkness of the living room. The ladies were still there, filling the audience indefatigably; the master of ceremo-nies hopped up and down. Now and then, he called some woman up to the stage. The woman always came tripping up, mouth always open in a crazy grin of delight. The ladies in the audience went a little wilder and shrieked and laughed. Hymie preached the firm body, the clean ways of life, the dedication, the purity; he damned old age, the letting of one-self slip into a flabby senescence; he envisioned a world of clean, hard limbs, muscular thighs, great, bulging backs. And for Titanic men, he wanted women as clean, slim, and hard as statues too. She nodded understandingly as her eyes flickered from him to the television and back, and not once did she say, "When you get older . . ." He damned the soft, raddled flesh that preludes that sinking, the disappearance of youth. A woman bore off a prize. "It's very interesting, what you say, Hymie. One can see that you've given thought to it, deep thought. You know so much. It surprises me how mature you are, did you know that, Hymie? You're very mature," she said. He blushed; he could feel his latissimus muscles flutter under his arms, the spinae erectors in his back bunch with pleasure, and the intercostal muscles interfered with his breathing. "Whew, it's hot," she said and wiped her face with a handkerchief. She pulled the dress away from her bosom and dabbed the cloth to the top of her breasts delicately. "Do you suppose, Hymie, that exercise would help me? I mean, isn't it too late? Don't you think I'm just an old bag?" she laughed. His calves flexed and unflexed in uncontrollable reflex.

Hymie could hear the nasal, reasonable voice of Artie Kleinsinger saying, "Many people come to me saying, 'Isn't it too late?'" "No," Hymie told her, "but it needs a lot of work. Diet. Devotion."

"But don't you run to fat when you stop?"

"Why stop? Why ever stop?" he asked her.

"You're so serious, Hymie. A boy your age shouldn't be so serious." She stood up and posed in the middle of the room, on the rug, hands on hips, saying, "Well, tell me the worst. Where do I need it off?" She sucked in her waist and thrust out her chest and turned slowly. "I mean, as an expert." She slapped her hip. "Don't be afraid to tell me. Be scientific . . ." She squeezed her thigh.

She was closer; he could see her belly and the soft indentation of her navel through the white cloth. He heard the master of ceremonies yelling something about the grand prize. The buzzer sounded. The cowbell rang. He jumped up and away from her shouting, "Look. Look." He posed, tightening each muscle, making of his trapezius a protecting carapace. "You can be like this." Their applause came out of the screen like a pattering drumbeat, gaining in power and strength. Their silly cries of joy seemed like a thousand wild shrieks. She was closer and telling to see, to feel, that underneath time's riddled thigh-flesh there was strength, that the softness of buttocks were not meant to be hard, and didn't he think that hardness hindered? Think of a tough thigh, a stringy behind, a muscular breast, and a hard lip on a woman. He thought of it and washboarded his abdominals into an immortal, prize-winning corrugation. He imagined himself lifting a little more than he had ever lifted, a new personal record, going, for the first time since the beginning of the hot spell, past his sticking point. The wild shrieks of the women increased; the grand prize had been brought on stage; the orchestra and syrupy organ were sentimentalizing it wildly; the master of ceremonies was hopping up and down excitedly. Her skirt rustled up as she demonstrated a dark-stockinged, white-thighed leg. "Is that really so bad, Hymie?" He felt her breath on his cheek. An aimless stab of light showed bleached hairs above her soft lip. His calves crackled, his knees trembled, his thighs bowed, his whole body strained one more time. He assumed a special pose: head thrown back, arm, fingers clenched, reaching for the sun like a prayer, like a worshipping, like a flashing Praxiteles evocation. His ears were filled with the orchestra music's roaring and those shrieks mounting and the pattering of feet and drumbeats. "My, what muscles," her soft, hoarse voice whispered. He made his last stand. Speaker squealed, screamed, and shrieked, and those mad women bore down on him as if they were coming out of the screen to tear him apart. He turned and ran out.

The summer's heat had broken at last. Naked, he lay on his bed and felt cool in the rain-wet breeze that came in through his window. He could hear, far off, the thunder rumbling as it receded. He got up. He felt weak, as though he had been through a very heavy workout. He saw himself in the mirror. He could almost see dissolution setting in; each muscle didn't quite stand out as clearly as it had; age was smudging his chiseled perfections; he might look like his father. He started to flex his arm and stopped.

He put a towel around his middle and went into the kitchen to get a drink of Tiger's milk. As he opened the refrigerator, he saw a pack of his mother's cigarettes on top. He closed the refrigerator and took one of the cigarettes and the matches and went back to his room.

He lit a cigarette and watched fat, lazy curls of smoke hover over his head and rise sweetly till the breeze caught and dissolved them. He looked into the mirror again. He made a wise face at himself. He lifted one eyebrow and one corner of his mouth and his eyes narrowed knowingly. He turned his head to see his profile. He smiled at himself, understandingly, and, world-weary, he sighed. His mother was watching television in the other room. He could hear the silly gabble of those silly females scrambling for their silly prizes. He tried to make a muscle. He couldn't. He didn't have the strength. He didn't much care.

THE PASSAGE

THE young man stops on the way to the subway and says they should take a taxi. His wife looks at him and tosses her head; the raindrops spatter off her hair and her wet face flashes through the lamplight. He tells her they can afford it. She says she hasn't objected. The young man smiles and says it isn't every day his mother dies. Her fingers tighten into the black slick of his raincoat and she looks at him anxiously. He asks her if she is all right. She says she is fine—numb and floating a little—but fine; he shouldn't talk like that. He wants to know why not, because dead is dead and leave it at that and it is really better, considering; and he begins to whistle at the cabs going by.

Five empty taxis cruise by, hissing on the slick asphalt. The sixth stops, but the driver says that he can't be expected to drive all the way from Brooklyn to the Bronx, not on a night like this, can he? The young man shakes his head and says no, not really; he steps back on the curb under the tree where he waits with his wife. Her forehead is frown-cloven, as if she is concentrating. He strokes her back. She smiles at him and takes his arm and leans against him. The next cab stops. They get in and say they want to go to the Bronx. "Why not?" the cab-driver says, and starts off. "A lot of drivers wouldn't take you out to the sticks, not on a night like this; but I say, why not? It's money. I mean there's no traffic on a night like this, not this late anyway. Why not? I have to say you're a long way from home."

The young man tells him that they live here, in Brooklyn.

The driver turns half-around and says, "It's none of my business, but what are you going all the way up there for at one in the morning?"

The young man says that his mother has just died; his wife squeezes his sleeve again: her cheeks bunch up, drawing her upper lip up, and her teeth shine moistly . . . and the young man whispers to her, asking her again if she is all right.

The driver, twisted more toward them, drives down the broad, empty street, beside all the black-doored stores and empty, tin-patched houses. He says, "Listen, I'm sorry to hear that. I didn't mean anything by asking. I mean . . . I've had so many losses myself, so I know how . . . Listen . . . how old was she?"

The young man says that his mother was sixty-five. He sees the brightly illuminated identification card which says Sam Ferkauf. The meter clicks. The tires slide on the rain-slick. The motor is missing and the pistons make a putt-putt sound.

"That's terrible. You have to bear it. Listen: she was a good woman; she worked hard all her life; she led a full life; may she rest in peace." And seeming to think he is not heard above the sound of the motor, leans over sideways and says, louder, " . . . in peace." He sits up straight again and shakes his head.

The young man looks at his wife; she stares at the back of the driver's head; her face relaxes a little.

The driver breathes deeply and sighs noisily. The young man sees the driver's eyes, wide-eyeballed and staring, floating in darkness, flicking back and forth out of the frame of the rear-view mirror. The cab tosses over the boards they have laid down over the subway reconstruction on lower Flatbush Avenue and the tires barely grip. The driver keeps his eyes on the road now. He leans his head back, tilting it a little as if listening. They say nothing. They are over the boards now, driving past the darkened theater marquees. They run past a few lots, a few public buildings, under an elevated-train structure on which a huge sign shows perpetual daylight in which a man and a woman, one behind the other lying propped up on their elbows, smirk broadly over a vase-glass of beer. The driver takes in a huge breath of air and sighs again, this time louder. The young man watches his wife; he sees her dare to glance at him out of the side of her eye, but not move her head.

The young man slumps down, puts his feet up against the back of the driver's seat, and stares out of the window; his eyes are level with the lower ledge; he stares at lights blurring in the shimmering raindrops. The driver starts to sigh a third time but, as he begins his ascent over the Manhattan Bridge, says, "Listen. We all have to go. She led a good life. She had a full life, you know what I mean. Were there any more children?"

The young man looks at the back of the man's head, fiercely limned in the approaching bridge-lights. The motor putts louder as the car crests and the driver half-turns his face and asks, louder, ". . . children?"

The young man remembers and says no.

". . . father alive?"

The young man thinks for a second and, before the driver can repeat the question, says yes.

"At least you're not alone. A family is very important at a time like this. Still . . . sixty-five . . . still. Listen, we all have to . . . That's not so bad. But what can you think when a kid dies, nine years old? I mean he's seen nothing of life at all. Oh, I have three more. I have a house out on the Island. A good wife, couldn't ask for better. My mother, bless her, she's seventy-five and with all her teeth, would you believe it? But a thing like that makes you think. I mean in your time, like your mother— it's sad—but nine years old . . . ." The metal-grill surface of the Manhattan Bridge, always unsure, is now wet and more unsure, making the cab undulate from side to side. The driver leans over the wheel: his hands clench hard: his head is thrust forward and his long thin neck juts far out from his round, hunched shoulders. When the car is in control, the driver's head turns a little more to the back so that it looks like his head is resting on the wheel. "I mean go explain it. What did she die of?"

The man tells the driver that his mother died of cancer.

"God rest her soul. That's terrible. It's fate. But what do you think of a nine-year-old boy killed by a drunken driver?"

The young man starts to say it is terrible. The driver says, "I mean you have to think there's just no justice in this world. You have to think a thing like that."

They catch up to a slow-driving truck ahead of them and fall behind the row of red warning-lights bobbing and mounting to the bridge's apogee. "They shouldn't allow these scows on the bridge." He turns a little more. "He was nine years old. He was so bright I couldn't understand him half the time myself. I wish now I had. We got the house on the Island with the insurance money from the accident. I mean I have to work a little extra to keep up the mortgage . . . you don't want the place to look like a sty, do you? But at least the other kids won't get run down now." He shakes his head. They are descending now.

"He was very bright; I couldn't tell you how bright he was." The driver turns around, looks at them, and turns back to look at the receding bank of red lights. To the side of them, whisked in and out behind the pillars, girders, and cables, the massive wall of downtown lights always flares gaily. "At first we thought he was retarded . . . he didn't talk for the first three years . . . you know what I mean. Well, my wife and I, we thought it was God's curse. I admit I wanted to get rid of him. I admit it." The light, shining through the windshield wiper's wash, throws streaky shadows on the driver's cheeks. The young man looks from the rain-fractured window to the driver and shakes his head mechanically. ". . . admit it," the driver says, louder, and his voice mixes with the engine's imperfect sound. The young man sits up a little straighter and his head shakes three or four times more vigorously.

The taxi skids slightly and the driver's hands adjust automatically. "I always said they should concretize the surface here. You could get killed. Then, one day, he was three and a half, mind you, three and a half, and he begins to talk like he was twenty, like he had done nothing but talk: but brilliant. Whole sentences. Some kids are like that, you know?" and he turns around. The young man and his wife nod together. He reaches in the dark for her hand. She finds his. They squeeze hands. She takes her hand away, reaches into his raincoat, and takes out a pack of cigarettes, starts to put the matches away in her own pocket, remembers, and gives them back. Now they are both looking at the driver and try not to look at one another.

They come off the bridge and the car turns eastward in order to get onto the East River Drive. The driver is talking and the young man and his wife nod and say yes from time to time.

"He knew," the driver says and comes close to sideswiping a car. "He knew," and his voice breaks a little. The young man and his wife shake their heads. The driver corners violently; the taxi pitches and yaws and the meter clicks for every turn. It seems almost as if they are headed back the way they came. The young man looks out the window. The driver leans his head back and says, out of the side of his mouth, "You have to navigate it right. You get to know an awful lot. Miss the lights this way. Driving twenty years." The young man nods and continues to look at the hollow black apartment windows through the raindrops.

The taxi heels over and rocks them together and he sees her face; it is tight again; her frown is back. He asks her how she feels. She tells him she feels nothing.

The driver hears this. "You just have to carry on. I know. I've been through it many times. The things I could tell you . . ."

The young man supposes yes, there are a lot of things the driver could tell him, what with having driven a cab so long. . . . "You hear all kinds of stories, but the strangest always happens to you, I say," the driver says. They curve swiftly up and round a long, semicircular ramp and then descend suddenly in a long swoop. At the bottom they run through a sheet of water which sprays up and splatters the side windows in the back. The couple draw back from it even though the windows are closed. "Listen," the driver says; "my kid, he was bright; almost a genius, you know what I mean." The young man starts to yawn and it is stifled by the driver saying, "All right, he had one arm shorter than the other and only three fingers came out on that hand. But you didn't notice that after a few minutes because he had a smile could break your heart. He could have been anything; a lawyer, a doctor, an atomic scientist . . . anything."

And they are on the drive, going north now, beside the East River. The motor is loud again. ". . . anything," the driver yells. Dim ship shadows float down the river. The reflection of a barge, heaped high with broken automobile bodies, is pulled slowly against the downriver ripples. Across the river, far away, the lights of Brooklyn and Queens flicker. The raincloud bank does not extend all the way across the river. On the other shore the air is clear and moonlight stains rooftops and spires shades of blue-silver. The great Domino Sugar sign flashes yellow reflections in the water and towers recede sedately through that light-filled air. The couple stare across the river at the peaceful night. "I mean there are more things . . . they don't know everything, you know," the driver says.

The young man says that is very true, that they don't know everything. His wife looks at him. He knows she is looking at him, but continues to look out the window.

The driver says, "Listen. Explain this. I had a sister, God rest her soul. She had one kidney. You know how it is with one kidney?"

The young man says that of course you have to be very careful with only one kidney.

"She loved him. It was as if it were her own child. It almost broke her heart when he was killed. She always loved him . . . from the first. She used to say, 'Sam, you don't know what you have in this child.' Well, she got sick with a kidney ailment and had to go to the hospital. She was there for a year. She almost died, I don't know how many times. Then she got better." The driver half turns around now. The taxi begins to edge from the right side of the road to the center as if his hands on the wheel overcompensate for possible drift. "She's on the step of the hospital. She's shaking the doctor's hand good-bye. She keels over, falls into his arms and never comes out of the coma. Go explain it."

The young man sighs and says it is inexplicable.

"I ask the doctor, how come? He says, what can I tell you?"

The young man says who knows. The driver turns back, sees that he is almost on the center divider and veers, almost ramming another car. They curse one another. The other voice, a distant yelp, floats to them through the window, dim, vituperative, wavering. They pass under a foot-bridge and are silent for a while. Riding lights run past in the water.

"Things turn out funny, you know what I mean? You plan. You plan, but it happens another way. Cancer? I'm very sorry to hear it. Did she suffer?"

The young man says that his mother didn't suffer too much. His wife looks at him and understands that he is sparing the driver because his mother had suffered a great deal.

"It's better this way. It can be a blessing. For all they know ... they don't have all the answers ... they can only shrug their shoulders and say, let's wait and see. I went to the biggest doctors. They couldn't do a thing for my kid's arm. Well, you can't complain. You know, he always wanted a house in the country, as he used to call it. And that it should have swings in the back. You want to know something; when we got the insurance money, we decided, my wife and I, all right, let's get out of the city: let's buy a house. All right, it has a mortgage and I work extra but at least there are no drunken drivers to kill innocent children. You have children?"

The wife says they have no children.

"Well, you're young yet. You'll see. They can be a blessing and a curse. We went out on the Island and looked around and one day we see this house. It's not too expensive. It's big enough. It's in a good neighborhood. We fell in love with it. We're set on buying. We look in the back."

The young man sits up a little and says he is sure it has swings in the back.

The driver turns around, almost three quarters full round. His right arm is along the back of his seat and he tacks excitedly through the puddles as he drives with his left hand. "Clairvoyant. Yes. Go explain it."

The young man says please, drive carefully and that there are more things . . . and he couldn't begin to explain it. His wife nudges him. The young man sits up a little higher and tries to see the photograph on the driver's identification card, but the taxi is running in a long curve, going up the bridge to the Bronx, and the young man is leaned away toward his wife and can't see too clearly. He has an impression of a plump-faced man wearing a cap. "They don't have all the answers," the driver says.

"You never know how it comes, or when it comes, but when it comes it comes."

The young man says that it is certainly true; he says he had a friend who was only thirty-five, or six, or four, who died of a massive heart-failure, arteriosclerosis, now who would have thought that a man so young . . .

"You never know," the driver says.

No, the young man agrees, you can't explain it. His wife nudges him and says that it is very true. They are speeding under an arcade of lights into the Bronx. Far beneath them the light reflections bob.

"I mean he used to say the craziest things. I wish I'd understood him. One day he tells me he's not like the others. I thought he was being sensitive, you know, and I disagreed with him. And he tells me no, not on account of the arm, or the leg, or his eyes, but *different*. I asked him how. He said to me, 'Don't you see it, Daddy?' Just like that; 'Don't you see it, Daddy?' My sister, she knew."

The young man's wife says that the good always . . . The young man glances at his wife. Her face is calmer; she bites on her upper lip. And so he tells a story of someone else he knew who has died, someone young and full of promise. He makes the case much more interesting than it was. His wife nods and keeps saying yes, yes, and adds a story of her own. The driver keeps shaking his head. They are off the bridge and down in the Bronx and the driver sails around the bends; the meter clicks and the young man, who knows the way, wonders if the driver is just trying to lengthen the trip: he has never gone this way.

The driver interrupts, "Oh, I've been to my minister; I've had psychiatrists and doctors in my cab, intelligent people. I've asked them, how come? I mean your mother, God rest . . . she lived her full . . . three score and five. But a child of nine. A gifted child . . ." And the cab wavers a little and, since it has drifted to the wrong side of the road, the driver beats around a turn, drives up a wrong-way street, turns again, and is on a broad highway going the wrong way. He says, "You'll have to pardon me. I remembered," and he drives off the highway, turns a few times, and is back on the other side of the highway, going the right way.

The young man says to be careful, or . . .

"That would be funny," the driver says and shakes his head. The man's wife tells of the death of an uncle. The driver remembers funerals of prominent people and discusses the size of corteges. He is off the highway and is going along small, dark, side streets. The meter ticks again. They are all talking excitedly now, caught up in the exchange of stories, each of them discussing the wonders of death, unable to stop. The driver turns a few more times. The young man knows now that he is being cheated, but wonders if he should say something about it. They keep exchanging reminiscences. The car keeps veering wildly and they almost crash a few times. The man and his wife grin at one another when the driver isn't looking at them and continue to tell stories. After a long while they have nothing to say to one another. They lean back, exhausted, silent, somehow satisfied.

It has stopped raining. The taxi drives along a last stretch of drying highway. The driver says, sleepily, "Go, explain it," and stifles a yawn.

The young man says he cannot. They are silent for ten minutes.

The driver yawns. They drive through the moonlit night. They drive over and under rows of lights. Overhead, the sky no longer reflects the city lights. The driver yawns and cannot stop yawning. He says, "These night jobs get you. If it weren't for the mortgage, believe me . . ." The couple sit there, holding hands. She asks him how he feels. The young man says he feels nothing at all. They drive off the highway and down a few streets till they are in front of his mother's house. The young man gets out, helps his wife out, turns, looks up at his mother's building and sees that there are lights in her window. He turns to pay the driver who is leaning across his seat to the window. The price is much too high, the young man knows that the meter has been run at least a dollar too high. He wonders if he should say something. He decides not to because his mother has died and it is not much money and it seems not proper. But he decides not to tip, to let the driver understand that he has been taken.

The driver's face is at the window. He needs a shave. His thick black stubble leaves a circle of white flesh and the white lips are barely visible; his eyes are distended with the strain of his position. He says, "Did you notice; not one stoplight. Not one. I'm sorry for your loss . . . may she . . . My kid, he said that day, 'I don't want to go down and play.' My wife and I, we look at him and say, 'What do you mean, you don't want to go down and play?' He says, 'Just that. I got a feeling.' Clairvoyant, you know? We say, 'What kind of feeling?' He says, 'A feeling.' I say, 'Don't give me foolishness; go down and play.' He says, 'I don't want to.' My wife says, 'What's the matter with you? You sick?' He says, 'I don't feel right about it.' We say, 'What's wrong?' He says, 'Nothing. Nothing, but I shouldn't go down.' 'What kind of talk is that?' we ask. Listen. He shrugs his shoulders and says nothing and I say, 'You want a beating? Go down and play.' 'All right,' he says, 'but I'll see you sometimes.' I say, 'What do you mean by that?' And he says, 'Nothing, nothing at all, but I'll see you sometimes, Daddy.' 'Listen,' I tell him. 'Get the hell out of here.' You see," the driver says, "he knew. Clairvoyant."

The young man says, "Go explain it." The driver's face and hand are at the window. The man gives him his full price and adds a dollar tip to it. The driver says something about being sorry for . . . and drives away.

They stand there for a moment. She says, "You shouldn't have," and begins to laugh and laugh. A long way off a dog barks. The young man says, "The bastard," and begins to weep for his dead mother.

94

THE BIRD-WHISTLE MAN

ONE warm May Sunday, strollers in the park were startled to hear the singing of fantastic birds. The birdcalls sounded familiar but no one could imagine where such birdcalls had been heard before: certainly not in the Jersey Marshes or the Catskills, and they were unknown to the Connecticut shoreline. The birdcalls were rich and tropical and had an almost echoey sound, as though sung in hothouses. After a long while of neck-craning, eye-squinting, or forced, casual sophistication, everyone discovered that a smiling man—he had flesh pouched around his anxious eyes and gray hair—was making the sounds. After another ten minutes of admiration, they accepted the ribald, musical jungle cries as they accepted the insane plumage of the beats, the fluttering rags of the bums, the folk-song *jongleurs,* and the Italian street singers: they moved on and didn't notice.

The whistler had been a civil servant, an elevator operator in the Municipal Building, who had come to the age of retirement. In these times of plenty he was lucky to have a pension and so didn't have to worry or get another job. True, the pension was small, but then his mother, with whom he lived, had money from a candy-store and rents from a few apartment houses: she gave him spending money. Since he lived at home and paid his mother a nominal sum for food and rent, he could live within his budget. The problem was boredom. The elevator operator was intelligent and knew that when the time came for him to retire, he would have to have a hobby, or he would go quite mad. As it was, he went to the movies; he read three newspapers a day; he visited relatives in Brooklyn once a week; he went to the neighborhood coffee houses; he sat in the park and watched people go by. But there was a limit to how much time he could spend in the coffee houses, and since his stories were all bureaucratic and institutional, and he knew nothing of women—it disturbed him to hear such stories, no matter how humorously, how triumphantly told—he had the sense to know that he would bore the coffee drinkers.

At first he thought he might take up an instrument: the accordion, for instance. But his right wrist had been made too stiff by gripping the ascent-descent lever and his left hand was clawed from pulling back the folding iron gate, which had not been oiled in the twenty years he had been on the job. Not being mechanically or electrically minded, there was no hobby along that line he could enjoy.

One Sunday, before his retirement, he strolled in the park and saw the Italian street singer with a little crowd around him. Now he knew and had seen the street singer a thousand times, certainly every sunny, warm Sunday for eight years. This time, instead of watching the singer, he saw the faces of the listeners. They listened with smiles on their faces; they swayed to the music; they hummed; they laughed at the singer's quips; lovers' heads were pressed together. The civil servant wished he could make people as happy. He failed to notice that while everyone enjoyed the singer's smiling face, his strutting, his happy, strumming hand, he perspired with the effort and his never-still eyes were cold as he watched the faces of the listeners to see how they reacted to his music; for their reaction was his reward since he never took money.

The civil servant wished he had a hobby like this. He wished he could make people happy. He saw himself, smiling, dancing, singing, plucking at a mandolino: most of all he saw the happy, admiring faces, the hands beating in applause.

One day a clerk brought in a little tin bird-whistle to work. It was small and concealed under the tongue: it gave off three sounds; a trill, a high shriek, and a laughing, demented call. But the whistler was a joker and used it only to whistle at the girl clerks. It sounded marvelous. The civil servant saw himself birdcalling and the center of an admiring crowd who would love his art. And so he bought a tin bird-whistle.

At home, in his room, he practiced softly, chirping to his mother's old cat to see if he could make it pounce; but quietly, so his mother, who had headaches, wouldn't hear him. The cat, used to conversing for long times with the civil servant, knew the whistles to be false, unbelievable, and turned his back on the metallic sounds. But he could whistle with his lips alone and discovered he could flutter his tongue and tremble his lips and vary, in a number of ways, the column of air in his throat: he found he could do better than the tin whistle. He began to practice and produce sounds that were much more authentic.

At first he reproduced the sounds of domestic birds: sparrows, starlings, pigeons, canaries, a few others. But he found that they were too simple and hardly bound to entertain at all. In fact he did them so well that everyone took them for the real thing. So he began to learn the rich sounds that jungle birds make. He was quite wonderful. After a little while he sounded like some rich, fantastic aviary, full of gorgeous and rare birds. Of course he had never heard any real jungle birds: he got the ominous sounds of the birds out of jungle movies. These strange birds were the birds in Tarzan movies, sinister paradise birds to be heard in the stalking scenes of Japanese guerrilla warfare movies, or the interlude birds heard in expeditions-into-Darkest-Africa movies. However, try as he would, he couldn't get rid of a little hollow sound that made the bird-music resound as though whistled or called under a glass roof. He also barked at cats and meowed at dogs.

But now that he had tried the bird-whistles out the first warm Sunday after his retirement, he saw that it had all been for nothing, because after a short while no one paid attention to him. The Italian street singer, about a half-block away from him, was prancing in front of a crowd while lovers of European street songs danced and watched out for the police. After a while the bird-whistle man began to chirp and trill and flutter shrilly at the girls who went by: it was good for a laugh and the strollers and sitters grinned every time a passing girl's confident stride was broken as she turned around to look for the strange, unfamiliar bird who sang at her.

But the bird-whistle man found he had one audience he hadn't counted on: the children. The children loved him and understood that his bird, if not to be found in nature books, was perhaps more allied to the odd birds of the fairy tales; so they came running to listen to him. He would take them, turn them around, and point up into the trees where the branches drooped with mystic birds which were, obviously, to young eyes, enchanted into the shapes of mere pigeons. The children especially enjoyed a call which would start with a little cluck, a chirp, and go trilling wildly up and up the scale to end with three victorious clear calls like pebbles dropping into a still pond.

He would sit on the bench, bend over, and hold the child around the waist. Their faces would be turned the same way as they looked intently into the branches while the marvelous sounds came singing down: that the sounds crescendoed when a pretty girl walked by was unnoticed by the children. Sometimes the bird-whistle man would pretend that the bird was in their bellies and he would put his ear to their bodies to listen while they giggled and laughed as the inner notes tickled them like hairs. And everyone smiled to see the children having such a good time.

One day the bird-whistle man unveiled a new sound; it was a musical kind of macaw sound: it laughed or cried, almost—though obviously not—human in its emotions. It was so real that the bird-whistle man could almost see it himself; red-, green-, yellow-, and purple-feathered among the lush fronds, with a great, cruel beak and a whimsical, beady eye. An old naturalist was passing by and stopped suddenly, spellbound, and looked up into the trees for this unheard-of bird. He was a city naturalist who delighted in finding an abundance of wild life in the city, proving again and again—in letters to the *Times* and in the writing of unread books—how rich and forestlike the city really was. And here indeed, he thought, was some wild treasure. His head was thrown back, his mouth was open, his little old eyes looked up.

The bird-whistle man, seeing this, stared up too. The old man looked around him and saw the bird-whistle man peering at something and so followed the gaze. Others, who by now were bored with the bird-whistle man, seeing the old man gawking, understood at once and began to stare into the trees. Soon there was a little crowd, all laughing when the old naturalist's gaze was elsewhere, all looking fixedly into the trees. The birdcalls fell down and sounded out, more baroque than were ever heard in any jungle. The old man looked into the trees with all the people till his squinting eyes watered. He asked everyone where the bird was; all of them, understanding a good joke, pointed up into the trees and told him, "There." The bird-whistle man ran up and down his repertory, outdoing himself: he laughed, he cried, he shrieked, he carried on a tragic discussion, he performed a bird-mating. The old man circled backward, his head in the air, looking: he became dizzy and awkward and almost fell over trying to see what everyone saw. After a long while the old man walked away sadly, never having seen the bird that everyone so palpably saw, though he pretended, because he was ashamed, that he had at last seen it. That Sunday was a success for the bird-whistle man.

But on the next Sunday he enthralled a little girl with golden hair who was dressed in a yellow organdy dress, a red sash, white socks, white gloves, and white shoes. His face was pressed against her red sash while he pretended to hear the rich birds singing in her stomach. But the mother pulled the child away, disturbed by the man's hand around her child's waist and his unshaven face next to her. She called the policeman, said that he was molesting her child, and signed a complaint. The policeman, though compassionate, told the bird-whistle man that it would be better if he didn't sing that Sunday. Since the bird-whistle man had just sat down for his day's work, he was very disturbed. He ran to the Italian street singer and complained to him. The street singer sang a sad little song, danced a little, and stared anxiously to see if everyone enjoyed the mockery. In a few minutes the police came and chased the singer away too, in spite of the fact that he pointed out that he took no money and the audience's reaction was his only reward: so he blamed the bird-whistle man for the bad luck.

And since that time there was something wrong about the whistle; something untrue about it. The adults never noticed that there was anything false about it. And even the children, if they were not too near the bird-whistle man, didn't notice anything was wrong; but as soon as they came close to him and he took them around and whistled, they would break away and run. Some of the children became quite angry. One little fat, petulant boy became outraged and stamped on the bird-whistle man's foot and punched at him and then, red-faced, indignant, ran away. The bird-whistle man would whistle out and call to any passing children, "You want to see the bird? Look. Look. Come hear. You want to hear the bird?" And chirp hysterically; but if they came near him they would have to tear themselves away and, frightened or angry, run away.

Once a fight broke out nearby and he encouraged the two men beating one another by whistling shrilly, mockingly. Most of the time he just whistled at the girls.

He worked hard to perfect his whistle again to please the children. He even thought of buying a tape recorder to find out what was wrong now, but the complexities of the machine were beyond him. No matter how he practiced, his birdcalls were not the same.

In autumn, Sunday, he was sitting in the still-warm sun, among the falling leaves. Everyone was bright in their first winter wools. They were released from the bondage of the heat and walked rapidly. The bird-whistle man called to the children. He chirped at the girls. He hissed at a Siamese cat on a leash. He imitated a dog whimpering. Three dogs passed. The first dog was a puppy and so, too self-involved. The second dog was a Tibetan lapdog and so, couldn't speak the language. The third dog was a large German shepherd in the prime of life. It understood instantly. It leaped loose from its master's unsuspecting grip and tore the bird-whistle man's throat before he could do anything.

The bird-whistle man can talk well enough after his operation. His talent is not totally gone: he can still imitate the owl.

TARANTELLA

ALL through the summer and into the fine autumn weather the mandolino player entertained in the park every Sunday. He placed himself on the busiest crosswalk and played Italian street songs, sweet songs of love, double-entendre ditties, and some of the melodies made popular by New Wave movies. He always came at two in the afternoon and began to play at two-thirty. He would try to play till five or six, but the police always chased or arrested him for creating a nuisance by blocking the walk: after all, wasn't there a place set aside for players in the park? Sometimes friends would accompany him on guitars: once an accomplished accordionist's lugubrious chords underscored his sprightly tunes.

He would plant himself under the network of leaf shadows the sycamores cast, wait, perhaps smoke part of a gnarled cigarillo, look anxiously around to see if he was recognized, talk and joke till enough people gathered. In time he would be surrounded by a crowd of well-dressed sightseers, for the folk singers ignored him (he was unauthentic) and the beats listened only to sphere music.

His audience would all stand there, smile, clap, nod their heads, and tap their feet, keeping time. The mandolino player would move nimbly around his little arena: sometimes he would go boldly forward, with his body bent; or half dancing backward with gliding steps, he would sing soulfully; or side-step, his head cocked to the side as he sang risqué songs; or simply stand and sway in ecstasy ... though he didn't keep this posture long, for his anxious eyes flickered restlessly, looking for one who did not enjoy. Then he would circle, his mandolino pointed outward like a weapon, looking anxiously into all faces. When he met the one who looked persistently sad, he would pause, play very hard, sing his songs, even dance a little, till a smile appeared. Happiness would increase ... faces would be less compressed by the usual anguish; all would, from time to time, rock as a group, or chorus a refrain. But as he played, his face would always appear more soulful, his eyes more restless and alert, as if tortured by what he played; but he always played better.

Now and then he would pause and make a little speech. He always said, "My pleasure is your pleasure. I do not do this for money. My big hope is to play a whole day without the police chasing me. I only do this for entertainment, for what can lighten the world's heart better than a little music?" Then he would make a few jokes. And he would play his tunes and sing, in Italian, for instance, about a virtuous cuckold, while his expression indicated that the song was much more prurient than it really was.

One brilliant autumn day, when the sun cast a hard lace of leaf and sun dapple, he was playing as usual. The mandolino player was at his most delightful; a huge crowd blocked the walk completely and extended not only behind the row of benches, but onto the lawn itself, making it only a matter of minutes till the outraged police must come. A little girl popped out from among the legs of the watchers and was suddenly in the arena with the mandolino player. She clapped her hands together and hopped twice with both feet held together. She was about six, or seven, wore a little white blouse, a red velvet swirl-skirt with red suspenders, white socks, red shoes with a little red strap across the instep. Her hair was curly black and her eyes were big and violet and staring. Everyone immediately said "Aaaah . . . how cute" and "Wasn't that darling?" because she had an oval olive face with a small, pointed chin. She curt-seyed. She wore a hearing-aid plugged into her ear, the wire of which was gaily striped and disappeared into her skirt. And everyone said, "How sad . . . so pretty too . . ." She wore a bright brass and colored glass spider at her waistband where the wire went. Behind her, on the outskirts of the crowd, her grandparents stood. They had taken her for a walk; they took her every Sunday. They were both huge people, the man being about six foot seven and very wide, and the woman about six foot two with grandmotherly white hair. They were easily able to see over the heads of the crowd and smiled because their grand-child was very beautiful.

At first the mandolino player didn't notice her: he only saw the flicker of distraction in the audience's eyes and heard the sounds of the people's voices and wondered what had gone wrong, or thought perhaps a drunk was creating a diversion. The child ran up to the mandolino player and plucked the skirt of his jacket. He turned and looked down at her, threw up one hand, and made his eyebrows go up, his eyes clown-wide, and his mouth oooohed into an aaaah; and he made sounds in general to show how pleased he was at the presence of this lovely little

105

child, and at her love of music. He danced a few comic steps, toes pointed inward, to amuse her.

She said something, but her voice was unclear. He bent down and elaborately cupped his ear with his hand. His other hand, ever unstill, fluttered the pick lightly over the jangling strings. Her words were garbled, for she had probably learned to talk after she had become deaf, and so spoke almost as if half her tongue were cut away. The crowd made more pitying sounds and some said, "How sad it is . . . so lovely . . . how darling . . . how sad." The mandolino player didn't seem to understand what she wanted, but everyone called out that the little girl wanted to dance to his music. He smiled, nodded, patted the girl on her hair, and kept on playing, nodding, bowing, as he danced away from her. She followed after, telling him that she could dance, that she wanted to dance, that she could do the most modern dances—having seen them all on television— and he kept smiling at her and interrupting his songs to look at her and say how pretty, how lovely, *bellissima!*

Seeing that he didn't understand what she was saying with her garbled voice, she stepped away from him; she was used to not being understood. She took a position. Her arms were held out, her fingers together, as if she were about to snap them— though she didn't have the power to make a loud noise—her hip thrust to one side, and she began to do a dance to his music. Her tongue stuck out a little at the corner of her mouth and her face frowned. Her head was cocked a little to the side, the hearing aid nearest the mandolino player. Her eyes seemed to see nothing but the mandolino player's face.

Her hips began to shake back and forth rapidly; each hip-thrust kept beat to each note while her whole body swayed from side to side at a slower tempo, almost sinuously. At first

106

the dance, violently American, was incongruous with the delicate European glissandos. Her skirt flared to the side, lifting till it was an oscillating circle of shimmering red (her red nylon panties had an agitated white nursery figure on them), showing her surprisingly muscular legs, bare and shining. They all laughed and applauded. The spider she wore on her skirt seemed to shuttle from one side to the other. And soon the music and the dance meshed, as the two of them, watching one another, couldn't help working well together.

And seeing this, everyone said again, how cute it was, and applauded, and smiled even more, and clapped their hands loudly to keep the beat, in case she didn't hear the music clearly. The mandolino player, trapped by the enthusiasm of the crowd, knowing that there is nothing as pleasing as a child, kept up the beat for a while. She shook to a Neapolitan street song while he picked the rhythms, his pick flashing rapidly over the strings.

At first he thought her attention would wander after a minute or two, but while her body shook and her feet wove complicated patterns, her eyes never left his. Then he thought it was a matter of getting the lovely child tired, but she had inherited a monstrous stamina from her monumental grandparents. And after a while of this, the mandolino player looked down at the child and saw that she parodied a seductive appearance while she danced: her face was thrown back a little, her eyes were elevated half up into her heavy, dark eyelids, and her moist mouth was slack. But her eyes showed that she merely appeared so because they were really alert and anxious as she watched him. Then, understanding, he knew she could dance all afternoon and that no one would stop looking at her. He circled, facing outward, looking into the faces of the watchers, singing loudly, making droll expressions to indicate how lewd his lyrics were. But they stared past him as if he didn't exist, looking at the child spinning in the center of the arena.

He turned, and standing at the periphery of the arena, altered his rhythm; she kept the beat, speeding up. He stopped, changed, and went into another song. She called to him, trying to keep up, "Faster. Faster"—at least that's what it sounded like, only the vowels being clear. He slowed the tempo. He began to walk around, trying to look as if he were merely playing, she dancing, and they enjoying themselves giving pleasure. He turned himself between her and the mandolino. She, without missing a beat, danced over to him and plucked his jacket. He turned to her and looked down. He smiled. She looked up appealingly and the audience was charmed and clapped and murmured. He had no choice but to play for her a while longer.

Seeing she had won them, her hip movements became more violent and the expression on her face more seductive. The audience was further delighted. Seeing that he had really lost them, the smile on the mandolino player's face became a grimace; he began to alter his rhythms rapidly. The little girl barely heard the changes but met each innovation. She was breathing heavily now and her face was covered with little drops of perspiration. Every time the mandolino player changed, she changed. Her skirt swirled higher; the muscles in her legs tightened; her mouth was open and her tongue was out a little more, flicking back and forth over her lips, making them look red; her hip was thrust farther and farther out and the nursery figure had shifted its position till it was over her belly; the beat of her hip became dogged and commanding. They stood facing one another, dancing and playing.

The mandolino player moved nearer to her. She danced away a little, turning her back to him: she—her ear with the hearing-aid was nearest him—looked over her shoulder at him, burying her chin. The smile on his face was fixed. He did little dance steps too, but no one noticed. He changed his music now to something slow and sentimental. She changed too and was doing a slow, amorous little dance, as she glided along softly, and they all laughed uproariously. No one noticed him. He turned toward her and followed her closely. He changed his tune to something harsh and jangling; a march. She did a high knee-kick, drum majorette's dance. He moved nearer to her: he was almost treading on her heels and his knees rose under her skirt, almost bumping her rump. The red panties were now lifted high and bunched tightly between her buttocks. She looked back and up, her head to the side, her face gleaming, smiling. His hand flashed in and off the mandolino face, seeming now to spin in and out of the strings as he came still nearer. His hand made wide arcs as he made elaborate motions and his knee bent and straightened and he rocked back and forth to his music. No one noticed. His hand flashed out: he whirled away: as he turned, bent, his behind bumped her bare behind.

The pick, in turning, got caught in the wire of her hearing-aid. But instead of the hearing-aid being dislodged from her ear, the pick sliced easily through the wire. The two ends fluttered apart. For a second the crowd didn't notice and kept beating time; all of them moving as one, enchanted. But she was not able to keep up with the rhythm at all now. Her movements became jerky and had nothing to do with the music. A hand shot out aimlessly. A hip bounced. The skirt flared. A foot almost slipped out from under her. The head fell into a lolled position. The mouth kept widening and narrowing. The arms seemed almost to double back on themselves as if the joints worked both ways. It seemed as if only the violent motion kept her from collapsing on the floor. Her head heeled over almost to her shoulder and she grotesquely danced off to one side till she came in contact with one of the watchers and then, bouncing off, went off in the other direction.

The mandolino player became alarmed at what had happened, watched her anxiously, and tried to alter his rhythms to keep up with her. People began to notice and someone said, "That child. What's wrong with her?" The threads of the hearing-aid wire kept flapping and were beginning to unravel and everyone saw that it was not wire at all, but gaily-colored string.

The mandolino player, seeing the looks of the audience, became scared. He tried harder to keep up with her motions. He had to play jangling, atonal music now, harsh, strident, and arbitrary to match her movements. The spider on her dress seemed to dart aimlessly along. The nursery figure had disappeared. He played a long run that did not sound true, but merely went on and on, rising by odd quarter-tones, following her movements, and then broke off into little mutterings and thumpings on the wood of the mandolino. She hopped and her body flipped from side to side. People began to frown.

The child's grandparents forced their way through the crowd. The grandmother picked her up, kept kissing her wet face, and straightened her clothes while the little girl thrashed; the grandfather fumbled with the edges of the string till they were woven together. And when they were one, the little girl smiled her charming smile and relaxed. And she said, her voice thick and unclear, that she still wanted to dance. Her grandfather said no, she was tired and unstrung, but she pouted and insisted, her voice growing thicker with frustration till it sounded only like sound. The grandfather, towering over the little mandolino player, said that he would play one more tune for his grandchild and then they must go. The mandolino player tried to play a saccharine tune, one that pulsed slowly and was to be accompanied by a steady, vibrant trill. She began to dance. But he kept striking the wrong notes, notes that jangled, and soon everyone drifted away to listen to the folk singers or to watch the beats listening to unheard music. The little girl was taken away by her grandparents; she left with the promise of an ice-cream cone.

The mandolino player continued to play all afternoon. He played as he had never played before. But now no one stopped, for his music was dissonant and discordant, and for once the police did not chase him away.

SOMEONE JUST LIKE ME ...

IN Union Square, the crowds viscous out of the subway and off the busses in the morning move along the flanking streets, through the Square crosswalks, among the slices of crumb-littered scurf, into the office buildings. Aimless Old perch along the benches; winos flow out of their seventy-five-cent caves and ten-dollar-a-week roominghouses. The first slackjawed shoppers come, all with the transfigured look of inattention. All flow around, or through, passing unknown to, even unseen by, one another.

. . . manclump in Union Square Park talks all the time; a synagogue agog to visions unseen to scientific eyes. Two main disputants are its nucleus: glosses addend and it fifteens fat with vehement, antiphonal additions: or it dwindles to three or four as some cancel out in deviation: or it buds off free-arguing, secular groups. It apparitions out of the Fourteenth Street Automat seven or eight (depending on the weather) in the morning and keeps on (depending on the weather) till night: late in spring, summer, and autumn, early in winter. Continuous creation of it-doesn't-matter by antientropic *minyan* (not dependent on the weather at all).

Going on for many years now. ("Listen! They were here when the Indians came down off the land bridge and they'll be here after when the Bomb goes off . . . you ask me, there are those who know how to avoid work no matter how. Right?") Is on the side nearer Klein's, the almost-Universal Giveaway On The Square; left over from the great Athenian days, unencumbered by agoraphobia, or -philia: discussing trivia. A telephone company truck has pulled up near them and a repair man has opened a manhole cover, moving them away from it, and is descended to make restitutions. Warning-pink pennons flag out from the portable guardrails, yellow rubber cones surround, and a batteried yellow eye on a stick winks over their heads. The sky is gray. A chill wind blows in, focusing through all the passes between the buildings, vor-texing in the Square, chasing around the flagpole, sedimenting fallout in the friezecracks; but it is not noticed because the talk is specially good. Wind, spirits of vapor rising, exhaust of smoke genie-ing up in roiling masses from the ConEd coke-fires truck tailpipe comments of derision, monoxide fart-quanta, heretic brake screeches. But, persistible through years of oppressive duration, it solves, always, such problems as the tax death of the West, the sex life of the Pope, what rabbis carry in their beards, what priests and nuns *really* do, did Napoleon have a Christ-complex and did Christ have a Napoleon-complex, are the rich really unhappy, and are the happy really poor. But an Astrologer (sunflower seeds, the Body Revealed, *Arcana Coelestra,* changes his dwelling once a month impelled by the irate spirits of malign Landlords, wishes he had the nerve for a little anthropomancy) notes the mold-grown shadow and chokes as he is about to say, "Do you really think she didn't . . ." spits it out, has to leave. He ran from the malicious influence he felt debouching out of Cancer, from the north side of the Square, rudely slouching . . . Invincible Old Rational begins his reasonable plaint . . .

Not *too* odd to look on, Mannie Davidson velocited into the Square. Feet trod through ashes and grit and cement, and the left hand held onioned shopping bags (his all) hissing against the hornpalm, as did the right; shaghead in a gray fur felt with a stained black ribbon to remind him . . . great knuckly fingers held the fraying strings, the little treasure, taken always from room to room. Leanhead, scrawnneck, thin-shouldered, torso fattening out to plump hips on pylony legs: like two; mounted on his own arse. Green field-jacket and gray sharkskin pants let down to fulfill his enormous height, each wrinkle where late the cuffs were, like time's service marks, two, three, and four rag-end times . . . he hunted for his unwinders. His footsplay floor-kicked through the bitter wind and made the leaves titter along the cemented mica.

"It was not that he was so special," the socially secure says, "but, rather . . ."

Fifteen stories above the Square, the boss had her spread on the cleared blotter on his desk. Her skirt was bunched up around her waist, tangled with her slip. The sight of parts of her white, strap- and deskedge-cut buttocks splayed out, that shock of seeing thigh-backs, stockingtops, the unbusinesslike vagina among the pens, cartonmarkers, invoices and order pads always excited him the more. Her panties lay beside the left side of her head, white against the mahogany shine; on the right, the pallid face of the boss's wife and his two simperfaced children beamed out of the rococo glass frame, staring at his hairbacked hands kneading her big breasts. At first her sheen-sheathed legs had hung down over the front of the desk and her head hung down over the back. She was a tall piece of goods; he, a short man, was sure he would never have made out, especially because of her perfect oval of a self-contained face, and her blond, cool, center-parted hair, but it was surprising how easy it had been. A word . . . these days, he thought . . . Next door, in the outer office, the typewriter of his other secretary was tattering the minutes; he tried to be quicker and quiet so the other secretary wouldn't know. On the floor above, his machines were toystamping, vibrating everything. He leaned over her, solicitously, as if concerned about her, as if he were causing her unbearable pain; he put his hands above her shoulders and his arms and shoulders trembled a little with the strain. Her head hung lower over the back of the desk; her hanging hair was rippled by the motion; one longer lock brushed back and forth, making marks in the dusty floor. Her eyes were a little above the windowsill; she seemed to look down into the Square itself. He couldn't see her face clearly and wondered if it remained as cool and smooth as it always was; was she, an icy piece of goods, beginning to buy what he was selling her? He leaned over farther. The typewriter stopped for a second. He stopped, his breath sucked in. There was a faintly heard rattle of paper, a clicking of the platen, a rolling ticking of the space bar, a smash of the tab key and carriage travel, and the typing began again. He started and stopped; the machine made a funny noise, as if something was not right, as if it were chewing down an unmalleable lump of metal that refused to toyform. The machine resumed its smooth, floorshaking movement and the boss proceeded a little faster, bending closer. The blotter slipped back and forth, sighing on the newly waxed desk, and he realized that all he had to do to laborsave was to move her back and forth instead of exerting himself. Her head tilted farther back; she seemed to look out over the Square with intensifying interest. Her breathing remained slow, orderly, insulting, having nothing at all to do with the rhythms he had been using. Gripping the slight plumpness of flesh at the side-joints of legs and hips, he complexified the motion with a slide-to-side swing. Her jawline jutted farther up. The typewriter kept going. Her legs drew slowly up till her ankles slicked back and forth against his white collar. An intense light came up from the Square where someone was welding; it came from somewhere to the right and below the Klein's sign, blazing around the flagpole edges, came from the right and under the point of the decanted carpenter's-angle sign, and attracted the boss against his will: he could not seem to look away.

But, as Truth spits it out, stating the insight ("He's come." "He hasn't come yet."

"He's come, I tell you."

"Maybe, but not in the way you think."

"He's come."

"He's coming."), all turn away and are looking, for a second, past the guardrails and down into the manhole where someone welds something. Meekish mawkface of the repairman blanded into no expression by his mask. Intense blue light obscures and leaves caroming particles dancing. Spark of weld leaps a gap and intenses heat like new, young suns to unite several voices. Turn back and continue. "As I see it, there were thousands of petty little prophets running over the face of Israel at that time. Read your history. The miracle of birth was really the miracle of choice."

"Then what was so special about *Him?*" a reverent voice asks triumphantly.

"Nothing, really. Randomness. If you win the sweepstakes, how are you special? And yet it makes you special. The Romans made him an example to bedevil the Jews and to keep them in line."

. . . debouched into the Square, Mannie Davidson. Paused a glace-age in the North Broadway side. Came through N dimensions from here to here without passing through their there. Two jabbery women, who had not gotten the scent of cheap, good things yet, were passing him; he galloped away. And came, for a second, to the group and saw that he had beaten them . . . they, far behind, walktalked down the railed aisleway and it would be years yet before they reached here. He stood there, turned slowly, and surveyed ComUnion Square; black-velvet pile sky shading away just a mile till it was lost behind the Greco-Roman ConEd cap, where they tear your living heart out if you don't pay for the Light. Shifted the bag cords back and forth . . . bleeding palms? Not at all . . . not even a pain to tell him he had suffered and so he had forgotten long ago what he had never felt and hated the thieves for stealing what he might have been. Passcard in his pocket from Mary, Mother of Madman Hospital in Brooklyn, though long expired and wrinkled like an old man's face and as irrelevant. He edged closer to the group when someone says (a little fanatic without a chin and a shineline of drool intensing the crease beneath the full lower lip), "Wayatawnabow? The Virgin Mary, Slick and Mild, Hefts forever the chic Christ Child." He is answered with a look of I-wouldn't-bother-to-dignify-that-with-an-answer stare by a man with a widebrim homburg hat and a stain and polkadot scarf of silk. But Mannie's head jerks around as he heard a scream. Pigeons scattered up into the sky . . . they all heard something too.

Lost in a slow, portentous pleasure, she saw not so much him above her, looking greedily down at her, or felt yet the presaging pressure impaling and expaling her with frenetic predictability, but stroked the little fringe of backneck hair which tingled her fingers, and the smooth sunlamped gloss at the top of his head. Her expectant jaw thrust up and the weight of her head itself, hanging down, opened her mouth wide so that the foretastable column of air tingled her lips and wagging tongue, and the exquisite weight of her hair and annunciating rhythm, slowly, began joining one and all, the blotter shifting back and forth on the smooth wood of the desk, and the laboring inchinch of the ConEd clock hand, and the auguric and puffy procession of premonitory clouds across the sky, and the prophetic movement of the cars in the street, and the beat of her own heart, and the ominous beat of the toystamping machine above, which vibrated the desk, the blotter, the little man frantically thumpthumping in her, and the tripping of the typewriter, and the electric hum of all the myriad timepieces—counterpointed by the approving though timeless stares of the boss's wife and two children to quicken her. She stared out the window at the world reversed, and looked up at the light. A pencil clattered to the floor. His movement stopped for a second, but her pleasure did not, as she looked at that intense light omening up from the square and blinding her to all except itself, making everything else around look black. There was a little shudder, a brisk jerking, and a punctilious stopping of everything as the man finished and pulled away. Her face contorted with agony and the lingering of the light made spots dance in front of her, poxing his face, and she could have screamed in anger. She would have slid backward and off the desk as he withdrew suddenly, but he caught her by her ankles, threw her legs down, and her heels flamencoed on the desktop.

"No. An obvious paranoid schizophrenic with delusions of grandeur."

"You college kids; you think you know everything," a whiskery gent with a whiskeyry breath snaps.

"Reason, after all . . ." Emaciate and hooknosed little bird, head full of chess problem solutions, no flesh to his pectorals, sandwich crumbs on the mouth-borders, myoping up with a triumphant got-you-there grin.

"If you ask me . . ."

The image shifts and shifts with blinding rapidity . . . Mannie left them and began to walk away. He passed a coming pretzel lady on her way, during her break, to join conversation. She liked to hear them talk. She nodded at him as he passed. He was too busy to see her, searching for them: odd quest (memory or dream); three hoods who had waylaid him and stolen three of his Precious and Beyond-Price. Now they were oned in his prescience. Conscience came back to him as Reason, the small, still Normmaker's voice, telling him, "Emmanuel, you can't resent forever in the past." "Why not?" he had asked.

The passing bargain-hunters looked at him. He had rushed by them before, but they didn't remember him because you meet all kinds . . . and here he was, running the other way . . . past their hair domed into puffy lacquer-shells, one, bullet-shaped, the other like a globe, its bottom scalloped out . . . He passed the little temple (now a public urinal) where late the orators spoke to those impassioned laboring hundreds and now the pigeons cooed to sleep those echoes. Cars rushed by. His uplook eyes saw the windowfaced flame (where a suddenly pulledback spy-face had peered down at him) on top of old ConEd. He strode, sedately, splayfooting through the Square. And passed in a whirl. His gaze flared along the graphlike edges of the building escarpments, upping and downing along the heights and the deeps, searching the border between her and sky, but seeing only the windcracked snaprags above the Square's center and over Klein's gay and Universal Giveaway, looking merely barred, squared, and starred, all gray, because that was one of the things they had stolen from him. All was litter under his bumbling footstide as he rushed, fragmented by other people's old and excremental myths.

Maskfaced, the huntingwomen shopstalked . . .

Drifts a little to one side, edging away from the warning-stalk and evolved in a slow spirals to meet the limpy pretzel lady's approach as, in her noonday break, she came to the gathering to contribute a little of her own . . . salted halos circling in immutable and linked o's, changed, and were transmorphed by the democratic visions of one and all (to some, disturbing, but), as by a rising vote of consensual vectors, agreed on and carried: acceptable as gifts. Wool watch-capped, beadeyed, somebody's mother too, sole support of her crippled daughter, she gathers Culture with great minds. She sees Him as the Universal and Compassionate Son-in-Law for her child. But the light from the welding in the manhole disturbs her just a little bit, that bluewhite fire fountaining up, and looks away to the soothing and impartial green of the telephone repair trucks, and away, because there is an obscene sign seen on the panel: Mercury, snaketangled, poised forever on a Princess phone; and it seems as if the wiring down into, or back up from, the manhole springs out of the decal on the truck.

. . . shoptalk and sniff the air, their heads nod or shake violently and their mouths twist, giving cruel finality to mild topics . . . and, blue-ringed, their keen eyes stared through marcasite-crusted harlequin glasses which lewded their innocent and searching gazes into something knowledgeable, entranced; from Klein's Only, the sign enticed them on. They talked and skirted the disputatious puddles of silly and arguing (men! what do they know?); a thousand Aged, like complaisant gargoyles cast up and wracking their wake, were passed by . . . and these impervious and triumphant matrons sliced through all the half-formed emanations with the sheen of their stockings on their still good legs. The rimmed mask-eyes blazed toward, and their greasedwhite lips gaped at, and they saw Jerusalem across the Square. A huge skewhead, half in their way, appeared and flicked away when they were (honestly! they should do something . . . woman isn't safe . . .) annoyed.

Mannie, a little dizzy, swore that they were maenads hunting him down. And, he thought, following their cruel stares —at Klein's where, under the wreck o' gnomen, the names in light announced . . . well, half a cross is better than none.

. . . and turns away from the truck and turns and ones into the intellectual clones. She feels the shadow of a blot on the sun, sunspot or eclipse, nibbles on one of her pretzels as one says ". . . but really, you can explain him biochemically, genetically; what he had was a condition, and that was what made him a little the way he was . . ." Calculations and chemicals make the Christos.

"As I see it . . ." the meek voice tries again.

". . . because, diploid, overloaded, like a mongoloid, epileptic, anything, I mean the fact that he didn't lead such a special early existence merely indicates that something temporarily recessive in his genetic programming unspooled to its tragic hour and went off . . ."

"To the potlatch on the cross . . ." the Economist says.

"But what about the Star, and other wondrous signs?" an Astronomer-Royal asks.

"Coincidence. There was a so-called wonderous sign and they had to come up with someone to explain it all. I mean, if you'd pay attention, we're all mosaics and some of the pieces become fulfilled in time, some now."

And, damask, He dances . . .

Mannie, back, sees something flicker over their heads and under their feet, and he turns and began to run. And ran past the two of them, their mouths going many to the minute (and if she thinks for one minute she can get away with that . . . well, I told her plenty . . . believe me) while their whole becomings are attracted to that moment . . . when a crazy lunk, birthscar along the temple, the mandible, and down the side of the neck, rushed by (they let more and more of them loose . . . what do *they* care? . . . that's the fifth we've seen today).

. . . dances, wearing a white field tunic, flashing . . .

And for a second the boss felt great, all pain of being anodyned as he delighted in her look of inutterable ecstasy. He stood away and clear; and felt the chill on his bare legs and on the Naked, pricking out of his decaltaglioed shorts. He pulled up his pants quickly, peering at the place where he had just been, gaping at its swallowing muscles taking a little of his own, personal interest (he sniggered) . . . He was finished, stuffing in, and zipping (almost catching it in the zipper's teeth) all before she sat down, her legs sliding to the floor as her heels clicked and she worked her skirt down over her oval thighs to her smooth knees, and her hands made the cloth-wrinkles smooth with patting, motherly motions. Her face was still oval, composed, her big eyes cool, heavylidded, enticingly elliptical—probably dazed, he thought—and she had begun to chew on her gum. He pulled out a cigarette and lit it and turned away. The light of his lighter merged, for a second, with a glow from below, in the Square, where they were welding, and the smoke caressed along her smooth face. She left. He turned, looked, and saw that she had left a stain on his desk blotter. It was limned by the unmarked green and given form by the unwet portions left by the lines of her garter belt; a bird shape, or was it a head? He took out the blotter from its holder. He fluttered the blotter—even though it was dry— and found himself, stain side out, making a pirouette on his leather heels, as though the blotter was a cape and he was Veronicaing a bull. He stopped. He smiled. The dreams one has, he thought, even at fifty-three. He went over to a steel closet, unlocked it, and put the blotter in with about four or five hundred other blotters, all interestingly stained, locked it, went back and put a fresh blotter on the desktop and was ready for business.

"In the thirteenth, greatest of all centuries, they knew how to appreciate and love him," the professor of sentimental history said . . . In the quorum's heated words, coalescing with fire and love, purple forever in the yellow East, embedded as topaz and coral and emerald, laughing in the rose window's glow.

They clicked across the Square where, above, the doom signs in lights circled forever, announcing that today there was to be a Persian lamb fur coat sale (for heaven's sake . . . it's just like them to let you know when it's too late . . . do you think *they* want to give anything away? not them . . . if I had known I would have been down here in the A.M., dawn even). And though talking about neighbor trouble, and child trouble, and the trouble of growing old and plainer, they hastened their steps, having caught the scent and sighted the quarry.

Mannie ran past three Forlorns, unsexed and detimed by drink. Lines of winos laughed at him. And their seductive words sang to him, but he didn't have the time to stop. One made weaving motions and the other *pliéd* compulsively with legs lolling, as it exposed its crusted All to the quickening, chill winds; hot hind parts trying to do the obsolete mare bit, stopped by the tiredness of custom and so ungenerated by the world's exhausted Wild West Fart. They sang timelessly as Mannie, floating, took days to pass them. Two hardfaced and contemptuous babes, burn-eyed, passed too; their spike heels rushing things for them, almost into sobriety, but they were passed on the way to the miraculous bargains (how do they do it? how do they stay in business, I'll never know . . . a profit in pennies, believe me) in the store.

"There is a Christ for all of us. There is a Christ Scientist, Christ Accountant, Christ Artist, Christ Chiropractor . . ." Images shuttle back and forth with bewildering rapidity as Mannie came running back. He remembers the second thief who forces open the hasp of his head, and something flies out and into a waiting net. Does he hear the words, or dream them? Someone tells his mother, "Oh, it'll straighten out . . . they always do. They all have their head skewed from the

124

forcep's grip." But is there restitution? There is not. And so, for a long time, he worries about the soft whisper of cobalt running down and ruining him, and counts the drops of blood left in his heart, and he worries for busses and never steps on cracks. He leaves.

Three winy convivials sang to Mannie, "If tomorrow comes, can today be far behind?" Topers shivered in the chill air, old men moldered in the malair, and all the signs blinked and blanked in the fair air. The faces of all the institutional clocks were hazed out and the sadness of gray alltime affected them barely. The Forlorn presented its face to the stars behind the face of the world roof itself; they kissed through the clouds. The third, drunk and drunker still, probably paretic and with a liver psychosis, made opening and closing motions with the fingers. A bloatbody in a primavera mother hubbard bobbled on spindle legs, pavaning up and down in a mysterious hexagonal, for drink or love.

She went to the ladies' room, checked her appearance, came out and went to her desk. She passed him as he was bent over the other secretary's desk, seductively waving an order blank. He was old enough to be her father. She sat down and put a sheet of paper into the typewriter.

The Sign enticed and beckoned. They lived for the moment when they would get in through the revolving doors. Some clown rustled them with his smirchy shopping bags. Bebleared eyes of men, drunk with age, lifted a little, as at a memory, when they passed. Nothing stood in the way of their dare-they-buy-it gray, Magian lambskin coat, a bargain (believe me) if there ever was one, and they could almost feel the thrill of it . . .

A cohort of young hoods assembled near and around the

little temple. They wore starred leather jackets, tight black chino pants, and all carried pocket radios, easily mistakable for cigarette cases.

Around, and talking back and forth over the hole, they look down for a second and see only the welding mask's face. They even forget he is here, so deep are they in talk, and it seems as if he is always here.

Mannie dances around the outside, almost upsets the eyewink of the golden warning light, halfknocks over the gateway protecting the hole from pedestrians, almost stumbles into it himself, rights himself, and circles to get a better vantage point. Someone gestures argumentatively with a left hand . . . and Mannie remembers: his mother made him righthanded and the benedictions of this world can only be given with the left hand. If not for that (all pawned for presents by those thieves) he would be like "Christ Dialectician, Christ Weightlifter, Christ Pretzelvendor, Christ Cardpuncher . . ." It is the excuse he has to accept in order to get away from the bin: that his mother does it to him in order not to upset her table settings. That, and with the long exhausted Sane pills, and the advice long absorbed into the blood, or that he is aboriginally bloodpoisoned, and helplessly, "An agrarian reformer who, among so many, I tell you, fought the class war." Christ the Reaper to Christ the soldier, form in the air, leading the downpressed and disconsolate minions who seek to try their hands with Rome's might.

The weld hisses up again, out of the manhole, and Mannie Davidson shifts a little because it is strong in his eyes. Faceless man with two sly look-into-you eyeholes looks into the world's and the weld's intensity. They have closed the doors to multifoliate visions of existence, closed, one by one, by the pardoner's

126

art, one by one, done by the damning Understander's all-encompassing love, like turning pages down on the dead past and the deader future, leaving only the always-living-beside-me, abide-me, limitful and dreary and unreceding present. Compensating schiz, nonservomechanism. The sky, now that he sees it more clearly, is not so much drizzleveloured, but coffee-grounded smoggrit into a kitchen sink . . . and the sun is a pale washplunger.

. . . old poet, still wearing a tweed uniform and laborer's chambray shirt, says, "Some of the greatest poetry the world has ever known is in the King James version." Sure. Washed in the blood of the iambs.

. . . the thrill of softer than steelwool curls all over their goosey flesh, even under the perdurable thighcut of their shape-maintaining corsets.

Her head is to the side and tilted a little forward and she looks down lovingly out of lowered lids. And, as she types, her mouth makes mysterious motions as her sly and immutable smile surrounds the cudmovement of her chewed and re-chewed gum. The Boss had come out and said, "Come in here and take a letter, Miss Farbotnik," to the other secretary. Who did he think he was fooling, she thought; well, let *her* be bored.

The sun's light came now from under the grand and unchanging bank of omnipresent clouds. The crowds hesitated, stopped, reversed themselves, and started to flow in the other direction, going down into the subways, coming out of the stores, beginning to leave their work and to go home.

The cohort had formationed. At the word, their right hands had gone up and pressed the radios to their ears; the second word had turned on the radios; the third word started them doubletiming in place; the fourth word began their knees high,

127

doubletime march in perfect unison (almost a run) around and through the Square park. They keep perfect formation and run around and through and over every walk. Their faces will be blank and intense as they will listen to their pocket radios sing Hosanna, with steel guitars, voice wails, all in echo chambers. The hundred radios yammeryammer epithalamium in the corner candy-store as they brisktrot around at sunset.

. . . and, of course, their word for it was a breakdown; multiphrenia which fractioned the vision like a beeseye view, or like a detached retina would; world seen through a mad mosaic of once useful, now antiquated inherent matters which drugs supported in a ready-to-be-shattered imbalance, and a therapy might make better from moment to moment. "Now go home, Mannie boy," the Shrinker said. "Go home and seek the healthy environ. Report, dear heart, but once a month to the rehab clinic and adjust your heart out." In the pocket he had tracts on the Good Life by Social Workers, clothing on his back from the Salvation Army, moneys from Welfare Workers, slouched into the carrushed bedlam, a slow-thought and rude beast, but all of it couldn't contain his fury because the skew-head sight haunts him from the mirrors of every gum machine from here to the Bronx and out to Brooklyn.

The revolving doors to Klein's gently nudged their behinds, inviting them. They rushed in (did you ever see such crowds? honestly), and lived for the moment when they would posture in front of mirrors.

"When did he leave?" someone asks and they all see that the telephone repair man has come out, packed up his stuff, rolled back the cover, and driven away the truck. "It is wonderful, how, after all these years, this man manages to interest us. And I'll tell you why. Not because he is like all those things you said he was, but because, if you ask me, he was like me. Someone just like me, or you," the mild, little man, swaying back and forth, finally manages to get out.

"Balls, he was," Mannie screams.

"Then, all of a sudden, this jerk, he looks up and lets out a yell, and begins to run after I don't know what."

As he roared by, the lips, leestained into a tiny prisskiss, pouted in delight and promised; a whore could give him what the passing houris had not. A dregsdark and drunken Negro cackled agreement.

The woman from the Bronx will get into an argument with her friend over the quarry, the last Persian lamb coat (marked down) in the store, and which just happens to fit them both. They will begin to scream shrilly at one another, friendship forgotten, and pull at the coat, in spite of the protestation of a floorwalker and two salesladies who will attempt to pry them apart. And before they are done, they will have torn the lambskin coat apart from its sleazy seams.

The hophead thinks he sees St. Easterisland Statueface emerging from the white noise, but it is only the drunken old Negro.

"Not again," Mannie shouted, running. "This time I'll find you." Shock, scop, reasonable words, head pats, a little insinuating insulin, consolations of Normal being, medicine, all make it false dawn; and he ran, his feet clumping through the walks and streets, among the shriveled trees which, bare, bough out in intricate weaver's warp to reimplicate him here. "Houris! You hear?" he shrieked at the laughing Forlorns and ran on. They cackled and reimprecated him with finger curses.

The secretary, sitting at her typewriter, a little sleepy, will watch the setting sun being bracketed lazily between the build-

129

ings. She will listen to the heraldic sound of the machines on the floor above, beating rhythmically, pressing out toys, *not* typing out of spite and amusement, because she knows that the boss will suspend all action till he is sure that everything is "going on as per usual." But after a while, she will be drowsy, almost to the point of a selfsatisfied little sleep, her oval and blondframed face reposed and her smooth cheeks glowing, she will begin to itch violently between her legs, and looking around, though there is no one else in the room, she will scratch herself through the fabric of her skirt with the eraser end of the pencil And, almost stupefied, she will see the great ConEd clock come close to culmination, feel the shudder of the subways con- and diverging, shudder laxedly to the rumble of the traffic, and the comforting tromp of crowds homing, and feel shocked, as though all the electricity moving all the city clocks will crackle through her body, and begin, suddenly and violently, as the setting sun rays catch a portion of a railing bar, far below her, in the Park, and laser up, to orgasm worse than earthquakes: her fingers will spasm in passionate surges on the typewriter.

The cop will panic, and shoot the big loon. Well, what would you do? Officer N'Malley will ask. He'll come screaming and tearing up the street, shoppingbag handles in his hands and a wake of junk a yard wide and a mile long behind him as he runs past the Consolidated Edison Company Building, screaming—Officer N'Malley won't know what—something like, "Stop, thief," crazy as they come and why do they let them out? His mouth will be open and the snaggleteeth yellow against the black maw of bellowing panic, about six minutes before it is the cop, N'Malley's quitting time, and if only he would be past, one could shout, Stop. Halt. Or I. But running clumpfooted, he will be bowling them over like pins (even the hightrotting boy hoods, leaving them a tangled and sprawled mass, the noise coming out of their shattered pocket radios, a little less heavenly) and his arms will wave and he will loom larger than this monolith, N'Malley, in blue in his way, and it is just one second (twelve yards) to reach (when there will be nothing for it) pull and aim and fire. And he'll spin and fall and lie among his own detritus, one foot kicking up and down on the concrete, and blood will butterfly out of the head-hole and his pelvis will thrash and thrash ecstatically till the sound of the sirens come and the curious come and it's all right, all right, who is this bastard? But it won't matter because he has an almost-effaced passcard from the bugbin and he has been having, dangerously, what they like to call a psychotic episode. Look at the size of the crazy fucker; what did they expect me to do? N'Malley will almost weep. Around him there will be old cartoon books, pieces of mosaic tile (obviously from a tabletop), some crusty and moldy sandwiches, papers, dank dirty and stinking laundry, five hundred wrinkled dollars in wretched bills that some of the wise guys will already be getting away with, and how can you chance it? Officer N'Malley will ask. Look at him. No loss. No relatives. The telephone truck he will have been trying to catch, released by the green of the next traffic light, will go on, the driver blandly whistling, not even knowing what will have gone on past him.

Discuss till late night. ("He's come."

"He's coming.") Stands around and on the teetering man-hole cover while fabricating spirit in argument. Agreeable ghostly exhalate of words, passions, chilled breaths, cigarette smoke, di Nobili fumes, till, waxingwaning ("Maybe he's *here*."

"Aaaaaah. *I'll buy that*.") It being too late, go out of the

Square, down Fourteenth Street, swaying a little in ordered walk, and adjourn to the Automat where they argue till ("He's—how would you like a punch in the nose?—come."

"Christ Mathematician. Christ Charismat. Christ the Tiger. Christ . . ."

"He's—and how would *you* like a punch in the eye?—coming.) in sweat, fetor, dandruff wisps, Muzak, eructations, steaming carrots and chicken croquette odors, the nagging, badbreath voice of the manager—swaying till it is time to go back to the Square, Dawn . . .

NOT WITH A WHIMPER, BUT . . .

"WELL, what did you expect to see?" he yells against Miss Kaley's fatlid eyes. Naked stands he on the crumbly door lintel, waves his fist and rages. His nakedness is a shield against her; her balefulness does not frighten him.

She splutters, "But no one answered . . . something might have been wrong . . ." and, pretending to look at him, she slys a look past, through his door, through his kitchen, to the bed in the front room. Afternoon sunlight hazes a blanketed bunch on the bed. Then stares at his face (furtively down look, thinks he, triumphantly). Her mouth's wide enough to frame a small lemon; her jagged lower teeth fang up.

"I'm not your prisoner. I'm a free man." He steps forward. His nakedness becomes a weapon now, forcing her back. She breaks, pivots swiftly on sensible shoe, and retreats. "Where are you going?" he roars.

"I had no idea," she says, over her shoulder, halfway down the corridor.

He follows farther into the hall, stands there, looking at her stiffback retreat, and shouts, not caring that he is naked, for he is fit still, and a man, "What do you think we are? Mother-Dad clowns?"

At the end of the landing, her hand hovering the balustrade-post, she must turn; her jaw thrusts and its lower edge is tension-scalloped by tautened neckstrings. She is growing old too, he meanly thinks. Her prim nostrils pinch to prevent the unsocial-worker sniff: it all cancels out her generous bosom. "Go back inside," she says.

"It's a free country."

"You are naked."

"Naked and a man, Miss Kaley," he shouts. The door at the other end of the hall opens a little. He yells, louder, "Naked!" His voice cracks; "A man!" The door closes. "Stop looking at me as if I was something dirty, Miss Kaley. Do you think it stops? Do you think it ends? Sixty-five; a pension; clip clip?" he leers at her and makes snipping motions with his fingers around his groin.

"I will come back when you are not acting so infantile, Mr. Billig."

She clatters down the stairs; he laughs (too loudly), turns, pads (uncaring: his footsoles are hornhard enough to shun splinters) triumphantly on the chill hall floor, goes back into his apartment, slams the door grandly, marches through his kitchen, stops in the doorway between his front room and his kitchen. Stillness: time pooled, ready to breach and leak away; he has to move; she is still heaped under the summer quilt; he has to rewoo because his work's been undone. He steps in a little more. Her face is beginning to surface from the quilt: tousled hair, scared eyes, red face, shamed look: pitiful, he thinks, and a little ridiculous. He understands. How can he make her stop being ashamed when he is still full of the same feelings himself? He hopes she is not too humiliated. He turns away and glances at two mirrors on the wall, faces them fully, looking at her reflection, listening. She looks as though she is about to cry. He has to do something or it will be over before it has begun. He is almost too tired to begin again. Let her go, let her go back to Miss Kaley, let her dream, he thinks, you can control that. But he thrusts his chest, squares his shoulders, sees muscles (do credit to a young man) tighten through the slack of old skin (can't help that). He laughs now. "That's telling the bitch."

She says nothing: she looks ahead, staring at the closed door. He looks at her again through the mirror; will she cry? "All right," he says, "I wasn't nice."

She says nothing.

"Baby (how silly it sounds: bravado), can't be nice. Don't respect you unless you raise your voice. Shows you're still a man. As it is, they get you coming and going."

The afternoon stillness thickens as the hot sunlight pours down over the roof-edges across the street; voices clamor outside . . . high-pitched Puerto Rican argument; fainter scream of children; transistor antiphony of high mob-voices chanting dadayadadayadayadaya with boombeat: meant "I love you, will you be mine" these days . . . "I will."

"I know what you're going to say. I could have been nice. Doesn't hurt to be polite. She was worried about . . . us. She bothered to come. I . . . we . . . might have been sick. She means well. All right," he states her argument. "That's *her* story." He doesn't turn to face her directly; she might cry. He can sense it already: she will go. He will be alone again. He turns in front of the mirrors as if watching himself nonchalantly, as if examining his body. "But *does* she mean well? No! She's a part of them . . . it . . . No. I'm not crazy tea?" Does he see her smile through the haze in the mirror? Pretending to look carefully at his face, he sees that her face is still ashamed; that silly sense of humiliation: why? But he knows why. "Anyway, I don't think she saw you. It was crazy, wasn't it? But why did she come? Baby (still a little stammery to say), ask yourself that. Who needs her snooping? We don't belong to her. Go where I want; do what I want." And, stepping back, looking slyly at her, he yells, "NO!" She is startled, looks at him, or, rather, his image. He stands with his feet spread, his body bent back from the waist, hand raised, his finger pointing to the mirror-top: an old, declamatory gesture. Billig likes the pose. "Remember elocution?" Right hand up high now, left hand on his diaphragm, head back, he roars, "They get you coming (makes a gathering motion with his left hand), or going (with a grandiose away-motion.)" He comes very close to the mirrors. Their images seem almost to kiss, and he says, "She's jealous. That's what she is. Wants us back tea?" And if he doesn't detect a smile on her shamecolored face there is, he is sure, a little relaxing, an acceptance. He hasn't won her back, but he's made an opening. He assumes yes. He pads back into the kitchen.

Fussing around the stove he can see her through the doorway in the mirrors. She leans back into the blaze of afternoon sunlight, at repose, thinking about it: her gleaming face bobs indistinctly in the light pouring onto the bed. He fills the kettle. The sound of water rattling hollow in the aluminum is comforting. He sets the kettle on the flame, puts spoons of tea into a shiny brown pot (can't stand the instant stuff, bags, or juice, never could: extravagance, but worth it: jasmine) and keeps talking at her through the doorway. Her hands are clasped on her lap under the cover, making a little mound below her belly. He talks, taking care to avoid angry oldman talk, full of those petulant justifications, reminiscing softly while waiting for the water to boil, trying to amuse her, trying to make her look up at him from out of the afternoon light.

The old man wants to know when do we become old? When's the first time he really knew it?

Perhaps that one winter afternoon: he was lying down; had a dream or a reminiscence, couldn't be sure. Once upon a time he was in a field of some kind. Long time ago. He used to run toward a sunset behind red-edged tree limbs, running right into it . . . and he was light, child-light on his feet. In those days he floated just above the tickle of grasspoints under his feet (was he always barefoot then? and who was laughing? some neighbor now? or had there been a girl?). He used to feel a wind, hear the laugh which forever came at him through those branches, out of the sun itself; perhaps. He would feel the wind bringing the sweet smell of crushed grass and ran harder to catch . . . the laugh . . . whatever it used to be. He was always young, strong in those days. He hadn't learned what it was to be winded. And he could run for just about forever. Where had that been, when? Was it even him? The air was always fresh: he breathed deeply; his chest could take it all in, never stop expanding: and the everwarm sun was hot always on his face and he woke to coughing, choking, and sat up, a little feverish. Couldn't remember where he was. Looked at his gnarled hands and what had happened to him? He almost cried to see it; tried to sleep and go back then, there, but he was in his small two-room. There were unscourable mottle-streaks on the winter sink, flaky liverspots on the wrinkled stove enamel, and his windowpanes agued in the December winds.

She says, but not looking at him, "You shouldn't walk around like that. You'll catch your death." He pretends not to hear or care: let her worry.

The long winter days passed slowly yet were quickly long-gone.

Certainly he hadn't become old the day he retired, did he? "Did I?" She doesn't look at him but she shakes her head, not agreeing or disagreeing. Her mind is on what has happened. "And would you believe it, eyes actually got better; far-sighted; common phenomena. No, really (as if she is contesting it), just threw my glasses away. The optimist (she doesn't smile) . . . optician, whatever he was, he explained it." And, nearing, peering into the mirror, pulls down the skin from his eyes: they are blue, clear, shifting, looking from themselves to her image to themselves. "Billig had plans. Visit museums, all the monuments, read books, go to concerts, even see a few plays. Had a little laid by, you see. Went down to the Social Security. Friendly, but a little disappointing. What did Billig expect?" She shrugs her shoulders, still staring away. Should he go over and just yell at her? Be gentle. Be cunning. Woo; woo and court. Mr. Billig expected a fanfare, applause, celebration, a hymn of welcome and . . . maybe a prize of some sort. They were merely polite, routine. " 'Hello, old man, hello Mr. 112-16-1752, glad to see you. Proof of age? Forms filled? Check'll come soon.' What kind of way was that?"

"Everyone goes through it," she says.

Ahh, he thinks. A friend of his, gone now, "Heart attack," shook his head knowingly and said, "Get a little job. You'll be bored. Nothing to do."

"Not me, friend. I'm free," he said.

The friend shook his head knowingly. Couldn't talk to that type; meek clerk's look, thinned hair, temple grayed, bald spot showing, age freckles. "They respect you more if you have a job. Besides, you never know what's going to happen."

"Not me. Morris Billig is free." And he moves his hand in a wide, flat, expansive gesture, a little comic though. He feels that though she is not smiling, she is perhaps at least interested. Shall he go to her? Strike! Strike! he tells himself, go up, grab her, love. The memory of pensionee Billig tells him, not yet.

His day came. Free. Check in the mail. Free. Tried to sleep late, but his body was imprisoned in the old habits, still job-vigorous, not old at all. Give it time, he told himself; he'd be able to sleep till . . . eleven o'clock . . . go to sleep at three in the morning too. The alarm didn't go off, but he got up feeling overslept, logy, five minutes later than his six-thirty usual. Sat. Looked around. Odd stillness in the apartment; time didn't ripple it. Went to the window. Looked out. Saw passersby streaming to work. Leaning on the windowsill, he watched them for a while. Felt wrong, felt . . . guilty; comforted himself by saying they looked like gray-faced drudges: once he must have trudged like them. He thought of going back to bed, but he moved around; wasn't used to it yet. A little bored, though pleased throughout the long morning. And: breakfasted *before* dressing, cleaned up; floors swept, dusted, things moved around and replaced, listened to the news on the radio, shaved carefully, going over the white stubble two times. "Funny how my head-hair is dark, not one gray hair, you see, and how my beard, if I let it grow, is all white. How do you think I'd look in a beard?" And he looks closely at his smooth cheek. Do her eyes stare toward his jaw?

When will that kettle whistle? He held off decrepitude with a pair of five-pound dumbbells; raised it to ten apiece when he retired. Then he did some shopping. Went to the library.

Those days are gone now; a thousand little errands dissolved and unremembered. "And I have still to get up to the Museum of Natural History." He laughs. She looks at his eyes in the mirror looking at her. He thinks she smiles, but is not sure, for the light flowing down from the hot sky obscures almost everything. Prices rose slowly; his bank account bled away; Mr. 933066 was dying. So he took to using teabags twice, washed and ironed his shirts himself. The kettle begins to whistle. If, when he goes to pour the hot water on the tea leaves, she gets up, dresses, gets ready to leave, he will have lost. He anticipates the empty days again. But her clothes are all on a chair, five feet from the bed; will she expose herself? "A little something in your tea? Jasmine and brandy, my love?" Only it isn't brandy: whiskey: cheap at that. He pops his head back from behind the door lintel; she's still in bed. He wonders; what would she say if he pads over with the liquor bottle, tips it, wets his finger, touches the finger to the hollow under her collarbone? If she'd get up and leave . . . If she'd pull the covers up high . . . Or, better, she might just let the covers drop till her breasts . . . and he would liquor-moisten and kiss her breast-tips. She, giggling, would admonish coyly, finger wigwag (for she was a retired school-teacher), but he'd say, "Old styles are the best," that's what he'd do, bow, and caper away, his white, bushy chest-hair ruffled by the breeze of his movement. No. Miss Kaley's presence remained; he might be left; he didn't do it.

But old he felt when he got sick. Walked six blocks to the library against the wind; six blocks back, caught in a freezing drizzle. Caught a cold. Couldn't shake it. "And me, hardly sick a day in my life." Cough. Feverish. Wouldn't go away. A month. Two. Debilitating. And he got panicky; after all, he was alone (had a daughter in Hamtramck; a son in Los Angeles). Outside, fresh snow coffeed into slush in an hour and stayed brown a long time; tires wheezed, trying to grip. Got better. Had a relapse. Phoned the doctor from the candy-store downstairs. " 'I'm sick,' I say, 'hundred-and-one fever.' 'Come to my office,' he says. 'A little fever never hurt anyone.' " She clicks her tongue: sympathy. When Billig got there, the fever was up to 102; 102½ from waiting in a chilly reception room. He was giddy, drunk, slow-moving, and by the time he saw the doctor all he wanted was to have gotten home and been in bed, long asleep, and if he was going to die, he wanted to die at home, though he was too sick to care. But the doctor wasn't the angel of death; he had a toothbrush moustache. The old man got peered at through a pinwheel of hazy steel halo. "A little chest fluid; not dangerous; La Grippe's left you in the grip of a mild bronchitis. Aspirin, penicillin; fever will go. Heart's fine. Everything else's fine. You're fiddle-fit. Dollar-sound (though what's the dollar worth? ha ho)." But he was too sick to hate the doctor's way of talking. "Funny thing though," he says. "I used to like a doctor who joked. It made me feel easier. Not anymore. Maybe *that's* being old?" "Not what you used to be, but that's understandable. Age. Age. Take Take codeine and Turpin hydrate . . . Stokes' Expectorant . . . gargle: Dobell's solution . . . now don't drink yourself to death. Ha. Come back in a week."

"You know how you get?" She looks. He sucks in his sunset pinkened cheeks and looks, eyes outbugging, sad, sick, old: feels the expression is right and steps over to look in the mirror

141

and is surprised to see himself naked: he forgot. Doesn't like the image and hardens his face and it looks younger and he laughs. "Sick to well in one second: miracle cures." She smiles wanly, though she is not looking at him.

Convalescence was a sense of clogged sini; being closed in blocked internal passages; slow fading: inside, sections rattled in the hollow, unlike flesh, his or anyone else's. And, not able to move well, not caring to, he slept in the days and coughed through the nights and watched the car headlights swing smoothly despite the puckered ceiling. He heard the sirensong of windwhistle coming in and the sigh of steam heat leaking out, and he crawled around, stuffing the leaky windows with rags, promised himself to plaster it all when he got better . . . if he got better . . . He listened to the radio a lot: hard to find good, soothing music . . . so much of that wild noise, savage, wordless, passionate, alien (he almost begins to diatribe against the age, but stops). And Old Grandfather Billig got seasons greetings and pictures from his son in L.A.—fatfaced, balding youngish man, kid-surrounded—and his daughter in Hamtramck—a plumpish middle-aged woman, like his wife had been—all strangers now, strangers wishing him the warmest, Patriarch's children and grandchildren, but there was nothing to feel proud about, nothing comforting about it at all. "I never saw the grandchildren, you know."

"I see mine once a week," she tells him.

"Do you?" he asks.

"There are pictures in my purse," she says.

"I'll look in a second," he says and goes to turn off the waterwhistle; it is becoming painful. He starts to get the cups and saucers ready: sturdy porcelain, Navy surplus, a little thick for the lips, but seven cents a set. He hears the bed creak. Footsteps pad and floor-creak. He stands there, holding two cups, unable to move because he can't forget those times.

Because it seemed as if his hearing had become more acute. Sounds began to bother him now. He heard fights in strange languages, Spanish, Southern Negro, Middle-European, a couple who listened to the television set, gleeing (he hadn't thought there were so many funny programs) in high giggles: when had they moved in, all these people? Dreams worked in the sounds too. They made him jumpy, crotchety, raging. He hears a feminine tinkle from the bathroom: silence: the soft, ladylike gasp of a fart: silence: paper gently ripping and crumple-crackling: silence: the toilet flushing—but really, he thinks, could she leave now; could she?—her footsteps moving. And now the bed creaks again. He clacks the cups together and is aware that his chest is pounding terribly. Careful, careful, he tells himself and chills one cup against his ribs before continuing. It seemed impossible to move without a great effort. He kept coughing, bringing up stuff, and felt, irrationally, that there were gear wheels inside of him, their ratchets worn down, spinning furiously till they caught and there was meshage: great clatter: rumble: echoey coughs. Sick and well, up and down, but seeming to lose all the time he was recuperating. Still, because he had begun to think about it more and more, he began to become afraid of certain kinds of deaths: it wasn't the dying he was afraid of but having some kind of stroke, lying there, noise and roaches crawling all over him. He went back to see the doctor even though he couldn't afford the five dollars.

"You gave up," she says. He looks though the doors, the mirror, at her. He holds the rinsed cups. Water drips onto the floor, onto his feet. She forgets for a second, giggles, and says,

"You look silly standing there like that." She laughs. "One thing you have to say for Miss Kaley is that she sure snaps you out of it," then stops, remembering. The old man sees he has lost ground. He turns, goes back into the kitchen and starts to pour hot water on the tea leaves to steep, and hot water into the cups.

The doctor auscultated his chest: rumblings, measureless caverns inside a thirty-six-inch chest: cough and clatter, broken and barely functioning machinery lying around. "What's in there to make so much noise?" he asks. "The pacemaker's only a small machine." "I've read a little," he proudly tells Baby.

The doctor liked that; he laughed and told the patient that he was taking it like an old trouper. When he laughed, two maloccluded lower teeth showed; they matched the cutoff points of the moustache, as if the doctor used them as shaving guides. "After all, you're old. Hand-grip weaker, bodyweight less, more spiritual (laugh, chill nudge with the stethoscope), bloodflow to brain down, maximum work-rate slipping . . ."

"I'm retired."

". . . but being old is the price you pay for civilization. In nature, the life of man is solitary, poor, nasty, brutish, and short short short. Be thankful. You have the insides of a man ten years younger."

"Don't feel it."

"Oh, you should live a long time yet. Listen: civilization has given you this time. You'd have been long dead if. Enjoy it. Coast. You're retired?"

"Yes."

"Well, you're free then. No work, no routine, less gonadal activity so less passion (which is a headache anyway), less everything. You're free. Enjoy it. That's the best prescription. This time is a matured investment; owed time. Enjoy it."

"I'm retired," he said and the doctor looked at him carefully, but decided he was being funny and laughed, showing his lower teeth.

The old patient went home. He began to think about what the doctor had told him. Couldn't get it out of his mind. How did you know you were old . . . and when . . . He tried to imagine the way he had felt when he was young. Aside from the fact that he was sick, he couldn't tell the differences. He got up and went to look in the mirror. He didn't see much: pale face, but he was used to that face. Wrinkles here and there, but nothing serious, nothing *too* old-looking. He thought about it more and more, got curious, and then he got undressed.

"You didn't."

"I did." He pours the hot water out of the cups. He pours the tea into the cups slowly, carefully, making sure that it flows in evenly. Then he slices a quarter of a lemon in two.

But one mirror hanging on the wall wasn't enough. He only saw his shoulders and chest down to a little below the pectorals. He got another small mirror and propped it below the other. They both look at the mirrors, still tandemed there; he from the kitchen, hidden from her direct sight; she from the bed. The shadow has risen so that her right hand is in coolness. Their eyes look at one another. He stood straight, squared his shoulders, firmed his muscles, and went through a whole posing routine. He saw a strong neck, legs still muscular, fatless trunk, though there were some skin-wrinkles around the waist (had he lost weight? from illness, or age-shrinkage?). Not bad. Where was he old then? "Less gonadal activity," the doctor said. True enough. He looked down at his penis. How different? Not different at all, unless to the expert's eye. Quite like a young man's; he would swear to it. Is she sneaking surreptitious peeks through the mirror? He turns himself a

145

little so that she might see, but not so that his face seen might embarrass her. Then why did he feel this way? Sickness? To be sure. Weakness? But that was an illness-concomitant. Weakness of aging? He touched it. No response. Old man's stranger's appendage. He thought of his wife; he couldn't remember her, only his daughter in Hamtramck. He thought of girls, naked; ahh, a little lift, a minor stiffening at pale, abstract fantasies. Was he indeed old? Billig turned away from the mirror.

Then there was a knock at the door . . .

"There wasn't."

"There was." It attentioned suddenly into an achy rod.

"It didn't."

"It did." And yelling, "Just a minute," he tumbled here and there, trying to dress, stuff his shirt into his pants, catching his penis and his shirttail in the zipper . . .

"You didn't."

"But what I'm trying to bring out is that I did" . . . and felt (age, sickness, nevertheless) a young man's pain in his not altogether useless For Pissing Only. He went to the door, half doubled over. It wouldn't go down.

She is giggling now. He pours a little whiskey, a drop really, into the tea and bears the cups in, telling her . . . A tall, slender woman in a tweed suit stood there. "Miss Kaley," Baby says, amused, reminded then and so, sad, humiliated again, but she takes the tea saucer. Miss Kaley looked at him bent over in the Old Man's Crick; she gave Billig that Oh You Poor Alone Old Man look. "I'm from the Borogrove Golden Age Group," she said, forcing sweetness through a clenchsmile. He adds sugar and stirs; she squeezes lemon in and stirs. Their submerged spoons scrape hot whirlpools. "How'd you find out about me," he asked Miss Kaley. The tension slackened; it limpened; he straightened. Crippled or courtly, he stood aside in a half-bow to let her in. Advancing her instep, talking about the Boro-groves, she came in. They would be honored by his recruitment.

"What for?" he asked.

"Life is not over, Mr. . . .?"

She knew very well who he was. "Billig. Who said it was?" And he smiles, sharing his secret with Miss Baby in the bed. She lifts her cup, sips, and shares with him that sad secret. He hopes their tea will give her a little strength against Miss Kaley. Miss Kaley smiled at him as if to say, "You're not hiding anything from me." "Social activities . . ." Miss Kaley began and outlined a group program that included Social Dancing (though not the Twist, the Hula Hoop, folk dancing, the Limbo Rack, the Hully Gully, Frug, and Watusi), stately, digni-fied, uncrippling dances. "Now you've got to face the fact that you're an old man" (Had it been here that he had learned it?) when they were seated ("Tea?" "I should be delighted." And he had used a new teabag for her), facing it for him, grabbing the old bull by his dulled horns, candor-calling it, dis-armingly, with a brave little adjustive smile, sighed, getting it over into the Now We Have It Out In The Open . . . was that so bad?

Miss Kaley was quick-moving; bangles tinkled on her wrists; she wore dangly earrings: they were misleading; her adducted hands danced, but her elbows were held tightly to her slender body; her outgoing feet were disfigured by big, social-worker shoes which made her legs, shapely, seem sticklike. She wore a heavy, squaring-off tweed, but it didn't seem to hide too well her surprisingly big bosom. She wore glasses which tended to slip down her bony cheeks, raising her eyebrows a little, giving

147

SOMEONE JUST LIKE YOU

her an honest or amused look. Her mouth, however, was bent inward so that the pink lipflesh barely showed. "We're here to help you."

Her right hand holds the cup; her arm is all bared now, soft in the shadow which has risen farther to the left till it touches her neck and cuts down her shoulder and chest and seems to disappear under the cover. He is seated, now, in an easy chair, his body partly hidden from her by the arm of the chair. The cloth feels strange, exciting, on his behind and the backs of his legs and where his privates touch there. His cup clatters as he tries to find a comfortable position.

"It's kind of you," he told Miss Kaley, staring at the tweed bulge. He gestured at her unsipped tea. "A little coffee instead? I could brew some . . . don't care for the instant kind."

"No thanks," Miss Kaley said and stirred her tea. "I like it lukewarm," and she laughed, looked around, took stock: pictures, books, radio, bed, mirrors (he blushed and felt a light tingling there again), curtains, but all cleanswept. He could see she was thinking "Old Man's Room," and wondered, quite surprised, seeing it through Kaley bulge-eyes, had sixty-six years left him only this? "She does make you feel like that," she says as she sips again, smells, stops, looks at him. If she drinks it, it will be a commitment, this old seducer tells himself. Miss Kaley made fast moves with her hands, shaking her bracelets nervously while her head teetered the earrings and her feet danced adjustively, though her steady bright eyes pinned him to her expectancies. It annoyed him but he was too tired to get angry. He declined the whole thing. She left after a while, telling him she'd be back real soon. When she was gone he realized that it had been a very long time since he had anyone to talk to.

"You've put something in it," she says.

"A touch . . . a sweetener . . . baby (cloysound, he forces it out) . . . sweets to the . . ."

She sips it. Ahh, old Billig thinks.

Then, finally, one day, he had three dollars and twenty cents in the bank. He was reluctant to close the account; had it . . . thirty years. "My God. Thirty years." The pension wasn't going to be enough to live on. So he applied for relief; old-age assistance.

They sent a young, but balding investigator: man in his forties; plump; wrinkled gray flannel suit; upcurled shirt collar; smooth pink face; judicious lip-purse; had a spinsterish order of doing things; high nasal voice; and he sat by the radiator.

"Relief, Mr. Radaman . . ." Billig started to say.

"Assistance, Mr. B. Please. Assistance."

"I hate to do this; I hate to take charity; never been dependent . . ."

"Now now, Mr. B. It's not charity and it is no shame." Mr. Radaman spoke loudly, clearly.

". . . but what I'm trying to bring out is that I just can't make it."

Mr. Radaman worked figures in a notebook and primly said, "After all, you've paid your taxes. You're entitled."

"I didn't eat for two days last week waiting till my pension check came."

"Why didn't you come in to see us," Mr. Radaman said accusingly and asked questions: management, legally responsible relatives?

"Oh, I wouldn't want my children to know. I haven't seen them for . . . must be ten years now. She lives in Hamtramck

149

. . . what do you think of that for a name? I wonder how it got a name like that. I must look it up . . ."

"I'm sure I wouldn't know, Mr. B.," Mr. Radaman said. "But . . ."

"And she's married; no income of her own."

"We'll write to them, of course."

"Do you have to?"

"Procedure."

"Don't want to worry them."

"Now the way I compute it is that you are seven dollars and twenty-seven cents short every half month, Mr. B."

"Is that all? Only seven twenty-seven? It felt like more. Do you have to write them? Maybe I can get along . . ."

"It's your funeral, Mr. B. After all, it is more than you think."

And he knew it was. "I'd like them to think I was independent."

"I certainly admire your spirit, Mr. B., but procedure," Mr. Radaman said, puffing out the P, purring the R, stressing the O, hissing the SSS, lingering on the EEEE and UUUUU sounds, projecting it as if he were talking to someone about five feet behind Mr. B. So it was final. And Mr. Radaman accepted the case contingent upon Mr. B.'s exhausting his bank account, departmental procedure. " 'Well,' I said. He says, 'Mr. 933066 R.I.P. Long live Mr. OAA 7, 933, 822.' " She giggles at that.

Mr. Radaman, conscientious, visited only a little more than he had to but, to Mr. B.'s way of thinking, rarely. He found he wanted to talk now, but Mr. Radaman said they could always chat after the required interview. But after, it was a case of looking at his watch and saying, "Oooops. I have to run." He hated himself for looking forward to Mr. Radaman's visits.

The check for $7.27 came twice a month; the loneliness was there all the time. He planned ways to engage Mr. Radaman, keeping him talking. He strained his memory, trying to find what had been interesting in his life. What had he done? Been a draftsman and a parts-lister, high-class engineer-type clerk. Not much in that. But he felt that if he could . . . entertain Mr. Radaman, it would in some way provide a justification for Mr. Radaman's having to come, having to ask his questions, for his case being so cut and dried; it would be a way of earning his $7.27 semimonthly. That was what he told himself. But he does not tell this to Baby either. They sit and sip tea, immersed in the silentness. She doesn't look so agitated now. A faint film of sweat slips along her temples and pools in the hollow where the clavicles meet.

So he ordered the events of his past in fiat series, trying to recapture the memory feel, the passion of a past moment. He only succeeded in budgeting events, item by item, chronologically. He half-remembered what had happened: the First World War, Lindbergh, the Crash, the Depression, Pearl Harbor, the first year the Dodgers won the pennant, popular dances. They were events he had been near, but not in: dull, abstract, tasteless, March of Time, everyone's memory, someone else's memory. What he did remember wouldn't have been interesting: a furious argument with his wife, a mauve dress with shiny costume jewelry she had worn to a dance. He tried to give it all as riders to the required information but Mr. Radaman, polite, skilled, elicited only the litany of institutional question and response, picked what was required out of linger-dates, backtrack corrections, the windy, boring crotchets and canceled out the rest with an "Oh hell, that really isn't pertinent," and ignored the angry But It Does Matter, as well as the self-anger (for Mr. B. heard himself being boring).

A few warm days came. He got better. He went out into the streets again. Bones ached a little, sense of a little fever that the thermometer didn't show; moved slowly; even made him breathless; false spring winds hit him viciously: he moved through syrup. "What I'm trying to bring out is, *that* is age; *that* is being old." She nods; she understands; she sips; they have all gone through it. He went into a square-park nearby. Wherever he went he saw nothing but old men come out to sit a while in the watery sunlight; blinking, blinking. Where had so many old men come from? He didn't remember them. Drab rows of them all perched on the circling benches, dull to see; crowds of them standing around; hordes of them around the public *bocce* run. Many old were in wheelchairs; palsied others shivered perpetually; others were twisted and crabbed along, helped or alone. Old winos—the Respectable Retired gave them a wide berth—soaked up the sun. Coats draped loose; caps were too big on shrinky faces. Angry Old; white-limned faces barked at one another, arguing through the difficulties of loose old logic, false teeth, trembly memories about events that might have been (you could look it up), vindictively cackling out fact backed by years of I Know What I'm Talking About. Not him. He strode by, feeling stronger than them now, different, and, to prove it, went in to waste money on a youthful black and brown houndstooth Professor Higgins hat, very rakish. But where were the young? He looked for them. The hat didn't help him. All gone. Nowhere. Millions of oldsters, though none with a Professor Higgins hat. Suddenly, setting the cup and saucer teetering on the arm of the chair, he gets up and goes to his closet, gets it, puts it on. She smiles, funny sight, clownish. He raises the hat; she giggles and looks at him a little longer. He grins, comes back and sits down. "Eight dollars it cost me."

"You didn't."

"What I'm trying to bring out is that you have to." And she nods.

But hard winter set in again . . . his sickness came back as a low-level fever. He lay around now, doing nothing, watching the plaster sloughing off, wondering if he should decorate the house to keep busy.

And one day Miss Kaley came back. "She doesn't give up." They have finished their tea and look at one another. He is sweating lightly. How long did she struggle, he wonders, before Miss Kaley got her? Never asked. Must. "Finished? Good for you. Hot drink in the summer cools you."

"You're a romantic," she says.

"One of the old school, baby." Silence. "Don't be a schoolteacher all your life. Free yourself." She wags.

Had he thought of joining their little group? He hadn't. Miss Kaley urged him to. Something about her attitude bothered him. She assumed too much; he couldn't penetrate past what she saw . . . but what did she see? An Old Man. That was it. When had he become like an old man? "No shame in being old, is there, Mrs. Kaley?" he asked.

"Miss," she said. "None."

No shame in being Miss either, he thought. "But I don't feel like it, you see," he lied. "Like a young man. A little short in the pneuma, but then I've been sick lately. I could get a job, man of my talents, but I wouldn't give them the satisfaction. Principle. Retired. I've earned it. Freedom. Chance to be myself. In the old days . . . well, it was work till you died—you could read about it—and you died young. Now . . ."

153

"But I understand your position thoroughly." Her head moved; her earrings nodded; her eyes noed.

"Don't feel it in any way."

"Now . . ." she said (he must have been raising his voice; angry, excited, shaky with fury inside, but he watched his hands carefully to see they didn't tremor). He caught sight of Miss Kaley's profile in the two mirrors: she was unconvinced, though leaning forward with an earnest, Let's Be Honest With One Another look, narrow in the eye behind those candid-making lenses.

"Now what do you think we're doing wrong in Vietnam, to say nothing of Taiwan? Or, for that matter, what about Professor Witfogel's theory of the waterwheel and tyranny?" he asked her suddenly.

She looked puzzled; thought he had flipped off into senility. He was going to explain, but she was giving him a You're Being Childish look; a woman's trick for equalizing the odds. "Now, now," she says. He stands up and takes the cup and saucer from her with one hand and with his other rough hand kneads the back of her neck, bunching the flesh on her upper back, looking down the space of cover into where her breasts cleave.

"Now, now," he mimics gently. His hand keeps her head from turning. Her avert-eyes look into the slanty bar of hot sunlight on the wall.

"That feels good," she says. Her white hair shines against his time-gnarled knuckle-flesh. He goes into the kitchen for more tea and . . .

"Look," he told Miss Kaley. He stood up and executed a perfect palm-touch to the floor without one little bend of the knee, no groan, no creak of the unoiled parts (his chest clattered, but she didn't seem to hear that) and, turning his head, looked at her from that position, smiling with most every one of his own teeth. He saw her smile a Humor-Him smile. He stood up and said, "Mind is flexible, Mrs. Kaley."

"Miss," she assured him.

"And the body is not dogmatic," and he laughed. "I'm willing to accept being old. That's years. But is age willing to accept me? I haven't the thoughts for it yet," he said. "So you must stop looking at me that way."

"What way?"

"Seeing what you've made up your mind to see."

She smiled at him a little more softly, surprised. Her slightly pointed teeth protruded a little below the upper lip, but she gerontologized a little less stringently, determined to be cunning. She said, "But that is why we want you in the Borogroves."

"Why?"

Surely you've read about "The Problem of Aging in Our" . . . a quasi-public, parti-civic, mutual bund of geronts who meet that Problem of Aging "Which I'm sure you know all about" by . . . Those Cast Aside, but Still Useful who have learned to make a most wonderful Adjustment and still have "a Future."

He told her he didn't care for it. He wasn't a joiner, never was: life was too organized as it was. It should be freer. "Organization for this, that, everything. Know all about the problem of aging. Sunday supplements; national photomagazines; news magazines; wherever you go; highly inspirational, but . . ." he says.

"They have teas for the ladies," she says.

"Painting. Linoleum cuts." He comes to the doorway.

"Needlepoint. Weaving." Her hands shuttle.

"Carpentry; card games; dominoes. Shuffleboard; painting," he says, taking off his hat and holding it high, stepping in time to each craft.

"Knitting, tatting, hobbies, crocheting." She sits up, then kneels, holding the cover to her bosom, waving with one hand.

"Crossword puzzles jigsaw puzzles songfests hobbies," he roars and dances in a soft-shoe routine.

"Rehabpurposeinliferehabhobbiesrehabhobbieshobbieshobbies," they both, throwing their arms wide, sing. And laugh. And then she, realizing, embarrassed, picks up the cover and holds it to her neck and says, "I shouldn't have come." He looks at her and goes back into the kitchen and pours the hot tea into the warmed cups and, for both cups, pours in a greater dose of liquor than before; he listens to the creaking bed, not knowing if she is getting out or sitting back. He comes in quickly, bearing the cups.

Well, it was a place to go; come out of the cold of small apartments and come flocking off the parkbench perches, but . . . no; it seemed terribly trivial, he told Miss Kaley.

Miss Kaley said, "It isn't healthy to shut yourself off. At the Borogroves you will find companions, men like yourself, women of your time of life. You could make lasting friends, not all of them merely old, because we have some *really* interesting people in our group. After all, warm relations have even matured into lasting ones."

He coughed.

"Marriage, even."

He laughed. "What do I want with an old woman?"

"You're not being realistic," she snapped at him, suddenly angry.

"Now a young one, that's different. Oh, not a teen-ager;

156

that's for literary or Biblical characters. Not a Jayne Mansfield —you see, I *am* being realistic—but what do I want with an old woman?" he said, scorning. But this is one of the things he doesn't tell her, but gives her the cup instead. She is a little calmer now and the incoming shadow covers three quarters of her now, making her easier to see. He sits down at the foot of the bed, crosses his legs, but takes care not to let the saucer touch his thigh.

"No. You're *not* being realistic," Miss Kaley said too quickly. "Why not?"

And her sudden look told him why not; a look full of disgust, quickly masked as she smiled, those teethtips showing, and moved, jingling her merry bangles. "Oh, they're the worst," she tells him. "Aren't they?" he answers. But he caught Miss Kaley's look and said, spitefully, "Oh, not a young one, but someone in, let us say, their thirties." Younger than Miss Kaley's age: the bloom of youth was there but the withering of age was frosting it (like Miss Kaley), and understanding was growing (but not like Miss Kaley). But he didn't go too far because he wanted her to come back: he was lonely. She left; she said she would come back: he said, "Do, please do."

She sniffs the hot tea-fumed whiskey and says, "You naughty boy, you've made it stronger," but sips.

"Best medicine in the world." She looks at him in that wise way teachers have; can't forget it, or help quailing before that look even now, and it is more than fifty years. He rises, saying, "A toast. Well, we're rid of her now, of good Mrs. Kal . . . oops; Miss." They laugh. She shakes her head, not so much refusing the toast, but at something else, and sips the tea. He sits down again and can rest the saucer on his thigh now; the heat has gone out of it.

Now he began to have bad afternoon-nap dreams. Each time

157

he woke uncomfortably, an old man with a young man's throbbing penis, and, starting out of bed fast, looked around to see if someone had seen him this way. But as he was awake, he knew he was alone. He was always breathless, tired, and he forgot just what it was he dreamed. Silly. Afternoon emissions. He wondered if his prostate was going tricky. He stumbled out to drink some water for his dry dry throat. He caught himself passing the mirror and admonished himself with a finger-shake. He tried to stop his naps. And then the apartment began to seem too small; he became restless and was driven out, more and more, into the cold streets.

Now the streets seemed always full of women; he hadn't noticed for a long, long time. Their cheeks glowed; their hair was piled in strange soft fluffs, or ballooned out, held by what magic in impossible sensual shapes, unhairlike, or whirled in exciting sinuosities. Their skins shone white, dark, brown, as he watched the lights along the soft curves. He stared at them highheeling past and turned to stare surreptitiously. He watched athletic calves bunch over flat heels as they rose on their toes. He became skilled at seeing and appreciating the bare sense of the flattest breast under the thickest winter wool. Once, a girl took off her hat and, shaking her hair, swirled it back and forth in the bright light and it made him weak like having dizzy spells. He had to turn away because . . . because they might see his hungry look. Young and old, women and children even, he stared and was ashamed of his new lust.

But he had to have his naps now and then, and so became shut away again. Once he woke, heavyheaded, to see a disembodied stocking-sheen in the half-light and, dizzied, sleep-drunk, he went close, turning on the light against the afternoon darkness. And he was almost beginning to caress what re-

solved to a marbleized shine of the washtub leg, cold cold cold
to the caress: shocked, looked closer to see how he could have
made that mistake because the fine varicosities in the porcelain
repulsed him. What had he been doing? Unable to sit around
and read now, he rushed back out, going into the chill evenings
and walked along past the pre-Christmassy windows, risking
pneumonia, wishing he had someone to talk to. He stared at
the mannequins in their sequined party dresses; they suppli-
cated with outturned hands and he thought they made them
much better than they used to.

A few weeks passed. Miss Kaley came back. He opened the
door to her knock and was shocked at the violence of his need
for her. He stopped himself and stood stiff, trying to find a
course between eagerness and prideful rejection. He admits all
this. He was cunning and talked carefully. He watched to see
that his hands didn't tremble, that he made vigorous gestures,
leading her to believe that he might after all join. He talked
fast, trying to interest her, bringing up the past: it was full of
Never-Dids, Almosts, and If I Had Onlys. He struck boldly
and said, as he was reminiscing, "So I said to myself,
Gesualdo . . ."

"I thought your name was Morris?"

"Gesualdo always sounded funny, so I took the name of
Morris. Billig, said I . . ." and he began to fabricate a past that
might be interesting for her; it was. She stayed. Not all fiction,
certainly much, most of it in fact, a kind of fact: you just had
to find the ways to talk about it. "We're all thrilling novels,
baby," he says. Miss Kaley stayed for an hour. "Gesualdo Billig
used to be a . . . a carpenter . . . but it didn't turn out to be as
dangerous a job as it used to be," he said. Miss Kaley looked at
him, puzzled, began to understand, and laughed at Gesualdo

Billig's audacity and said she would come back again. But she didn't get back for two months.

It was then that he began to go through a strange period. He blushes to remember it; it is something he hopes is far away, time-buried, but how long ago, really, when his life was full of longing and he was sure he was going senile and he could hardly walk the streets without being afflicted with sudden needs, painful shameful urges, and had to take to staying home and looking out his window only.

The cover has slipped a little from her shoulders and is lower now; the light from the window shines along the smooth curve of her plump shoulders; how surprisingly good they are, Billig thinks, for a woman of her years. If the cover slips a little farther, revealing the beginning of the division of her breasts, he will have won. From the tilt of her cup he sees that she has drunk about half. Perhaps one more cup of tea, a stronger dose . . . he is feeling better now. They smile at one another. Mutual sufferings: odd needs. The ever-present sounds from the outside buzz, far away now, half ignored. He feels vague stirrings, even now, as he remembers.

For he found himself forced to masturbate once in a while, as if to merely relieve intense pressures that racked his loins. Long afternoons spent in thinking what if . . . young girls . . . and then feeling disgust during, and remorse after, because it was always a case of the young fantasy girls who, somehow a little independent of his visions, realized what they were doing and turned away from him in disgust, fright, horror. And he, unable to stop, would continue mechanically and ejaculate without a fantasy and lie there, hearing the throb in his ears and seeing the room pulsate and then, after a while, thirsty, would first rinse his mouth and then drink and the old man would be disgusted with himself: unnatural practices. He tells her only parts; she waits for his story; her teeth click against the cup; dry sound on thick ceramic.

But one day Miss Kaley came visiting. Mr. Radaman came too. Coincidence. They talked; subject in common. Didn't dare mention Gesualdo: Radaman knew. At first Mr. Billig was flattered. Warmth in social-worker mutuality . . . Billig-sharing . . . jargonese leavened by psychologizing. Mr. B. waited for Mr. Radaman to leave. Mr. Radaman lingered. Soon, too soon, they were cozying a little; he was trapped into offering precious tea to Mr. Radaman. Of course Miss Kaley scorned Mr. Radaman; he wasn't a proper social worker. Mr. Radaman worked hard to overcome this defect; he had some courses in social work. They left together. Miss Kaley said she would return. The silence was especially heavy when they were gone. He was disappointed for, since they had come together, he had gotten to talk to neither one of them; two contacts diminished into none.

He takes the cups. "Tea?"

"No more," she says. But he fills them and stiffens the dose of whiskey. Not much left there; once gone, all done, last chance, he thinks. He comes back. She says, "No thanks," but takes the cup, her cover slipping more and more, showing her good skin, the hollows gleaming with perspiration, smells the whiskey and, smiling, she drinks it. He, holding the cup high in the toast position, faces her and sees, happily, that she is looking at him. "You're not trying to get me drunk?" she asks. He nods yes. They smile and drink together.

Billig's strange urges grew. He was masturbating more than ever. His afternoon fantasies became more elaborate. And many times he awoke in the mornings, aching, caught between the needs to urinate and have sex: it (strange now, almost not his), rigid. He came fresh out of dreams where, somehow, girls partially dressed ran through forests. And he, young, young, always chased them, caught them, caressed them, let them go, and chased again. He lay there and sustained himself in his dreams. His girls always had the faces of girls he had casually seen, never women he had known (except, oddly, for Miss Kaley now and then), never his wife, and once, before he was quite sure what was happening, his daughter as a young girl. And he used to lie there, stupefied, imprisoned, ashamed, trying to stop, saying this is the last time, or, just one more time, just once, but, compelled, it would happen and he was immured in a twilight world where shadows on the furniture were mixed up with leaf-shadows that forever used to flicker over stockings and garter buckles and brassiere straps: panties were loam-smudged; slips circled tree trunks. He lay there, laughing, rolling on inexplicable tire-tracks in the forests, or ran and plucked costume jewelry from shoetrees and caressed buttocks caught and held through trunk clefts. Then he would ejaculate and begin to cough and rattle and grind and after a long while, when he had long stopped, he would sit there in the dimness and look at his hands: rootlike, they always twitched a little and stopped: his phantom and shrunk-flesh gears would whine into a creak as he tried to reengage and move. Was he senile? Was he destroying himself? What was happening? Was it even possible? Go out. Go out, he said. What was the point, he replied, and hung around all day, an ancient man trying to leave off, but instead, caught, half dreaming, half compelled, he would begin it again and end it with a cough, rattle, and a cup of hot tea.

Miss Kaley, continuing her campaign, came back. Unaccountably, Mr. Radaman happened to come the same day . . . there were a few questions he had forgotten to ask Mr. B., or there was a form he had to have filled out: he was vague about it. It bothered Mr. B.; as a rule, Mr. Radaman came no more than he felt he had to and now here he was again, pretending interest, saying we must do much for poor old Mr. Billig. Special clothing; certain extras (all allowed, of course). What was happening? He watched closely as they were sipping the begrudged tea. "Wasn't it sweet, those adolescents?" he asks. And he thought that he, the man of years, of maturity, must soon prevail. But, like people of another nation, another way of life, they were talking above him, around him, through him. While they talked he tried to interpose the Wisdom of his Years, the Knowledge of the Senior Citizens. He heard himself talking, being boring, and stopped. Did Mr. Radaman, a pale smile smudged onto his round face, leaning forward, past him, hunger at her breasts while drooling social-worker talk? "Oh, she was his cupof; you could see that." He stared at Miss Kaley in a newer light. Did the investigator lust after her slim legs, the dainty outturned feet, the fast-moving, slender hands, the seductive arc of her long earrings . . . he looked at the carapace of stiff tweed on her big breasts and suddenly it happened; he saw her naked. "Had to lean forward to protect myself."

He demonstrates, going into a cramped position. She is laughing, drinking the tea, laughing again, at ease. "So I figured it this way. If he comes again a third time, they're using my place to meet. But she hasn't, you see, given him the OK to meet outside. But they were there to talk about me . . . it was *my* time and it made me mad, believe me."

He had begun to worry now. Supposing he had some strange disease which, at this stage, manifested itself as a great tickle, but would, in time, become, let's say, a cancer. He tried to read about it but found nothing in the library but desiccated tables about diseases of the old, sterile descriptions that had nothing to do with longing. Finally, he went back to the doctor, but was ashamed to tell him just why. Said he felt ill, and old, and needed a general checkup.

"You're dying," the doctor said as his beady eyes stared from the center of what looked like a shiny pit. Billig stammered. The doctor said, smiling and silly, "But you've been dying from the day you were born. Ever think of it that way? No, hah? Thought so." And his fingers crawled over the old man. "Bronchitis's gone. Fine shape. Declination, you see, but that's understandable; aging. Loss of tissue, shrinkage, less glomerular filtration rate, less nerve-conduction velocity, less gonadal activity and . . ." And seeming to understand something suddenly, he said, "Listen, there's nothing to be ashamed of."

Billig's discovered heart pounded and the stethoscope knew all.

"Lots of men your time of life come to me." Patting gesture. Reassuring nod. "But what do you expect?"

Billig hoped: was his shame common? If not, sequester this mad and dirty Old.

"I'd give you pep pills, but what for? Widower and well out of it; blessing in disguise; age's consolations. Fine, fine." And Billig, ashamed to say anything, went out into the streets to be driven mad by any passing woman.

Mr. Radaman and Miss Kaley met a third time. This time Mr. Radaman sought to help Miss Kaley persuade his client, Mr. B., to join and disport in the Borogrove Golden Age Group. "Wasn't it grand, those two kids; all concerned? What I'm trying to bring out is that I was running a social club here," he says. She smiles at him; her face is flushed. He sat, impotent, furious, watching their heads, turning from one to the other and then, still while they looked at one another, Miss Kaley's lips unpinched and Mr. Radaman lowered the volume of his shout. Their faces close, it was a regular Conference on Aging. From time to time they would remember *to* ask, "Well, in your experience isn't it so/not-so, Mr . P /Billig?" Miss Kaley, patiently, softly, understandingly, like to a little boy; Mr. Radaman talking to the people already of another country to whom it was only necessary to talk loudly clearly to make them understand. " 'I'm not deaf, Mr. Radaman,' I told him. And do you know what he said?" She shakes her head. " 'But as a matter of fact *I* am a little, you know. That's why I talk so loudly.' "

"He beat you there," she laughs.

"Well, I *knew* I lost that one, so it became a contest for Miss Kaley."

He got excited when she crossed her legs and her skirt slid a little higher, and he could see the inside of her crossed-over thigh. Then he talked. The past. He fabricated it into a richness of fight and tragedy. Unions; strikes; the hunger for education; the hard times of the Depression; the fight for amelioration; a little hoboing; love (certainly love . . . and how many women had there been than just his wife; the fantasy faces hung in front of him as he embellished). And then, the reading, the endless word-hunger, and the magic words, "Self-educated," and the rise to a station above manual labor, personalizing it all with a feel he derived from the sense of what-it-should-have-been-like. Almost his life: quite like his life. Mr. Billig pointed out that, in a way, the social workers' very jobs were owing to *his* fights. "They don't look at it that way, do they?" he asks. They hadn't. He made vigorous and punctuating movements of his untrembling carpenter's hands, showing how he this and that in the past.

Mr. Radaman tried hard to counter but lost. He was not, after all, a person who had as interesting a life as Mr. Billig. Merely a civil servant who had played it safe, never tried the big things, never been tempered by the bad times, a man, after all, Miss Kaley knew too well. Mr. Radaman was stubborn and they stayed a long time. Mr. Billig monopolized the conversation. She turned more and more to him. He finally routed Mr. Radaman when he said, "The trouble with those Florida places is that they are senilopoli (how she glowed at that word), not really places for the old, but places the young hope the old would like to be in. Tombs for the consciences. Not so; it isn't so; it doesn't stop," he said and looked at her knees. And they left.

The next time Miss Kaley came alone. And now she began to come quite frequently. She stopped urging him to join the Borogroves. He began to ask *her* questions; she consulted him a little about her Seniors; they branched off and discussed life in general. She told him she had been married, but it hadn't worked out: he had been . . . immature. "I pity the man," she says. He laughs and squeezes, gently, her thigh through the cover. "She told us about you before you came. She said that she'd met this wonderful man who had done . . . oh, so many things. For a while I thought she was talking about someone her own age. But when she said you'd be an inspiration to us all, I knew she meant one of us. She said you'd been a fighter, read a lot, were full of life, had done a lot of things." He smiles at her, a little fatuously, so she says, "But she always says they're either still full of life, or they're in serious trouble; you know, withdrawn: and it's up to us to pull together and help out."

"Well," he tells her, "I showed her that I wasn't sitting around waiting for, you know . . . it . . . stewing in my own juice . . . not that I have much left, you know." And he leers.

Her raucous hoot tells him she is a little high. She puts her hand to her mouth and giggles. "The way you go on, Morris . . . I mean Gesualdo."

"Well, what I'm trying to bring out is that it began to be a case of Gesualdo Billig, you see, and not poor old Morris Billig."

"Maybe she needed a father . . . that's what they're always talking about these days."

"What a dirty mind you have."

"Look who's talking about a dirty mind," she says, "parading yourself around in the altogether."

And for the first time he blushes a little, stands, lifts his hat, turns away, and goes into the kitchen to wash his cup, turns, peeks through the doorway to the mirror. She is smiling now.

He began to make a plan about Miss Kaley and the planning of it got him out of the twilight world. She came. They sat knee to knee. They had tea. Miss Kaley took it hotter; winter had come. He talked; he laughed; he waved his big, worker's hand generously; he told of the courting of his wife and made it funny and, somehow, exciting. She leaned forward and said, "I certainly admire your spirit. The others should see you, know you." And then they had come to the "Do you mind if I ask you a personal question?" stage.

Deep breath; not so candid; serious moment: hungered look on Miss Kaley's face: mouth a little open, pink inners of the white flesh there and the sparkling tips of the teeth showing . . . hungry to know, hungry . . . an important question, asked many times, he saw. He did not mind, he said, and prepared to give her solemn words of Strength: Wisdom: Endurance.

"Aren't you afraid of (breath) (sigh) you know (hand-pumping) dying?"

The cup rattled in his hand as he shifted a little. Miss Kaley crossed her legs. His hand was inches away from the long time since he had touched a fleshed-out stocking, and he was like a young man, uncontrolled at the sight of her knee. The excitement made him sillyproud; the strength was in him and he felt a shock that made his body tingle in a way he could only remember while he, for one second, thought of himself and Miss Kaley in bed; and her, those breasts, those slender girl-thighs under his hands, those large large large breasts . . . He sought words of Consolation while everything swirled. "I'm dying now."

Miss Kaley gasped; her tongue licked her lips. One hand was pressing into her great soft breast.

"We are dying from the day of our birth," he said.

A great sigh bubbled out of her lips.

"Of course I'm afraid. Everyone is." He made it sound like a lie, but he is. "But if I'm not afraid of death, I'm learning to be, baby (it comes smoothly now, most naturally)." And he tips his hat gratefully.

The expression on Miss Kaley's face told him he had said the right thing, for she thought him braver now, vital; for she believed in facing things squarely, in adjusting to what must be. He shifted a little closer and leaned forward and patted Miss Kaley's knee, lightly at first, sexlessly, old man comforting girlish fears . . . and felt tweed and stocking and wished he could remember poetry or speeches of consolation.

"You have to have the knees for these styles," she says.

The cup tilted; a little tea slurped into the saucer. Miss Kaley watched his face; he watched her knees, as if in deep thought.

"And those social-worker shoes, they fatten her ankles and skinny her calves," she says.

The tea dripped from the saucer onto her thigh; the tweed drank it thirstily.

"But then, maybe she has flat feet," she says, charitably.

They noticed; she ooohed. He moved quickly and had fallen to his knees, set his cup and saucer to the ground and had pulled out his handkerchief and was dabbing at the wet spot on her thigh and then felt the slight curve of her slender thighs underneath, but firmer than the negating thickthread tweed. And bending to dab better, he caught quick, exciting glimpses of the inner curvings above her stockingtops where her thigh-flesh was jammed together. Miss Kaley was saying, "But it's all right, it's all right"; the hysterical note jangly in her voice, her hands fluttering bangles, pushing him away while he grasped one thigh firmly, her other calf, and pushed his face against her bosom and kissed from one breast to the other again and again while she panted a thousand rejecting platitudes about Old Age.

"Though, can you imagine being kissed by . . ." and she sucks in her lips. "And her breasts are too big for her."

She pushed him away. They were silent. He, facing her on his knees, looking up at her. Her tweed-flattened breasts heaved high, as though pumping red color into those pale cheeks. Out of pinchlips she said, "Mr. Billig, you must accept your age. You must accept my position. When a man gets . . ."

"Picasso doesn't. Stokowski doesn't. Chaplin doesn't. Toscanini didn't," he said.

"But these are remarkable men . . ."

"God damn it. That's the trouble. We have all accepted. I accept. The world accepts. You accept . . ."

"What do you mean, I accept? What do I accept?"

He cackled, getting to his feet; rough gears catching now, grating hard, harshening. "Look at you." He pointed to her breasts. "Tweedy unwomaning suit. Low, flat, sensible social-worker flats; makes your legs look like two-by-twos. Sexless caretaker for the sexless dying, that's you."

She started to say something.

"There are breasts under that, breasts. Thighs under that rough cloth. You're supposed to be a woman, so don't talk to me about acceptance."

She stood up. "I must go back. This is childish of you, Mr. Billig, childish."

He stood. He shrugged. Nothing more to say now. She left. The silence was contained again by the sounds outside. He had a headache; anger had made him breathe too hard; the blood throbbed in his thin ear-veins, shutting him in. He had taken a chance. Lost. Dirty old man. Fumbling hands over her thighs. "Some picture it must have looked," he says. She doesn't laugh. They look at one another.

But, after three weeks, Miss Kaley sent him a letter. Apologized. Addressed him as "Dear Gesualdo." Apologetic babble. Had to have him come around to the club. She said perhaps, perhaps, she had been foolish; perhaps he had been right. It wasn't said in so many words, but he understood; she couldn't come to visit; face-saving. He thought he must go and bring her back.

He dressed up the next day. Wore his Professor Higgins hat set far off to one side. Wore his one laundry-pressed shirt. Wore a tie. In the mirror his shoulders were set straight and his face shone; quite youthful, and he went out.

The local public school has given one of its rooms to the

Borogrove Golden Age Group. You will go through a door which has an elaborate handpainted announcement; done by one of the Oldsters, no doubt, he thought: Gothicker than Gothic script, with feathery curlicues, drapery, trumpets in purple announcing in a golden fretwork . . . You will go down three steps . . . not quite a basement, yet below street level. The door is heavy to swing open; you should push hard against the brass bar; it clicks down and then the door will open easily for you, as if it resists perversely only to test the pusher's desire. The club is in a big hall, electric lit, because it is always gloomy, no matter what the time of day or what the weather; houses across the way block the light and so do the heavy board-of-education grills on all the windows.

He paused on the top of the steps like a young and jaunty hero.

The gloomy hall is festooned with colored crepe-paper decorations (contributed by local merchants) which are hung from the frosted, marshmallow-capped light bulbs. There are tables around the room, easy chairs, easels, recreational equipment of all sorts. Oldsters labor at all of them. Some of the men play dominoes, chess, cards, checkers; some do jigsaw puzzles; others discuss long-gone sports games. Some of the women gossip; others do needlework and paint watercolors. A radio plays light music; shuffleboard sticks clack disks contrapuntally to Vienna waltzes.

They all turned suddenly and looked in his direction, as if they had been waiting for something. Miss Kaley, at the rear of the long, low room, saw them turn and turned too. She was wearing a spring dress; it was tight and cut a little low. Her breasts thrust out fully now, pushing brazen print flowers on a mauve cloth field. She was balanced on high heels.

171

"Funny thing, only time she wore that outfit," she says. He comes into the room again.

Turning to a nearby wall-mirror, Miss Kaley patted her hair and fiddled with her glasses and shook her wrist, settling the bangles. He smiled to Miss Kaley's smile in the mirror and saw she was wearing lipstick; it was as if she was expecting him.

"We all noticed it," she says. "Would too, because after all you can't expect her to work in spike heels and a flowered dress."

"Why not? Give the place a little tone."

"Be realistic, Gesualdo."

He sits down by her side. They do not touch yet.

Now all Miss Kaley's Seniors have been trained to greet the newcomer. They will put down their tools; they will stop their games; they will turn toward the door; they will begin to applaud and sing "For He's a Jolly Good Fellow."

Miss Kaley turned away from the mirror, still smiling, and adjusted her glasses again. Their old voices cackled upward, imperfectly tuned, coming at him. They got up from their seats. They left their games. They moved slowly out, coming around their tables. They came toward him, singing and applauding. He heard the dry beat of their withered hands: stalks rustling. He saw their false-teeth grins. He saw their stiff grins. He saw their stiff walks. He saw the looks of senile pleasure as they corroboreed their slow way across the big floor at him.

She, the originator of this welcome, started coming, still smiling. An old man, a designated greeter, took his arm to lead him down. A woman, wearing tight little purple curls, was at his other side and took his hand to lead him to Miss Kaley.

Miss Kaley, coming, looked at the three of them, and stopped; she looked a little surprised.

172

She pats his hand resting on the bed. He takes her hand and holds it.

Miss Kaley's smile hardened a little from underneath her glasses which caught the lights coming from the windows and grilled her lenses. She resumed her walk toward them, her face looking a little odd, strained; she squared her shoulders and kept coming, a little doubtful, as if trying to make up her mind about something. She stopped in front of him and, not knowing what to say, said, "Well, Mr. Billig," and kept on, saying the accepted words of welcome. "How nice it is to have you down here with us," she false-voiced at him now. Her face was pained now. He looked at her and didn't understand why she was talking this way. She displaced the greeter, took Billig's arm and led him through the wildly applauding and singing Oldsters. Her grip was sure. She said to everyone, "We have a new member with us today." They applauded and laughed. He said, "Don't bother, don't bother," but her grip became surer, brutal now. She turned and looked at him again. She was angry, though her mouth was smiling. Her glasses reflected him, the curvature opaquing her eyes, but showing him to himself suddenly; strange, distorted, old. She kept on talking, telling him how wonderful it was to have him with them, her voice becoming harder and harder as she went on with the speech she had spoken many times as they went farther and farther into the room. She told him of all the things their wonderful Borogroves had to offer, as if she had never said those things to him before. The others, still laughing, some of them actually crying with joy, dispersed slowly, shaking their heads happily, nodding, patting him as they passed back on the way to what they had been doing . . . He said he would merely look around. Miss Kaley said nonsense, nonsense, Morris, come in, come in. Perhaps Morris was interested in a craft, woodworking perhaps; or perhaps in games, yes in games, certainly Morris was interested in games.

She lies at repose now, one arm behind her head. The cover has slipped down to her waist. He sighs and lies down beside her. They stare ahead together as if seeming to see that moment when he and Miss Kaley contended. After a long while he sighs again, makes up his mind, turns to her, turning his back on it now, leaning forward to kiss her where her neck and shoulder meet, his arm slipping around her waist. The sunlight is left against the wall now as a thin, intense light-bar, broken only by small antenna-cast shadows. He kisses her. Her eyes begin to close. He stops, sits back again. They stare ahead again. He says, "Now why did she do that?" His voice cracks. He says, "Tea!" swings his feet over the side of the bed and starts to get up, but she takes his hand and tugs it. He sits back again as she lifts the cover to put it over him. She kisses him now, on his cheek, as they lie, she facing him. "It's about time," she says. "I was sure you'd catch your death."

"It's summer."

"Summer colds are the worst. And take off that silly hat."

He takes off the hat and throws it on the floor beside the bed. He settles himself. She slips an arm around his shoulder. "Now what happened? Why'd she change like that? Why'd she do that?" His voice is a little less questioning, a little less old.

"Did she change?"

"Well, what I'm trying to bring out is that she missed her chance," he brags.

"Sour grapes."

He shrugs, laughs, turns toward her. She kisses his neck,

he kisses her under the ear, puts his hand under the cover and squeezes her belly, low. "These grapes aren't sour." They laugh. "Better. Better. I wouldn't have been able to rescue you."

"Careful," she says. "You're a dirty old man."

"No," he tells her and puts his face against her neck. "I'm just a dirty man. Leave it at that. Now why'd she change? You could just see it happening right in front of your eyes."

"I was there. I didn't see anything."

"Oh, you didn't know. Why'd she change? What'd I do?"

She pats his shoulder. "I'm sure I couldn't imagine. Maybe she thought you should be a father-figure."

"Who's dirty now?" he asks and turning on his side, begins to stroke her face, his eyes closed. His mind is still on that day. She feels he is not excited yet.

"Careful, careful," she says, not laughing now, beginning to kiss harder.

They are quiet for a long time; nothing happens. He sits up suddenly and says, "Used to be that radio program, One Man's Family."

"I remember it. I used to listen all the time."

"And the father, he'd always say, 'Yes. Yes,' tired like, you know? and 'Fann-nee.' "

"I remember. I never missed a week."

"And she'd say . . ."

" 'Hen-ree.' It was my favorite program."

"And you could just picture it: glowing dadface and apple-cheeked momface, heads pressed together, sighing; sort of restful, comforting. I mean shuffleboard, checkers, and sewing just the whole day through . . . Now why'd she change?"

She takes his head, pulls him down, face to her breasts

(which, with her plump belly and the tops of her thighs, are still very good). She strokes his body as his eyes peer through narrowed lids at the stiff brown nipples of those fine-skinned breasts.

"Careful. Careful," he says, beginning to get excited.

DO THEY TALK ABOUT GENÊT
IN LARCHMONT?

"I'LL be with you just as soon as I finish this page," Angie said. She was seated at a Colonial secretary in the corner of the room, typing. A cigarette was balanced on the typewriter.

"I know the way," Gail said. She sat in front of the coffee table; her cup was held under the spout of the electric samovar; the coffee urn perked. "How's the story coming?"

Angie didn't answer. She didn't appear to hear. She squinted intensely through the lamp's smoke-wreath at the door glass. A staple-gun kept firing on the other side of the wall.

Gail clinked the cup against the samovar, turning the flow off. She swung a teabag over the water. "What's it about?"

"Shhh!" Angie listened.

"I don't hear anything."

"Be quiet. Please don't start in. Sleep, please sleep," she incanted.

"You're being jumpy."

"What a drag—I've lost it, gone." She stood, ripping the sheet of paper out of the typewriter. She crumpled and threw it violently across the room. She switched the light off and came to the coffee table. "As soon as she hears the type-writer . . ."

"How about *that?*" Gail said, nodding at the staple-gun noise.

Angie listened. "She'll never get over that cold if she doesn't sleep. She kept us up half the night. No, she doesn't hear that. Hammering, bombs, nothing; but like let me sneak a sheet of paper into the typewriter and it's Mommymommy-mommy . . . To bug: she does it to drag."

"So what else is new?"

Angie poured a cup of coffee. She walked around the perim-eter of the chair-circle, sipping and talking. ". . . first one gets the cold—and then the other one catches it—passes it back—and it's up all night—and Mommy, I'm thirsty, Mommy—my throat hurts, Mommy—eating into my writing time, sucking my life . . ." The steady second-apart sound of the staple-gun continued. "She'll sleep now. Once she goes off—she's like on the big kick . . ." She finished the coffee and filled the cup again. "Where are the others? How long does it take to drop the brats off? Too much. We don't have time. You know what they're doing?"

"Since when are you taking it black?"

"They're talking in the school yard. They just don't take it seriously; housewives sucking up a little culture . . . Since I started to look like a mother-goddess." Angie was chunky; her behind stretched the blue dungarees pale; her hard breasts pushed the chambray workshirt . . . the button-spaces gapped; her hair was cut very short. She sat, her legs spread wide apart, cup and saucer on one thigh, elbow on the other, chin on fist. "Look at me."

"It's maturity, my dear." Gail was a short, stooped, birdlike girl with a little girl's round face. She wore a shirt with a Peter Pan collar and her stretch-slacks bagged around the knees and calves.

"Too much." Angie listened.

"Men have confidence in the motherly type."

"What's keeping May?"

"Is he going to do that all afternoon?"

"He's building me a writing room. I'm flipping. I read the riot act. Either I have a place where I can get away from *them,* or I split; out. Like that. I was so proud of myself. I did it without coming on guilty. But you know what that cat comes back with?"

"We can't afford it."

"No. He says all right, I'll build it. Like that. Poor Morris. It put me down, man, the most."

"I wish Marvin was like that."

"Cool; anything to keep me hooked." Angie sipped. The bitterness of the coffee made her face wrinkle. "Sometimes I think like if he'd only like put me down hard . . ."

"Would that end it?"

Angie grinned. "No. I'd just have a good excuse for cutting. Maybe when the room is finished . . . No. I say to myself, face it, you're a square, a housewife turned on with being a writer."

"You know better than that. Here comes Mrs. Whine."

"So I say, be a good mother, accept. You know? I wish I didn't have them; never . . ."

They could see a long row of one-family houses through the window, each personally modified, each with a tree and lawn or flagstone in front of each house. A woman was coming through the door of the house across the street. The collar of

179

her heavy coat stood, covering her cheekbones; she pulled the chin strap of her woolen hat up before the diffused autumn sunlight and the icy rustle of windblown leaves.

". . . just wake up one day and like they never were . . ."

"Look at her, just look at her," Gail said.

"I'm so mean to Melissa, cruel . . ."

"Cold blood, cold heart, cold . . ."

"But you have to be . . . Last week my period was late. Like there was no cause for alarm, none, but I began to come on wild—like withdrawal symptoms, dig?—and I say what are you flipping for? Stay cool . . ."

"Do we have to have her? That stupid bitch."

"Actually, but can't a woman fulfill herself, creatively I mean, by having children, just?" Angie mimicked in a high voice. She looked at the long-ashed cigarette smoking out of her cupped hand, stubbed it and lit another. "Look at her. Mother square."

Even though the street was hardly used by cars, the woman paused carefully, looking up and down the street.

"Do we really have to have her, Angie?"

"No. Just go ahead. Clue her."

"Well . . ."

"Sure, Gail. Just say, Mrs. Whine, you're the end but like you're too much . . ."

The woman had crossed the street and passed out of the window's view. The door chimes sounded. Angie leaped up. "She's doing it to bug. She wants to wake her up. The spiteful . . ." She threw the door open. "What are you ringing for?" she whispered fiercely.

"But it isn't polite to just walk in," Eleanor said.

"Oh, man. Like how many years have you been making the scene over here? You know where to put your things."

"I think I'll wear my coat for a while . . . I have a chill."

"Have some coffee," Gail said.

"Coffee keeps me awake."

"Tea."

"Actually, but tea has *more* caffeine than . . . you don't have cocoa?"

"Take some water from the samovar; I'll get the cocoa." Angie went into the kitchen.

"I don't suppose you have milk?" she called. "How are the children?"

"How are yours?" Gail asked.

"I think Kevin's coming down with . . ."

"That's just the way mine are," Gail yawned.

Angie came back carrying a packet of cocoa and a half-full milk container. She put them in front of Eleanor. Eleanor's legs were muscular; she crossed them to bring out the contrast between the calves and the slender, taut ankles. Her hands were long, bony, wide. She had unbuttoned the flaps of her woolen helmet.

"Where are the others," Angie asked. "Like at least May should have made it; she's regular. Shh!" She listened intently, not looking at anything.

"Oh, is Melissa home?" Eleanor asked. Her voice sounded unnaturally shrill. "My doctor says there's a new form of the flu . . ."

"Lie still, for Christ's sake," Angie said. She listened. She shouted, "Now you just stop fussing around and get to sleep or I'll come up. You dig me?" Her throat tendons stood out.

There was no sound.

"I tell you I'd be better off without them."

"That's a terrible thing to say; what if they should hear you?" Eleanor said; she was pouring the cocoa into the cup

181

of boiling water; part of it spilled on the rim and into the saucer; part of the cocoa-dust drifted, settling on the table. "What a thing to think . . ."

"Sure. I tell them all the time. I don't mean *dead*. I like just mean *not*. Just neverwas."

"But that's even worse, actually. They *understand*."

The staple-gun, having sounded low against the baseboard of the living room, stopped and then, high up against the ceiling, began to work down.

Five of them were sitting in the circle; the sixth chair was still unoccupied. "We might as well begin. May must have a good reason for not coming," Gail said.

"But she's never late," Angie said.

"Don't worry."

"All right. I hope we've all made the scene," Angie said, holding up a copy of Genêt's *Our Lady of the Flowers*.

"I've read most of it; the rest got chewed up by Abner; he's teething," Gail said.

"I couldn't get into it too deep," Eleanor said. "But I saw *The Blacks*."

"That figured," Angie muttered.

"About a quarter of it," Rose said. She was a tall, heavy woman with great breasts; her nose was hooked and her chin was pointed and she had long, deep dimples in her cheeks that would be wrinkles in a few years. ". . . but who can wait till the white sales roll around?" she continued to talk to Janet. ". . . swear, it's as if they go through a sheet a week . . . would get them black, but so morbid."

"Supposing we go around. What's Genêt trying to bring out? Eleanor?"

". . . this audience participation thing, like in *The Con-*

nection—oh, yes, there was this cute junkie . . . long, curly hair . . . I mean he *played* a junkie—and they used masks . . . No. That was *The Blacks,* wasn't it?" Gail said.

"Frankly I prefer the old-fashioned kind of play. Did you see *Who's Afraid of Virginia Woolf?*" Janet asked.

"I wasn't sure *what* he was getting at. Actually . . ." her voice shrilled out suddenly; ". . . I mean being a homosexual doesn't shock me but you don't have to go to such lengths to . . ." Eleanor paused.

"To what?"

". . . and when he said, 'The doom of the West' . . . oh, that chilled me."

"Are you going to see *The Toilet?* That sounds like fun."

". . . well, I mean who cares *what* they do . . . does he have to spell it out . . . that just . . ."

"Disgusts?" Angie said, smiling. She puffed hard on her cigarette. She leaned forward, her elbows on her wide, crossed leg. "Man, don't you see? Like the point isn't sex at all. You're letting all your middle-class hangups run away with you . . . besides, they don't *make* it. It's just a masturbation fantasy . . . a symbol."

Eleanor lifted her cup of now-cooled cocoa and sipped and made a wry face and put it down as drops fell from the cup bottom into the saucer and onto her lap. She had opened her coat.

"Put this inset in so the straps don't bind you, seriously . . ." Rose said.

". . . poetry of his images . . ."

"Poetry?" Gail asked. "What's poetic about a fairy? They're pretty, I'll admit . . . but all this talk about . . . well, it's just a waste."

"That's not the point, no. The artist is far out . . ."

"I wish we were cool Larchmont matrons getting squiffed on cocktails."

"Why envy *them?* Do they talk about Genêt in Larchmont?"

"No. Those poor Larchmont ladies discuss poetic words like Bergdorf Goodman, Lord and Taylor, the Tailored Woman . . ."

Angie drew her sneakered foot up, resting the instep on the chair. She held her ankle and argued over her knee. "It's the suffering of the artist in our time that enables him to see what we can't see. Like it's the artist's different vision . . . you can't see what's true in . . . well, Larchmont, for instance. You have to be far out."

"Exciting things happen in Larchmont. Larchmont ladies are sitting around, perhaps at this very moment, arranging husband-swaps. Say, maybe *we* should try something like that?"

"Oh sure. Swap Marvin for Sid or Morris."

The staple-gun started on a new line and progressed downward, each beat precisely timed.

"Well, *you* manage to write and live a normal life," Eleanor smirked triumphantly.

"This is a life?" Angie asked, but she smiled.

"And you once sold a story to *Partisan Review.*" Eleanor hammered home her point. "And May has sold some poetry to *Jurgen* . . ."

"*Yugen.* Sometimes I don't believe it ever happened. That was so long ago . . ."

"Don't believe that seriously," Rose said.

". . . and maybe it would be better if it just never happened . . ."

The staple-gun sounded, shooting staple after staple into one place.

". . . because you have to make it alone—the solitary act symbolizes the saintliness of the sufferer." She squinted through the smoke; there was a slight smile on her face; she stared past them to the Colonial secretary.

"No one is above . . ."

"Beyond. No, *below!*"

". . . lets your stocking sag otherwise and you look . . ."

". . . degraded to a point where below is beyond, not *down,* but far out, wild, outside of the degradation orbit; out. Elsewheresville, the . . ."

". . . more coffee?"

"That kind of filth is pointless, infantile, like a little child, actually . . ."

"The beatification scene . . ." Angie's eyes were closed now.

"What's all this involvement with the church?"

". . . flinging feces into everyone's face. Yes! FECES!"

Rose leaped to her feet, rattling the cups and saucers. "Know what Candace came home and said the other day? This'll kill you." She moved out beyond the circle where they could all see her. She stood pressing her legs together, trying to stand heels-tight. Holding the edges of her flowered shift high, a little above the black borders of her textured stockings, she curtsied to one side then the other. She began to speak in a high, simpering voice, rolling her eyes as she spoke, rocking to each line:

"Shit in your hat,
Shit in your pants,
And you will do
The duty-dance."

They all laughed hysterically. The air was full of smoke now; Angie and Gail had to cough. "Couldn't you just die . . ."

"What did you say to her?"

"Thought it was so cute but seriously, she can't go around saying shit . . ."

"Shh," Angie said, listening.

Morris had discarded the staple-gun and began to use a hammer.

May rushed in. She threw the door wide; it slammed against the wall. Her coat was open. She was panting. Her face was red and shining from the cold. Angie rose and started to move toward her. "I'm going to have a baby!" May yelled.

"Welcome to the tribe," Eleanor shrieked, jumped up and past Angie, and threw her arms around May, pressing her cheek to May's.

"Wonderful. How are you going to have it?" Rose asked, bumping her cheek against May's other cheek: May's arms squeezed their waists.

Angie was behind May, trying to help her off with her coat. May started to answer.

"Get it over with. When I was having Moira, I was out from . . ." Gail said.

"Natural childbirth is the only way . . . it's the most beautiful experience . . . oh, this is wonderful."

"I have a carriage for you . . ."

"You'll need a playpen . . ."

". . . a maternity brassiere . . . Lord and Taylor's has . . . are you going to breast-feed?"

"What a hangup . . . thought of an abortion?" Angie asked.

"When is it due?" Eleanor asked, patting May's flat belly.

"Ooooh, frankly, I'm so happy for you. This calls for a

drink," Janet said, coming close, pressing her lips to May's offered cheek and patting May's belly.

"Thought of a name yet?"

"I'm about a month and a half gone," May said.

"A month and a half! Oh, that's wonderful."

May giggled, "I couldn't bring myself to face it."

"Actually I don't blame you. I went for six . . ."

"Is it too late for an abortion?" Angie asked.

"I have a whole layette left over from Jeremiah . . ."

"Can you feel it yet?" They all laughed. "Oh, I'm so happy."

"Shit . . ." Angie said. But she went to a mirrored chest against the far wall, opened the doors and started to take out liquor bottles and glasses. "I only have Scotch. We have to stock up. We should have peyote, or grass, or LSD . . ."

"I'll get ice," Rose said and went to the kitchen.

"I guess your poetry-writing days are over for a while," Eleanor said.

Rose came back with a bowl of ice cubes and two large bottles of soda; one was already opened. She put down the bowl and the bottles next to the lined-up glasses. Angie dropped cubes into each of the glasses. "Which is why, if it isn't too late, you should like avoid this bit." She poured Scotch into each of the glasses without measuring and sloshed soda from the already opened bottle.

"That's a horrible thing to say," Eleanor's high voice shrilled.

"That's a horrible thing to say," Angie mimicked. "Come off it. It's facing facts. Look at me." She passed a drink to Gail.

"Blankets with ruffles are cute but not smart thinking. They do dirty things on them."

"Having children is the first step to like going under."

"Having children is the most wonderful, creative thing a

woman can do," Eleanor said. "There's an art to raising them . . ."

Angie stopped serving and turned. "Sure, like the art of the bottle, the art of the aspirin, the art of Captain Kangaroo. Dig: *creative* persons shouldn't have a marriage or children. Can't you understand it's a bad scene?" May looked from Angie to Janet.

Rose passed out the drinks, taking the last one.

"A toast," Rose cried. "A toast. Ladies. To motherhood. To creativity. To May. Ohhh, I'm so happy." They sipped.

"Whee. In the middle of the week. Do we get to throw the glasses into the fireplace?" Gail asked.

"She doesn't have a fireplace," Janet said.

"Get that Morris in here to start one right now."

Morris hammered. He was working low. They felt the vibrations on the floor through their feet.

"Actually, pregnancy is the best time of your life," Eleanor said.

"You'll love it."

"Morning sickness . . ."

"And the feel of the baby . . ."

". . . gumming your breast . . . oh boy."

"Personally, I admit I can't see it," Gail said. "Besides, I think it ruins the breasts."

"That's just a silly superstition," Rose said. "Seriously, it's *good* for the breast."

"Their skins smell so sweet," Janet said.

"Especially when they have a full diaper."

"You just cannot get along without diaper service."

"Wash, wash, wash," Rose said. She held her glass high and said, "Wah, wah, wah," baby-wailing; and began to move around May.

"Piss and . . ."

"Loose . . ." Janet said. She put down her drink and followed Rose, clapping her hands.

"Gummy . . ." Angie said.

"Wah, wah, wah," Rose wailed. They joined the chorus of baby wails. The hammer beat: three light taps, four heavy beats tapering off into five or six very light touches and moving on to the next nail.

"Vegetably . . ." Angie said and moved to join the dance.

"THE DUTY-DANCE!" Gail cried.

"I think you're being very silly," Eleanor said.

Rose moved with those old creative-dance movements she had studied so long ago. Gail picked up a vase and holding it on her head, joined the dance.

"Vomity food. Wah," Janet shrieked.

"Loose food . . ."

"Dribbling, dribbling, spitting up; wash, wash, wah, wah, wah: oh, so cre*A*tive."

"Frankly, they're *never* clean," Janet admitted, panting.

"And noise," Gail yelled. "There *is* some noise."

May's smile was fixed. She drank fast and looked at them circling.

"Wah."

Eleanor joined the dance. She was a little clumsy in her high heels and kicked them off. She moved with classical ballet movements, hesitantly at first but still, after all these years, graceful.

"Baby cries; in the A.M. Wah."

"In the P.M. Wah, wah."

"In the midnight. Wah, wah, wah."

"And in the middle of sex."

"How do they *know*?"

189

May began to dance in the center, twisting her hips, smiling slightly, her eyes fixed almost inward rather than outward. Angie leaped into the center of the circle and, standing by May's side, began to do a wild Charleston while they all kept time with baby wails and handclaps; their leaps and stomps kept rattling the glasses and dishes in the sideboard.

Morris stood in the doorway. "Since when did the literary society become a creative-dance group?" He was grinning.

"May is going to have a baby," Angie yelled, not stopping.

"How wonderful. So you finally made the grade. Does Larry know yet?"

The others kept circling. Rose, the heaviest, led; she took two long strides, leaped straight up into the air and came down on a stiffened leg; each time she landed she smacked her forearm across her eyes and threw her other arm out, her great breasts bouncing.

"Just what the hell—is wonderful—about it?" Angie shouted at Morris.

"What's eating you?" Morris asked Angie.

"The same thing that's eating her," Angie said, and pointed at May's belly.

Eleanor, shrieking now, her eyes wide, unseeing, the flaps of her helmet winging around her face, grabbed his wrist and pulled him into the group. "Dance, dance, the duty-dance," and she wailed twice.

Morris was turned around. "Just let me put the hammer down . . ." Rose clutched him and threw her arm around his neck, pulled him to her, then pushed him away. May danced in the center; her face looked up, her eyes were half closed, her elbows tucked to her sides; she swung her hips; her hair was flattened in a shining arc, its ends whipping back and forth across her face. Janet stuck her arm against Morris's crooked elbow and circled with him, folk-dance style. She let him spin off and he stumbled outward. "Hold it . . ." Gail, her legs spread frog-wide, half squatting, her hands up, out, clawed and quivering, leaped along in front of him, making scratching motions at his face. His indulgent smile became wider. He tried to join in, dancing clumsily in his workshoes. Eleanor danced behind him, her teeth biting the air. They moved to the side. Eleanor whirled him, tearing his shirt. His hammer hand flailed out and caught a plate, smashing it. He tried to break loose to pick up the pieces. Rose danced up and plucked at his back, tearing his shirt more. From the other side, Gail pulled out the shirt, flapping the shredded tail over his head. She couldn't help laughing.

He was laughing too. ". . . let me get . . . you'll cut your feet . . ." They caught him and whirled him, laughing, shrieking as they shoved and pulled and pinched him around May who stood there, bouncing, her face transfigured. Trying to keep up, he stumbled as they leaped, stomped, passing him from one to the other, tearing at his clothes. Almost helpless with laughter, he reeled free of the circle. The swinging hammer banged, dented, and knocked over the samovar. He lurched to pick it up, but the clawed hands of Rose and Janet plucked at his pants as they dragged him back into the dance. He fell. Angie, her eyes wild, unseeing, charged through and was on him, straddling, pulling frantically at him. "You're tickling me . . ." He thrashed from side to side under her thighs, when a child screamed.

Melissa was standing on the stairs. Her hands gripped the banister poles. She screamed again and again. They stopped, looking at the screaming child, dazed, unable to understand.

Angie was up and running through them and bounded up three stairs at one jump and had Melissa in her arms. Melissa shrieked louder. Angie made comforting sounds, trying to stroke her head. Melissa threw herself around, trying to break loose, almost freeing herself and falling over the banister; her face was red.

They all clustered below, cooing and laughing and making comforting sounds to quiet the terrified girl. Morris got up and went over to them.

"What's the matter, baby, did you have a nightmare?"

"It was only a game, sweetheart."

"Were you frightened, were you scared?"

"Oh, the poor little dear."

The child reached for her father. "Aaaah. She wants her daddy." Angie tried to comfort her but Melissa rejected her more; she wanted her father. Over and over Angie said, "It's all right, it's all right, Mommy's here." Melissa kept screaming for her father. Morris took Melissa from Angie. Angie tried to stroke Melissa's face but she drew away. "Sweetheart, it was only a game. See, Daddy's fine. Just fine. I'll put her to bed." He stood there for a second, grinning. His pants were ripped, skirted; his underpants showed; one sleeve was ripped off. He still held the hammer. "Oh boy, you ladies," he said, and with his free hand he put Melissa's face against his and took her upstairs. They could see her looking down over her shoulder. Her eyes were still unfocused, shocked. Angie shrugged and came downstairs again.

The women were all relaxed now, sprawled in the chairs around the room. Only May still stood; her arms were folded under her breasts, holding herself. She smiled, her eyes almost closed. Angie turned a stiff-backed chair around and straddled it. "I'm not as young . . ." Janet panted.

"What time is it? We have to pick up the kids . . ."

"Time yet."

"We'll help you clean up as soon as we catch our breaths."

Angie didn't answer. She was biting her nails.

"This may be fine for Larchmont ladies but it's too rich for my blood."

"Your fly's open," Mildred said to Angie. Angie didn't seem to hear for a second and then looked down, nodded, and pulled the zipper up. She looked toward the stairs.

"It's all right. She's stopped crying. What was bothering her?" Janet asked.

"A thing like that could be very traumatic. You never know how they interpret it," Eleanor said.

Morris came down the stairs. He had changed his clothes. He was grinning. Angie stood up. "It's all right. She insisted on getting dressed. She wants to join the dance."

"Oh, isn't that darling."

Morris went into the other room.

May moved. "I have to go home and tell Larry."

They all put on their coats and prepared to go out. Angie lit a cigarette and squinted against the smoke.

"What are we discussing next week?" Gail asked.

Angie didn't answer for a second.

"What . . ."

"*Naked Lunch.*"

They went out into the autumn afternoon. Angie went to the window. She saw them walking down the street to Rose's station wagon. They were clustered around May, talking. They

193

walked through little windpiles of dry leaves. When they got into the station wagon, Eleanor came back across the street to her house. She paused on the stoop and looked down the street where the station wagon was driving off. She waved and went in.

It had turned a little cloudy but from far off, low bars of dusky sunlight came through the branches and down the driveways between the close-set houses.

Morris's hammer began again.

THE AGE OF GOLD

GEORGIO won the first round. He demonstrated to Philidor the first of what was to be a triumphant harmony. Even Carlin, curry-colored Carlin with his de-kinked hair frozen into waves, had to open his nasty eyes wide at the appearance of the hors d'oeuvres. They looked like hot dogs but were filled with hot chutney-fruits, spicy meats, nuts, condiments, and boiled rice; all ground together and put into deceptive red casings.

"Why Georgio, how very common . . ." Carlin started to sneer but had to stop at the very first taste. Georgio took one and put it to Philidor's lips: pale Philidor chewed lazily while he leaned against a black pillow, toying a golden tassel. How like a young Seti, pleased and passing judgment, Philidor looked. His indolent smile told Georgio he had succeeded: heritage told. How like a fool Carlin looked. As for Anthony and his rock 'n' roll punk, Dewey with the razored hairline, it passed completely over their heads. Anthony said, "Yummy, Georgio." He vulgarly aped Georgio by trying to push it into

Dewey's mouth. The warrior bit into it and averted his head; it didn't taste like a hot dog.

When they consumed all, the designs on the plates, pale blue Chinese stylizations on a white, delicate porcelainware, were revealed: obscure but *wildly* funny obscenities. Anthony's or Carlin's wit could not disentangle them for a second. Triumph not complete, Georgio tried to undermine Carlin once and for all: "There's the point of it," Georgio said, giggling while Philidor's appreciative laugh rewarded him. "You *do* see it, don't you? Carlin?" he mocked.

Carlin bent forward, his long fingers reaching for the plate.

"No, silly, don't move your plate: they're Chinese and *supposed* to be sideways. Chinese obscenities are best, don't you find?"

"Ooooooh," Anthony shrilled, jumping up and waggling his behind.

"I see it, Georgio," Carlin said.

"It's *meant* to be obscure. I mean one *must* be sensitive. One must *have* a sense of tradition. Isn't that so? Philidor?"

"It's droll, Georgio, *très drôle,*" Carlin said.

"How tasteful of you to *see,* Carlin," he said and went back into the kitchen to finish the ragout. Could he rest now?

They persisted in floating in, looking over his shoulder, trying to mar his perfections, offering suggestions, wailing hunger. Carlin plotted it. He shooed them out again and again, telling them they would spoil their appetites. Finally they let him alone.

He tried not to watch them through the open door. Carlin called, "Come out and play, Georgio." The spiteful note showed Carlin was hurt. Giggles: Anthony's shrilled through the room. They were planning something. Let them. He was

196

immune. His mother had taught him how to ignore the vulgar. Georgio hummed happily to himself. He sprinkled the final spices and herbs into the copper-bottomed cauldron. The blend was perfect so far, the smell almost excruciatingly tastable. The heat enveloped him, warming him, making him feel like it was an afternoon—almost any one of those old perfect afternoons—until he turned and saw them through the open door.

They camped on the floor in fair attitudes around the rim of the eating pit, leaning on thick cushion-clusters, looking at him. Except for Dewey. The bop rock had contempt for all of them, but not contempt for Anthony's money. He sat suspiciously on an ivory and hide stool and practiced a pretty sullenness, pricking under his nails with a switch-knife. Anthony, with his Benin-bronze face foolishly contradicted by gilded hair, looked adoringly into Dewey's face. The conspiratorial tinkle of their conversation caused him to be inattentive to the service of the ragout. The sudden and furious ways they flung themselves into those silly, affected friezes to please Philidor distracted him, forcing him to compete with simpers too. He closed the door with a show of bravado, daring Carlin.

The closed door protected. But there was nothing to do but wait for the ragout to come to term, and so the smooth, stained doorwood bred visions: did Carlin and Philidor, freed from his gaze, throw themselves suddenly together and kiss, their mocking elbows squooshing mauve pillows? Were Carlin's dark fingers ringed with Philidor's pale hair-tendrils? He could feel himself panicking and, not wanting to open the door yet, slipped away for a second; the heat baked and fused everything into one protecting shape that held all the moments together.

197

The lover comes. He comes twice a week, in the evening. In the evening he thrusts a cracker at Georgio. "Now you eat that and go out and play, you hear?" They hold cups to their lips, drinking whiskey, but they are impatient. They smile down at Georgio. His hand begins, reluctantly, to crumble the cracker: he hears the rough clamor of children, shouting outside in the dusk, calling. He is not like them; he doesn't want to leave this unravished stillness and go out. He delays finishing the cracker, trying to preserve that quiet moment.

The door burst open. Startled, Georgio jumped back. Carlin's persistently spiteful laugh sounded, shattering the past, despoiling the flavor, cracking and flawing his assurance. His hand hit against a thick bowl-shape. It was always in the way. Rough Dewey stood there, looking lumpish, embarrassed. "Mother"—he said it "Muh"—n'I have a cookie?" The words were strange on his thick lips . . . as if he had never been a child.

"Now you just get out of here," Georgio scolded.

But Dewey moved in. Georgio caught a glimpse of leering faces; they were standing just beyond the door. "I want a cookie, Mother."

"I'll mother you," Georgio threatened with a yew-wood ladle.

Dewey thrust him back, rocking plates, lifting lids idly, letting precious puffs of flavor waste up into the air. Georgio, ladle held before him, retreated. Dewey raised the lid of the copper-bottomed cauldron. "*Don't,*" Georgio screamed. A sphere of steam floated into Dewey's face; he pretended he was going to pick his nose over the ragout. Georgio moved to cover it; lazy bubbles turned spices up from the depths of the ragout; Dewey closed the cover, raised, shut, opened twice fast, pretending to send smoke signals. Their mocking faces clustered at the door and they made whooping sounds. He threatened with the ladle. "Now Mother, just you let this child have a cookie or he'll fade away," Anthony said. Philidor, smiling wanly, leaned his cheek against the mahogany door upright. Georgio stopped himself and stood still, letting their laughter sound, finding refuge in dignity.

Seeing this game could not move him, Anthony and Carlin moved in and, taking pots, began to dance around the kitchen; Dewey grabbed the thick huge bowl and joined them in the cruel dance with pots held high on their heads. They waggled their shoulders, bounced around, singing, kicking their knees high. Carlin held the ragout bowl with one hand, tilted far over his face. Georgio followed, reaching frantically to protect the precious bowl, last of his mother's service. But seeing Philidor bent over, his folded hands pressed between slender thighs, actually hilarious, his long, soft cheek caressed by the brown stain of the door frame as he rocked back and forth, he stopped. "Play, you children, just you go on having fun."

So Carlin bumped into Anthony, goosing him with his bony finger. Anthony beat back with his buttocks. The bowl dropped. The yellowed china shattered. Jagged shapes darted out along the floor. They all stood still for a second, Dewey holding the great, cruel African bowl on his head, gawking; Anthony lowering the faience; Carlin's criminally delinquent hands cusping emptily; Philidor's palm protecting the fingers of his underhand which rested against his groin. "I'm so sorry, sweetie," Anthony started to say.

"Don't mind it," Georgio said to Philidor whose smile rewarded him.

Dewey mumbled an apology; harsh sulk-sounds threatening

to become angry if, as always, they were going to blame him. His crude hand fisted on the rim of the huge African bowl as he lowered it. Carlin darted and grabbed the bowl out of Dewey's hand and offered the primitive thing mockingly; his taut face had the strength and dignity of Dahomeyan idols, his cruel teeth showing, his eyes almost empty, the tense cheek-muscles glazed with the hysteria of savage retaliation. "Take this chamberpot, baby," he said. Anthony couldn't help giggling.

"Now just you get out of here and stop your troubling or there'll be no supper. Honestly, just like children."

Carlin's face was close, amazed that he failed to show anger or panic.

Laughing, they went back into the living room. He closed the door behind them and permitted the heat-haze to rise, to protect him, to waft him away from this tragic moment. What would he do? He could have wept. What would he do? His feet kicked at shards, bumping them along the floor toward the wall baseboard, under tables, under the sink, under the refrigerator. He saw a spear-shaped piece; he could sink it into Carlin's face, just sink it *in:* he bent to pick it up and found the great primitive bowl was still in his hands. It was gross, squat, repulsive: it would never do. It was an earthenware bowl someone he once loved had given him, someone who should have known he wouldn't collect things like that. Too big. Usually he kept it off his shelves. Tonight, it would have completely overwhelmed the effect of any other bowl. Unwillingly, he saw himself for a second, carrying the ragout in that coarse, stony calabash, staggering under it as he tried to bear it high, his hands pushed downward by its terrible, asymmetrical weight, till he would stagger, like some tipsy priest, with it held against his chest, perhaps its crude planes even cutting into his face. How slender and ineffectual his whole body would look under its weight. How they would hoot at that. How their laughs would make Philidor smile at that. Carlin would take advantage of that.

He could sense the blend separating; he smelled the hot wine, the pungence of a spice, and saw a bayleaf floating serenely on the surface. He bent down to pick up the shard. He rubbed the yellowed smoothness of the piece against his dark skin: the feel of it soothed him. Which one? The heat, the beat of bubbles bursting, all told him it was almost ready. He knew the flavors were boiling away. He dared not delay much longer. He lowered the flame and re-covered the cauldron. Delaying tactics. He rubbed the shard more furiously against his face. The fragment could no longer soothe. He tried to make himself move. He hummed again.

Mr. Joseph had given his mother a great service and taught her how to serve. Twice a week Mr. Joseph says, "You are more gracious than ladies born to it." She inclines her head and her head is as graceful as a spout's neck. Mr. Joseph places a tea biscuit on a plate and offers it to Georgio. "Eat this." Georgio delays, biting only a sliver of biscuit. In her strong, brown hand the cup looks white . . . had it been white then? Mr. Joseph's slender white hand holds the yellowed cup to his fragile lips. He puts the cup down, takes the biscuit from the plate and puts it into Georgio's mouth, then gives him a sip from his own cup. Carlin's shrill laugh came challenging through the door, recalling him. The shouts of the children, the coarse laughter of the neighbors . . . his mother and the lover in their stillness, never seem to hear . . . "Pay them no mind, son," Mr. Joseph says. "What are they? Savages.

You know a savage by the fact he's loud." Leaning, his hand slipped along the table. The roughness of the clumsy bowl stung him. It reminded him and shattered again his reverie. Leaning, he wished he could go to sleep. The lover comes. He nods at her. She takes his coat. He brusquely asks little Georgio little questions while his mother sits, her hands folded in her lap, on a chair. He shoves the cracker at Georgio . . .

They go to the table. "Doesn't she do it well?" Mr. Joseph says, as if surprised at the possibility. The arrangement was timeless again and he knew that here, somewhere on the shelves, waiting for his hand to reach out and take it, was the bowl to best Carlin.

Carlin was wearing four brass buttons on his olive coat— he thought olive did something for his complexion—slim, slim black-watch plaid pants, a collar that curled like a mauve tulip petal, a thin, greenblack tie like a stab: he waved his hands to show off those scarlet enamel cuff links. Therefore, Georgio would use those delicate demitasse cups for the Turkish coffee. For the sake of Philidor, he could have settled for the austerity of Swedish shapes, those cylinders chilled with icy gray glazes; or those flat, short cups, looking for all the world as though they were truncated globes fitted out with handles and, in the shadow of which, the coffee would take on the aspect of some primeval fluid, gray-tinged, unpalatable to the look, unnoticed, not like everything (till Carlin had wrecked him) served before, triumphant. So Georgio had dashed out and bought a set (he could hear Carlin's high, lewd voice, penetrating enough to jar his stemware shelf . . . moving closer to Philidor) of cups before they even knew he was out and back. It would be a whiteness of little cup, fragile, not so much in its construction, but in its appearance, in the way they could, if they wished, almost see right through it. The faint age-cracks, like yellowed increments of tradition under the translucence, would ring the contemporary blackness of the coffee . . . a cup that only an aristocratic hand might hold well. It would look, in Carlin's claw, so exposing of falseness. Could they understand it? Philidor might. He turned.

Which one? On the table majolica plates were placed in front of them. Georgio turned again. His image was slendered in the shining glazes of splendid bowls. Swedish silver, slim as surgical tools, lay beside the plates; Venetian glass goblets gleamed subtly; the salad, greens and reds and purples and oranges, lay in the fruitwood bowl; slim wine bottles towered almost as high as the jutting trefoil candleholder. But he hesitated and turned, and turned again while he pressed the bowl-piece against his cheek. He bumped into the crude bowl, almost dropping the fragment. He had to take the bowl, annoyed at its thick heaviness, and put it out of the way on a little serving table. He saw, considered, and rejected the rose-colored bowl; it was whorishly utilitarian, doing nothing. Hurry, he told himself, hurry: he should have planned for emergencies. The tall one? Its sides beetled over till they threatened to fall, to collapse, till the base was ringed with shards. Its value lay in that it precluded any such collapse. It had a delicacy that was *expressed* by a series of incised swirling lines that bellied in the center, but flattened toward the top till they joined in a line that circled eternally, paralleling the foliate rim. No, not that one. The bowl had no intrinsic value other than its own; it halted no hour forever in itself; it could not act as a bank out of which events in his life could be withdrawn. It was too grimly artistic. Each moment should contribute, like glazings and overglazings baked and rebaked on, layer by layer, an epic never finished, forever being told.

Where? He turned. He fidgeted back and forth among the

bowls. He had learned, seeing how each thing she holds in her dark, sure hand demonstrates how subtly she makes each serving a moment of triumph to set her apart. And how appreciatively Mr. Joseph's white hand holds everything, receiving, then setting down while he smiles. "I learned from *him*," she proudly says, years later. "Isn't that something?" Mr. Joseph says, smiling contentedly . . . had he not accomplished much? She says nothing; her hand holds the teapot, waiting for his praise to be absorbed into the afternoon air. And if, Georgio thought, she was set apart, so was he—apart from the children he had to play with—apart from the others outside. He drew comfort from that, drew comfort that, despite the panic, he knew he would do the fit thing.

He heard vague shouting which intruded urgently into the hot, golden haze . . . it beat against his arrangements. Carlin was entertaining furiously, destroying what Georgio had done and was trying to do. He leaned against the serving table. Any one; any pot: Philidor wouldn't see it anyway. He held, for a second, the flat bowl, feeling the brown salt-glaze. As a shape it was perfect. He heard Philidor's laugh and thought of him lovingly: pale, aristocratic, slender, blond, wearing that simple gray suit but, because of what he was, somehow gayer than Carlin with all his garish finery . . . The brown bowl preserved happy moments . . . Was Philidor laughing appreciatively at something Carlin was saying? Dared Georgio trust Philidor not to succumb to Carlin's flash? Their negations— waved hair, blondined hair, straightened hair, razored hairlines, imitative clothes—affirmed all the more what they denied. Couldn't Philidor see that he, his hair natural, tight-curled, was involved in the best subtlety of all; seeming to affirm what he was? And his mother, who rinses each cup in boiling water before pouring . . . she is never other than what she is. How much *more* she is, Mr. Joseph tells her reverently. How everything worried. Pick *any* old pot. How he fretted; his brow was distressed by a tracery of wrinkles that despoiled the black symmetry of a head domed into hair unbordered by lines of cessation and beginning. The flat bowl would not serve: things cooled too rapidly in it; things cool warmed too quickly in it. He rejected it because if it did not sustain what he had begun, the important time-segment would be shifted back to that moment of little "Aaaahs" when the hors d'oeuvres had come, or forward to when the *meringue timbale* and the coffee were presented. By comparison the ragout would be flat, lose its taste; how clumsy and unbearable it would all be. His image was flattened in the bottoms of a thousand hanging cups till the lid-lifting steam from the ragout matted all the shines and protected him again. The black mood began to descend on him: he turned and turned.

Carlin would win. Carlin would win. The record-player—Carlin always played sophisticated songs too loudly—sounded, threatening to vibrate the cups and bowls and plates and shatter them. He strove to burst out of the bubble, forcing himself to hum, to move through the steamy atmosphere. He must choose. He dared not choose wrong. He gazed through his lassitude; through the closed door. Anthony, happy, held his head against the warrior's knees; the cool Dewey hood, stiff and sullen, picked with his knife and dropped pieces into Anthony's hair. "I learned from *him*," she slavishly insists. He shakes his head, turns and runs away into the street to play. He goes to the window to see his remembrance of them, sitting, cheeks of cups touching . . . the fatherly white hand holding the biscuit to his lips . . . His knuckles banged against the

African bowl; he sucked them. It lay there, like a flaw forever baked into his existence. He peeks through the window. Their cheeks were together . . . he was sure of it . . . expecting the dust to glaze and the afternoon haze to pale them both into engravings on the room's shadow and the window's gloom . . . He tasted blood from his knuckles. Any bowl. Just any bowl. Because those joined cheeks negate this stupidity . . . the dusty haze, the bed, his reflected face there, over, on, hovering, caught in their thrash . . . bright ocher figure crudely scratched through umber slip. Brutally beaten into shape, prickly to the hand, coarse, full of rough clay chips . . . He rejected the ugly, outmoded thing . . . He should reshape his belief . . . His mother, poised, stiff-backed, pouring tea into cups carefully. Her strong hand dark and comforting against the teapot. The golden afternoon sun blazes on the brown wallpaper. Mr. Joseph sits across the table from her. His fatherly hand places a tea biscuit on a plate . . . he bites the biscuit . . .

. . . and groped to find and know a piece of Steubenware . . . wonderful half-oblate spheroid his fingers fluttered against, laughing—if fingers could laugh—against the smoothness of the glass. Of course. It was thick and solid; its shape simplicity itself. It was tinted slightly red; etched with white lines: Greek temples . . . Greek men held timeless in golden sunsets. He turned off the fires. He put on a white linen apron cinctured with a faded-blue velvet cord. He poured the ragout slowly into the bowl. He wrapped a linen napkin around the lip of the bowl. Its grace gave lie to its massiveness. He picked it up and marched forward to the door, to the babble ahead. He kicked the door and he stood there, in front of them. They were already sitting in the eating pit, knees touching, elbows on the parapet.

Whatever they were saying was stilled.

"The lady is a tramp . . ." the record-player sang . . . thin, smart voice . . . Their faces were turned toward him, waiting while he stood there in the flickering candlelight.

"Here, children, here," he intoned.

"Ooooh, how lovely . . . stew," Anthony cackled. "Stew, Dewey. Stewey, Dew. Stewey, Dewey." Dewey's teeth were already ripping hunks of bread, dribbling sesame seeds.

"Oh, Georgio's to the manor born, make no mistake," Carlin sniggered. They all laughed, but they were impressed. These were the simple movements of a triumph. He stood, posed, his hands holding the chalice high above his head, feeling slender and erect under it. One foot was thrust forward, toe pointing to the side a little. The contents shimmered, red and mysterious in the dim glass.

"How beautiful. It seethes like blood," Philidor said, accepting.

"With a cracker covering . . ." Carlin said. Out of the corner of his eye Georgio saw Carlin's face. It was a yellow goat's mask, the eyes narrowed and jealous. Georgio turned his face upward, offering, and walked forward and slowly down the little steps into the pit.

"How well he does it, for a low Baptist," Carlin said.

Georgio saw Philidor's quite beautiful smile . . . He bore it to the table . . . *"Introibo ad altare Dei,"* Georgio chanted and knelt, still holding the bowl high.

"To *Deum* who giveth joy to *Juventutem meum,* bubby," Anthony responded. "He gets it right out of the Catholic missal."

"I have your missal, right here," Carlin said.

"Ooooh, a Black Mass," Philidor said; they giggled.

The glass distorted his face into something to be forgotten . . . Yet, if you took into account the distortions and canceled out the convex lie . . . something like . . . almost like Mr. Joseph. He felt the glass attenuate. His gross hands grasped the chalice tighter; below the napkin his fingers smudged the etching. He lowered it. His head-image, as if scratched in, trapped in, passed along the glass curve . . . cruel graffito caricature, juju mask, almond-eyed, ellipse-lipped, pendule-nosed; ambivalent squat goddess of fertility birthing a shrieking black baby's head beneath the crude, stuck-on phallus . . . he looked away. The glass whispered and moaned. His little scream was cracked off. The bottom dropped out. The contents spilled in a mess onto the prepared table. A gout of viscous liquid shot hotly up and spattered Carlin's hair.

Philidor giggled. Philidor laughed. They were all caught naked in Philidor's jabbed laugh. Dewey was bewildered; his hand touched Anthony's face. Sudden thin lines appeared, scratched into Anthony's cheeks, beside his nose, making him look old. He leaned away from Dewey, trying to sit straight and look dignified. Carlin's fists clenched; he looked at Georgio; their eyes were, for one second, sad, knowing, brotherly.

Philidor looked at them all petulantly, then quickly glazed his face over with a bored, tragic look.

And Carlin, quicker, pointed at the soggy napkin and the jagged glass ring in Georgio's hands and began to laugh and laugh, howling, "My, how terrible, how ut-terly terrible, Georgio baby."

"Wipe your hair, Carlin sweets," Georgio growled. "I can always get another bowl." And won because Philidor nodded at *him*.

... AND A FRIEND TO SIT
BY YOUR SIDE

I sit at my desk, trying to catch up on my dictation. The phone rings: 2:00 A.M., the classic time, you might say. I let the phone ring twice; turn to a new sheet in my case-book; three times. I pretend not to see the supervisor Mr. Radaman's dirty look; he'd rather I stay in the office and finish my reports. The phone rings a fourth time. I pick up the receiver as the fifth ring is dying away. It's better to keep them waiting. I've found that people never hang up during a ring: they always wait till the silence is complete. It's insights like this . . . but try telling this to Mr. Radaman. Dictation is what he cares about: dictation and his big four-color graph which shows the unit's progress.

I listen. Breathing . . . a little heavy, perhaps asthmatic: the faraway sound of a radio playing soft music: a tentative little cough. I don't answer yet. Some of the others, they talk right away. Bad. Some of them wait too long; they end up saying "Hello*hello*" frantically into a dead phone. I turn the receiver a little away from my ear so they can hear the sounds of the office; this way a connection is established; they know someone is there. Durgam is typing up reports (how does she manage to get them done so quickly?), Morton talks to Todd about football (I suppose *their* reports are finished) while they eat sandwiches and drink coffee. The rest of the workers are out in the field. A man's voice begins to say, "Is this . . . Is this . . ."

"Suicides A," I say.

Now the others, they say "Suicides Anonymous." Wrong. You can't say "Suicides Anonymous" and help sounding pompous about it. "Suicides A," on the other hand, sounds brisk, even a little cheery. It gives a client a sense of . . . well . . . *thereness* (I like that word so much better than *reality*); something unarguable. The person who calls for our help needs a sense of solidity. And, it is my contention, sound casework begins right here, in the office, on the telephone. You don't wait till you're confronted with the client. It's because of touches like this that they've let me stay on for an extra year, even though the ages for our job are rigidly prescribed, twenty-two to twenty-six. "Can I help?" I ask.

It starts slowly; always does. Hems and haws; hates to bother us. "That's what we're here for, Mr. . . . .?" The usual thing. Silences are long; have to be patient. Lot of other workers, they prompt. Poor. Can't be short with them. Can't panic. It's a . . . well . . . a feel for it: empathy. Not sure he wants to kill himself after all. I say, "I'd like to help you, if I may, Mr. . . . . ?" Silence. "Would you like me to call on you?" Throat-clearing. "Would you wait?" Mumbles. Starts to talk. You have to listen closely; to make sure, for instance, that they don't sound too young. The age limit is sixty-five. Arbitrary. *Anyone* should be able to call us up when they need us. But they say you have to draw the line somewhere. Well, at our last conference, this was one of the points I brought up. I brought up the question of further . . . advertising (all right: call it that: that's what it is), the point of the possibility of pre-suicide group therapy to extend the coverage of our inadequate service-staff, and the point that drawing borderlines was not only inhumane, but a violation of the spirit of good casework. The urge to commit suicide is, after all

("I don't know," he mutters.

"We're here to help."

"I feel like . . . a freak."

"Don't feel that. Please. Do you want to talk about it?"

Silence.

"Please, think of me as a friend. I want to help.") universal, not confined merely to people over sixty-five. We should help everyone. They admitted the justice of what I was bringing up but said, you have to draw the line somewhere.

"I'm a friend," I say. The coin clicks down; he doesn't have a home phone; he won't talk too long. When the phone clears again, the old man is giving me his name and address. Geshwind: East Twenties. Name rings a bell; I've heard it before. Well, when the client's done this, you can say that seventy-five percent of the casework is done. I tell Geshwind I'll be there in eighteen minutes; putting it this way seems to be a sign of concern. Hang up. But before going out I check our files for previous contacts. I find he's had workers to see him *eight* times and we've rejected the last two attempts to contact us. By rights I shouldn't bother. Obviously an attention-getter (we're plagued with these). But still, his calling us up, his persistence after two rejections, means that no one has succeeded in finalizing the case . . . there simply hasn't been first-rate casework done on it. Well, it would show Mr. Radaman . . . I mean dictation isn't the whole story . . . I mean it isn't *the* sign.

I come back to the desk, push everything into a corner (they

like things neat around here . . . typical bureaucratic nonsense
. . . letter, not the spirit nonsense . . . so wrong), put on my coat
and leave. I pass Durgam. She's finished with her report. I don't
know how she does it. She's talking on the phone to a prospec-
tive client, giving them that "Sooee-cydes A-non-ee-mus" tone,
just lousing it up. I want to take the phone out of her hands
and do it right; it's an old fight between us. Mr. Radaman gives
me a dirty look as I pass and says, "Are you caught up?"

"Almost."

"How many more do you have to do?"

"I have to hurry, Mr. Radaman . . ."

"Maybe you better let me send Todd, or Morton."

"I'll finish when I get back."

"Well, I don't know now . . ."

And I go. He'd really be mad if he knew who I was visiting.
I rush downstairs, get into my car and start the motor. Then I
remember I have forgotten to punch out. I go back. I have to
avoid mistakes like this; it could cost me the extra year. They
haven't given me a ticket. Since we're in midtown there's no
parking. Someday they're going to admit the work we do is
vital and build us a departmental parking lot.

It's a short drive downtown to the Twenties and just off
Third Avenue; a rooming-house district. I don't drive fast, no
rush. Give them time. Let it build up inside. And, this time of
night, each minute is long and anyhow, if they've given you
their name and address, it's a strong commitment. There isn't
any parking space when I get there. Life is becoming more impossible in this miserable city every day. I have to circle the
block twice and finally park in front of a fire hydrant. Well,
haven't we the right?

The client lives in one of those row brownstone houses. They'll ne going soon. You could almost predict the man, the way he looks, just how serious about it he is. The whole place will smell of moldy carpeting and strong antiseptic; it will be cut up into small one-room apartments, having in each one hotplate, single bed, chair, all in a space about eight feet wide by ten feet; the sink will be in the hallway; one bathroom to a floor, always. I ring. I hope it isn't one of those arrangements where he has to come down all the way to the door to let me in. I hate those; it makes for movement. Movement upsets equilibriums so painfully achieved. The client can be so easily pushed either way by the wrong act. He waits a long time before sounding the buzzer. I open the door and walk in. The hallway is like all of them; thirty-watt bulbs shining on shabby ornate; lots of shadows; a huge mirror with hat racks on the frame, but no glass; heavy balustrades with pieces of molding missing; utilitarian plasterboard partition; pay telephone on the wall. As I go up someone peeks out from one end of the parlor floor hall; probably the landlady.

He lives on the top floor; so much the better. The height of the ceilings becomes lower and lower as I go up. On the top floor there are three doors; one of them is open just a little. I go in without knocking. The client is seated on the bed. He is wearing striped pajamas with heavy, cheap gray socks. His face is bony, but the chin and neck flesh are loose. Usual. He stares at a table about two feet in front of him. There is little room to walk around. I don't see *it:* usually *it's* around where you can see *it:* they always want you to see *it* to show you they're not fooling around. I doubt that he'd consider jumping: too athletic for an old man. The radio, a cheap one, practically all dial, faces him: the case is cracked. He doesn't turn to look at me. I come in, close the door behind me; I close it briskly so that it makes noise. I pretend that the lock won't catch and fiddle with it. I turn my head and say, "Hello, my name's Kieran." I play with the knob. "I'm from Suicides A." I open the door, close it a little harder, catching the latch, breathe a slight sigh, as if of satisfaction. He turns to look at me. He has that want-to-talk look, *have*-to-talk look. "I must be some kind of . . ."

"It's mighty cold out there," I say, not letting him ventilate too soon. "Not fit for . . . May I sit down?" I ask. I don't give him time to answer. I take off my coat, reach for the case-book in one of my coat pockets, look around, keep smiling, sit down, pulling the chair along, screeching it, bouncing it on the rough, warped floorboards, moving nearer, fish for my pen, seem to remember, get up again, go through my coat pockets again, looking for a calling card . . . all till I know the eagerness is fading. I clinch it by looking at my watch. It's 2:38 now. I straighten my clothes by patting. I always make sure to wear new clothes, neatly pressed, with bright touches; the pocket handkerchief, the tie, red or yellow socks, always, always a white white shirt, sometimes a bright waistcoat, very shiny shoes with leather heels so they click quite clearly; it makes an impression.

The room is as I predicted; in four and a half years I have seen it a thousand times. No pictures except for a huge calendar with a naked, big-breasted, big-smiled girl, compliments of the Bonheur Liquor Store, Yes We Deliver. Cracks in the wall-paint and the ceiling plaster. A window which looks out over a backyard, though I can't be sure because it is dark out there and the shine from the plain, wirehung bulb makes the window mirrorlike. A stand-lamp with wrought-iron curlicues, a browned lampshade with an eighteenth-century scene (hoop-skirts, knee britches, post horns, coach, dogs, lawn) casts a forty-watt cone on the wall behind him. There is one of those institutional slat-backed chairs like you see in libraries. It's been painted over many times: baby blue, that cracked away, a pink enamel underneath: God knows how many coats it has altogether. Taking great care to hoist my trousers, I sit down, cross my legs, open my book, click my pen point into position and wait.

"Well," I say, "care to tell me something about yourself?" and begin to fill in what he has told me over the phone.

He doesn't answer right away. He's turned back to face the table. His eyes don't *quite* have *the* look yet, that staring, not-seeing look, the eyes almost flat, as though the muscles hardly function or, perhaps, the lids no longer flicker. Light will not make them blink. The face will be still. Even the body will hardly move, as if the breathing has stopped. Not quite ready.

"Are you a Catholic?" he asks. His voice is flat; the voices should always be flat, toneless, not even really interested in my answer.

"No."

"They should have sent a Catholic."

"Well, I mean . . . You didn't ask for one."

"How old are you?"

"Twenty-seven," I tell him.

"That's pretty young, isn't it?"

"Most of our workers are younger, Mr. Geshwind. May I ask how old you are?"

"Sixty-eight. Don't know why I asked you that. Haven't been to church in years . . . not since I was young. Not much point to it, is there?" And he glances slyly at me.

"I couldn't say, Mr. Geshwind." His head turns fully to me; his cheeks are sunken, stretched on the cheekbones, his upper

215

lip wrinkled. I look past his stare to the table, looking for *it* again. On the table, beside the radio, there's an ashtray littered with stubbed-out cigarette butts, a bottle of water, a plastic drinking glass, a newspaper. A loud alarm clock ticks, the kind whose dials gleam in the darkness. "Of course the church has its comforts, Mr. Geshwind."

"How would you know?" he asks. Something a little angry in the tone. Don't bother to answer, but smile as if to say it doesn't matter.

"Do you believe in an afterlife?"

"You're retired, aren't you?" I ask.

"Yes."

"You live on your pension alone?"

His face turns away and looks back toward the table. There's a box of tissues on it. I wonder if he's put it in there? I make a point of not staring. His bedcover is made of chenille; the bed sags deeply where he sits. Ammonia smell, strong, nose-tickling. His forward tilting neck is very thin, but his body looks big in his pajamas.

"What I mean is, do you have any other income? Home relief, for instance?" He doesn't answer so I say, "No, Mr. Geshwind. In all honesty I can't say that I believe in an afterlife. In fact I think there's nothing. Nothing at all." I take out a pack of cigarettes, pull one out, light it, put the pack back into my pocket and blow a great cloud of smoke which shoots out toward him, slows, drifts and encloses him. The radio is playing "Siboney," but softly, full of soothing violin sounds, Spanishless. I don't offer him a cigarette because I want to see if he will ask for one. He doesn't. Good sign.

He turns toward me and his whole body tends to turn too;

his eyes peer through the smoke and he asks, "Well, what's the point then?" The voice is harsh.

"Of what?"

"Everything. What did I go through it for? Listen, I've lived through some hard times."

"Mr. Geshwind, I have to get some information. For our records."

"I thought it was 'anonymous.'"

I don't answer this. He turns away, but he answers my questions. Old history. He is disinterested in what I ask and in what he tells me.

"I must be some kind of freak," he interrupts once.

"No, Mr. Geshwind. It's quite common, you know."

"Want some coffee?"

"No thanks."

"I can boil some water. Instant."

"No thanks."

"Beer?"

"Not really, thanks."

"I have some cans on the windowsill. They're pretty cold." His face is pleading, mouth a little open, lip trembling, hint of saliva.

"Thanks. Really."

He closes his lips, nods, and he stares again.

"Now your family, Mr. Geshwind. Relatives?"

He sniffs; that means he has relatives, but he doesn't see them. The ash is long. It falls to the floor, that is it looks as if it falls, but I have moved my hand a little to knock it off. I feel that he sees it because he starts to turn so I lean past him and stub out the cigarette in his ashtray. His wrists are thick, his

217

hands quite bony, liverspotted dry skin stretched between the bones, crinkled at the joint-knobs. His hands hold his pressed-together knees and look dark against the white and bleached-red pajama stripes.

"Your family, Mr. Geshwind?" I say.

"I don't know what's happening to this world," he says, suddenly.

"I don't see that there's much of a change."

He turns on me, body facing. His voice is querulous. "You're young. Why do they send a young man?"

"But that doesn't mean we don't feel, Mr. Geshwind."

"What do you know? Wait." His head nods.

"After all, I've had almost five years of experience."

"Let me tell you something," he bursts out; this is what he is leading to; old grievances come to the surface; the neglect, the aloneness. "Might as well be dead for all anyone cares." His eyes are alive now, fretful. "You might as well have no family at all for all the good . . ." And the connection between the two of us is broken for a second. Of course the thing is not to let them go on too long, crabbing. It depends on how testy they are. If they are really irascible, the best thing is to let them go on for a while, letting them run down. If the response is old, tired, ritual, it is better to interrupt them before they really work up steam. Time's another factor, of course; you have to watch out for the dawn. The best work is almost always done before the dawn comes; many a case is lost if it goes on into the daylight. For a moment I am afraid that the cantankerous fury that sets Geshwind's knees to swinging in and out will be enough to keep him going for a long time (they've almost always had it stored up) and it's almost ten after three now. I take a chance. I stand up and say, "Excuse me," just tap the bony construction under his pajamas. He moves his feet and bumps into two pairs of shoes, neatly laid together. I go past him, bumping his knees, to the window, touch it and say, "May I?"

He turns, looks at me, and though his eyes seem alive again, he seems not to recognize me. His head's turned on his spindly neck, the muscles and cords stand out with the turning and anger, but the wattled flesh of one side of his jaw sags. His mouth is open, caught in the middle; he's not wearing his false teeth. His ears stick far out from his skull because his hair is sparse, silky, wispy. His eyes are wide, innocent. He stops and says, "Oh sure. Sure."

"It's hot in here," I say. In fact it's a little chilly.

"Go ahead."

"I mean coming in from the cold . . ."

"It's all right. Go ahead."

And I pull the window up a little. There are a row of beer cans on the sill outside, chilling. What does he do in summer? I wipe my hands with my handkerchief; gritty soot smudges off. When I go back to my seat, I make sure *not* to touch him. "Now, you were saying, Mr. Geshwind. Your daughter . . ." He has been talking about his son; the ingrate; lives out on the Island; too lazy to come and see him more than once a month, sometimes only once every five weeks; no room to live with his son and his family; sends a little money; thinks it eases his conscience; and when he does come they sit around and look at one another or, rather, don't look at one another, having nothing at all to say. Usual. Hasn't seen the grandchildren in over a year, though who would want to bring children to a place like this and to take him out there must mean a trip of hours back and forth. I could have told it for him.

His eyes are back, staring at the wall over the table. *It* must be there, but where? His head nods as if agreeing with someone whom I can't see; a bitter agreement. It's a common movement with the old: means "Wait, you'll learn." "You hear this all the time, don't you?"

"No. Well, that is every case is different, Mr. Geshwind, every case is special."

"A lot of people want to kill themselves?"

"Quite a few . . ."

"More than ever, eh? It's the times . . ."

"I don't know about that. Of course we never kept statistics, but you'd be surprised . . . Well, put it this way, it's not at all uncommon. It's a way."

"Things are bad. I just don't know what's happening to the world. The A-bomb . . . them hood gangs . . . people just not caring anymore . . ." and Geshwind's lips move as he talks, making chewing motions, sliding softly over one another. The radio is playing a rich, orchestral version of "The Lady Is a Tramp," Mantovani-ish music, full of stringy crescendos which pervert that perky little tune.

I smile and cross my legs the other way and say, quite cheerfully, "Oh, come now, Mr. G. Things are not as bad as all that. Think back, thirty, forty years. You didn't have Social Security then, hospitalization, medical care for our aged. You would probably have been dead, you know. The insurance tables show . . ."

"I might have been better off."

I don't answer that but say, "Well, there are an awful lot of things to live for."

He doesn't answer. He stares. He takes a deep breath, about to say something.

220

"Besides," I chide him. "You don't *really* care about all that, do you, Mr. Geshwind, the A-bomb . . ."

"I hope they drop it."

"You don't mean that."

"I do."

"How will that help you?" There are a few small pots on the table; a few food cans, a can opener. Maybe *it's* in one of the pots.

He reaches to the table, takes his cigarette pack and pulls one out. I see he only has one or two left. He lights it, sucks in smoke, puffs it out slowly, and then begins to cough. I take another cigarette and light it. One hand grabs the flesh above his bony knee which shakes with each spasm; the other presses against his body, just below the ribcase, and pushes in as he coughs out. His face reddens; little veins purple in his nose; his eyes begin to water though the stare seems quite steady, unblinking behind the watery film; the cough grows worse and he looks as though he's in pain; he gasps; the sound is like gears grating; he doubles over more. Then, suddenly, he sucks air in deeply, holds it for a second. A slight line of drool shines at the side of his chin. The coughing stops. He wipes his mouth with the back of his hand and takes another puff, but doesn't inhale deeply.

"All right?" I ask.

He nods, not trusting himself to speak.

"You should give it up."

"I probably got cancer already." His voice is blurred by agitation. "This air pollution. Read the papers. Think they care for us?"

"You should give it up," I tell him. It's getting a little chilly in the room now.

"I should give it up," he says; and though his body and face are turned toward me, his eyes look toward the table. He nods again. I realize the time is coming close. I look around. Radio, pots, lamp, closet behind me with the flowered cloth door (*it* wouldn't be there), cool air flowing in between the beer cans, lamp, cone of light on the wall; I count them all again and wait. It gets chillier, and the music is "In a Persian Market": tremulo-ly.

"Have you wanted to kill yourself for a long while?" His hands are beginning to shiver the slightest bit. I take care to say "kill yourself" in the most normal tone.

He sighs; no more. His eyes stare. The wind rattles the window loudly. Then I see *it,* the poison, reflected in the shaking window, standing behind the radio, and at which he has been staring. "It's not uncommon at all. Some find it an answer. Some do not. You mustn't think you're alone. Some do it because of the pain, some because of the loneliness, Mr. Geshwind; it may be the best way. Perhaps it is," I tell him plainly, simply, as if it doesn't matter.

Outside there is a little growling, a whine, a hiss; two cats begin soft, crooning yowls that rise and fall and rise again. One cat's voice is a little hoarse, the other's high; they blend, curiously like angry babies crying. We wait. The wails come in through the window, almost as if they are just outside. "Damn cats," he says. "At it all the time. Fucking. All the time fucking. Won't let a man sleep. Fucking." But his eyes don't move.

"You've tried the other things? I mean, Mr. Geshwind, I have to say that life isn't over, not by a long shot. You know what they say: the golden years of retirement."

"Sure."

222

"Well, there are the Golden Age clubs . . ."

"I tried. Checkers. Cards. No point. I packed them in. No point."

And I keep enumerating the many possible expedients that the old might take to fill their lonely hours. I don't wait for him to answer if he's tried these things, but keep going through them flatly, matter of factly, as if we both know that it is part of my duty to suggest these activities and it is part of his duty to state, or at least imply, that he has tried everything. I check them off a printed list in my case-book.

"Everything. I tried everything," he tells me. He is not particularly angry about it.

There is a growl outside, a scream, a hiss again, a flurrying sound, a thump, and then the crooning wail begins again. "I've been thinking about . . . about . . ." and he begins to cough again.

I wait till he stops. "Killing yourself?"

He nods. "For weeks. It all comes to nothing."

"What do you mean?"

"I don't know how to put it. Nothing matters."

I don't answer.

"Well, does it?"

I don't answer. It's getting colder. He's shivering. Finally I sigh, shift a little in the creaky chair. He turns his face to me, as if I have said something. The keening is higher now, agonizing to listen to; it kills the radio music. His stare looks at me for a second and then, his eyes on my face but seeing nothing, he says, "But I feel like a freak. It's so wrong."

I don't answer.

"Can you give me one reason for living?"

I start to say something. I stop. I smile slightly. I shrug my shoulders, my hands held away and up. Stop smiling and look down.

He nods as if he has expected it. "Fucking cats," he says and stops and waits. He will wait a long time.

Finally I tell Geshwind, "Mr. Geshwind, you've called us ten times. This is the eleventh time. We can't come anymore. You understand that?" I say.

He sits, staring. I get up, sit down beside him on the bed. The sag of the bed makes our bodies lean together. I put my arm around his shoulder and look at him and then with him toward the poison. He nods, as if he has expected this too. Suddenly, he pulls away, jumps up and strides to the window. He throws it up all the way and begins to yell down. His high voice yammers out and his words are not distinguishable to me. The back of his neck is like two ropes standing out, close but cleaved deeply; his head is patchy and red. The cats keep up the lament. He grabs a beer can and throws it into the darkness, yelling; the can strikes something; he keeps yelling and begins to throw can after can. He stops for a second, holding the last can and then tosses it out the window with an underhand motion, almost a shrug. He is finished. It is silent. The cats have fled. He slams the window down. He comes back. He sits on the bed. We wait. He turns to me. His mouth opens. He does not speak. He closes his mouth. He nods again.

We wait. It is getting warmer. It becomes now that very pure moment when everything is closed in from the whole world and there is a nothingness here which is *more* than mere absence of sound, more than separation from all the world, a time when nothing matters at all and, in fact, it never has mattered. And if you're good at your job, you empathize, and I feel

224

perfectly that barrenness, that pointlessness that Mr. Geshwind feels. We commune silently. I feel and feed back the sense of emptiness, that attrition of everything when even every bodily annoyance is somehow no longer a part of either one of us. The good worker must feel as though *he* might even kill himself . . . not that you do, not that you do. Only I and he are alive in all the world, together though apart, as if alone in two vast and deserted cities. And when that moment reaches the point of unbearable ache for you, you say, "How were you going to do it, my friend?"

"Poison."

"Ahh. What are you using?"

He nods in the direction of the poison. I get up, pat his shoulder, go close, then pick up the can. It is a common poison, strong, but not strong enough . . . one they all use, J.O., really for vermin. I say softly, "But that's no good. It'll hurt you a lot. You don't want that, do you?" and pat his shoulder again and then squeeze it.

He starts to think about it but I reach into my jacket pocket and pull two capsules out of the change flap. "You won't feel a thing. In fact, you'll feel pleasant, like you're going to get a nice night's sleep with lots of nice dreams."

He looks at the capsules in my palm. "I don't want to dream. My dreams are bad."

"The first good night's sleep in a long long time, isn't it?" I say.

He takes the capsules. "I don't know now . . ." he says.

"You're not alone, you know. Lots of people do. More and more every day. That's why I'm here, as a friend, to help you." I go over to the bottle of water, pour some into the glass, and give it to him. We're not supposed to do this, but still, you can't stick to the letter of the law, can you? "You said before that I didn't understand. Well, you know, we at Suicides A know that we too will come to this time. We're ready. We under-stand. I'm your friend as I hope someone else will be my friend when . . ." He takes the glass, puts one capsule in his mouth, on his tongue, and leaves it there for a second, his tongue out, as if tasting it. Then, since he finds it doesn't burn, or taste bitter, he raises the cup, swallows the water and the capsule. He chokes a little, coughs, clears his throat and, with his mouth full of phlegm, looks around for something to spit into. I reach over and give him a fresh tissue. He spits into that, folds it carefully, and throws it into the basket. "A little sweet," he says.

"Yes," I say.

Suddenly, before putting the second capsule into his mouth (not that it matters anymore), he says, "What if I changed my mind now?"

"You could be helped," I say and step back a little and look at him. I look at my watch.

"I changed my mind."

"All right," I say and turn.

"Where are you going?" Geshwind asks.

"To get some help."

He thinks about it. "Don't bother," he says.

I step back to him and pat his shoulder again. I turn and lift the chair and put it close to him and sit down; our knees touch. "It's the best way," I tell him. "You know that," and I pat his hand.

He nods. "Listen. Could you stay with me?"

"Of course. I'll sit by your side."

He takes the second capsule and swallows it. This time he

doesn't cough. He sits there, holding the cup, its bottom on his knee, and looks ahead. "Funny thing," he says. "I don't feel any different."

"Oh, you won't," I say.

"No. I don't mean my body. I mean I don't feel any happier, or any worse. A little scared . . . But it's still nothing . . . nothing . . . nothing matters."

"Why don't you lie down?" I say. "You'll feel a little more comfortable."

"I hate to lie down. I cough a lot when I lie down."

I nod.

"How much longer?"

"Soon."

We sit there for about nine minutes and I know, by the position his body takes (just a shift really, hardly anything different), that he is asleep, though his eyes still stare ahead as they did when I first came in. I get up, take Mr. Geshwind's shoulders and put him back on the bed so that he lies there. He coughs once, twice, but without waking. His eyes close. He sleeps. His face is relaxed, thoughtful, amused, but quite dignified. He's even smiling a little now. I wonder what he dreams. Well, I hope that when my time comes (in all honesty, I have to say it), I have someone as good to help me over the edge. Do they realize that? Does Mr. Radaman realize that? Never. I look at my watch. He will never wake up. I make a note of the time and close my case-book.

I put on my coat and go out and down the stairs. As I leave, I can feel that I am being watched from the door at the end . . . 4:50 . . . it will be dawn soon. No one is in the streets . . . it's all quite deserted. I start to go to my car. I'd better get back soon and get rid of that backlog of cases; I'll never catch up.

But, still, it's chilly, quite cold, the wind comes right through the coat: I decide I might as well have a cup of coffee. I'm feeling woozy. That hot atmosphere up there . . . I walk over to Third Avenue. No one is on Third Avenue as far as I can see in either direction. A few blocks away I see the lights of an all-night luncheonette. I walk over there.

But when I'm sitting there, I get terribly hungry and have to eat. I order two hamburgers; lots of onion, raw, and relish, and tomato catsup, and chili. While I eat, I fill in the notes in my case-book. I'm tired; the warmth makes me feel a little sleepy; the facts become a little mixed up in my head . . . one case merges with another and I decide to have another cup of coffee to wake me up. The counterman is standing listening to some windy old man talking; he half listens, scraping at his griddle, nodding at the right places, moving grease and leavings from one end to the other, bored. I listen to the old man's tone . . . it won't be long now. I wish I had a card to leave with him, but so many people are against our work that we're not permitted. The time will come . . . I finish, go out and back to my car. Some bastard has given me a ticket. I drive back to the office. It's dawning now. The cold light seems to come not so much out of the sky, but out of everything around, the buildings, the asphalt streets, the sidewalks.

Damnit! I think that retirement rule is silly. All right. They've offered me a job as a training supervisor, but I'd like to stay on for at least another year, working in the field. I've pointed out, time and again, how good I am, how few cases I've lost. Well, tonight ought to prove something . . . eight failures . . . Mr. Spingarn, our director, says he understands, but as it is they've given me an extra year. Unprecedented. Though when it comes to that, Mr. Spingarn says that Mr. Radaman says I'm always behind in my dictation. Admitted. But still . . . Mr. Spingarn says he can't go over Mr. Radaman's head. Discipline. I pull up in front of our building. The streets are empty. They'll be full in a few hours when I'm ready to go home. I admitted my weakness to Mr. Spingarn. I hate to dictate the cases, but it's my *only* weakness. Mr. Spingarn understands perfectly and, to be sure, sympathizes, but says that as far as my supervisor's evaluation is concerned, it proves that I'm not the indispensable field worker. Wrong. And, he says, I might be affected by the work. Wrong.

I get out and leave the ticket stuck in the windshield wiper; the sons of bitches won't ticket me twice. I come into the office. I punch in. Mr. Radaman is heading my way with an angry look on his prissy face. Just wait till I tell him who . . .

"AND NOT IN UTTER NAKEDNESS . . ."

ELLIE dreams: there is like this hand, this like floating *hand,* dig? Big. A hand out of this black nevermost. It comes near her and softly holds her body. She wants to like cut out —too funky-scared—but then she learns to dig it the most. That feels like too much, this bobbing good hand, man: a part of her and she a part of it, even to the wrist whose bone and muscle and tendon granulate into night. It cuddles her and comforts her and it is the most because this good, this drift, it *is,* now and always. But then it gave her a squeeze and she felt a universal and endless power of hand, not good, not bad, but cool, and for one too shameful moment it seemed like her breast was caught in the folds of the palm and it was not a part of her but had steel fingers and nylon adductors and little clocks for joints (and if it's one thing she and Pops can't make, it is time). And she had like this *need,* to call "Mama." Mama? Too much. All wrong. Why not "Pops"? Mama she like put down years ago when she cut out from the home scene: and anyway, she is herself the mama-scene.

And the clutch squeezed and lets go and then squeezed and lets up and her legs kick free in the blackness and she has the mama-cries doll-squeezed out of her every fifteen minutes and it is like the too bad end. But then she wakes. It is dark, black in their studio-loft, except for where limns gleam from the sky-light, the carmine warning-bulb at the long studio's end, and from Pops's weld-sculptures (which glow with an inner fire because he always puts a drop of his blood and a drop of her blood in with his solder). The walls pulse a little in the radiant light. That time is coming on strong now. Her hand-tips begin to tremor, but she remembers the months of training and cools it.

She nudges Pops. He sleeps with a kid's faceup, despite the scraggly blond beard, and that frightens her for a second: is his beard only pasted on? How can he loose the tendons, bend back those fingers? Only a kid. The anguish of the constricting dream is still immanent on the grains of darkness and frightens her and she feels very much alone. But Pops has been with her since he took her in, three months hungup, making the whole scene, reading all the how-to books with her. She shakes her head; the great hand is not a hand of darkness, but a hand out of herself and her trashed past, and she smiles lazily up at the night and at the dimly seen ricepaper scrims floating over the mobile and pipeware and the stamped-in ceiling. And when she's cooled again, she nudges Pops and whispers, "Man, that time has come." Her hand reaches out and her slender fingers (she's glad she's not all puffy like some other mothers and proto-statues) stroke in his beard.

"Mam-o, I'm too like beat now," he burbles and starts to turn away.

She giggles and digs him harder and says, "Like *now*, man;

this cat's coming down," and she taps the blanket over her womb.

Digs it! Jumps up and switches on a dragon-shaded, I-beam lamp and fumbles around all over the place and is saying, "Gee, I mean it's here, isn't it? Don't move, Ellie. Are you in pain? Don't panic, Ellie baby, I'll take care of you. Don't be afraid, honey," doing the panic-faced Spokane Wash. bit. His pants are on, covering his long, skinny legs, but his field jacket gives him flap-trouble covering the long bony white torso and he is flopping around in a circle, his scared eyes always on her while his shins are banging and his strong hands are flailing and a few *netsuke* are clattered to the floor off the fruit end side tables, and monumental and as yet unjoined sculpture shards are clanged and his long feet are in sandals and he's saying, "Now honey, there's not a thing to worry about. I'm calling up. We're going to have a ball, sweetie, you and me . . . the big moment. Don't worry. Remember. Cool it."

She giggles. He digs. Smiles. Cools it too. Face calm now, dignified; nods in her direction, lids half-closed, barely deigning to look at her: the Man: acceptance. And she turns away so that he shouldn't see her grinning face. He goes to the sink at the other end of the long studio, bends over, turns on the water, splashes himself, looks at his face in the little shaving mirror. Bares his teeth: they are strong, yellow, long, except for where a few blood flakes show around the gum lines, as if he had bitten into something too hard. He fills his mouth with water, swoozles it around, breaks it through his teeth and lips. He turns: looks at her: soft sickle and spear shapes shadow shining face in the calm lamplight. He lights a battery of welding torch-tips under the long waiting kettles of water. Then he goes to make the telephone bit.

She makes herself get up, throws the black cover neatly back over the bed, and walks over to a wall mirror. Slender, thin-faced, big eyes; the full breasts (she digs the most because usually her breasts are small) sway. The baby-sac itself is like a small, neat ball which distorts only her belly. And she does a low-low squat and stands up and raises her arms high and her head lifts and her long hair pours over the lilt of her pert behind. She lets her hands fall slowly to cusp over and under the cute womb-bulge and she sighs. And goes to bed. Pops is telephoning wildly.

Now Ellie is on the bed, naked; her knees are high, her feet apart and outturned: she is in the center of the encrowding; around her own Happening. The bed is solid, wide, but wheeled, tends to move. The water cauldrons send up a steady cloud of steam which pulses and intersects the blazing lights all over the studio: spots send off beams of light, some of which fan out, some of which are narrow, some intersect in throbbing nuclei of brightness, others dance over pools of dark . . . they shine out of all the hidden places and everything seems out-lined; the people, the sculptures, the paintings, the furniture. The sound of the creaky freight elevator and the clanging of coming feet on the cast-iron emergency steps is constant.

Starkie sits on a wild-painted old wooden kitchen chair, play-ing his guitar. Somebody bangs on the door. More people are let in. They say hello to everyone and come through to Ellie and Pops. "It's here? Crazy. It's come." And before they scat-ter to get drinks, they contribute a little something to Pops's and Ellie's layette fund, throwing bread into an Army helmet-shell ("the purest kind of shape there is"). Someone con-tributes a bottle of rye whiskey to the pool.

233

Starkie's strong dark fingers strum softly; loosening-up blues to cool anyone who might be bennied up to high or grassed-out to wide. Widmer, who sits on top of a ladder, makes two-minute cartoons one after another, not drinking. He tosses them down to two painters: one splotches ropy color neurons of carpaint from his Unconscious; the other portraits bubblegum possibilities of the notcome baby. The newest and purest art form there is; a going back beyond abstract expressionism, Pop-Art-Op, unanchored, hard or soft-edge, to sketch and paint a Make, once-only life as it happens, but together: one scene: one canvas. Marty Gerelstein is running all over; his Speed-Graphic, the Leica, the Poli, the Rolli, the Hasselblad, all flap like silver and black fruit; he shoots everything a hundred different ways. He accepts a paper cup and drinks without tasting while his eyes coldly frame out irrelevancies. "Oh daddy daddy daddy, free my spirit and do-on't put me down no mo-ore," Starkie sings.

Two girls greet, pressing cheeks, and then stand, talking, side by side, arms around one another's waists. "Long time no . . ."

"What a place, in the middle of nowhere."

"But don't the factories lend a spectral beauty to the moonlight . . . how quiet."

"But you should see it in the daytime . . . a susurration of endless trucks . . . twine carriers and junk-piled, rumbling . . ."

They giggle, part, and go on, Aviva and Wasileska: it is an old game with them.

Children, come with their parents, play games in and out of metal tunnels or hide in gunny sacks, odd corners, up and down the stairs.

Seated on another bed-couch, three mattresses piled and covered with a Navaho blanket, Hodge hefts his eyes inward

234

and upward and around till only moonslivers of white shine through the pod-fumes wafting up from between his fingers. A fallen angel, he wears an Ivy League wool suit, tie, the whole acceptance bit, not paying any attention to the long-leg square chick who is trying to ignore this happening by talking into Hodge's unhearing ear. Hodge calls to Pops, "How many pains is that?"

"Contractions, man. There is no pain to childbirth. It's their way of putting you down. Look at the Tikopia. Look at the Urundi."

"Negate the ideology of pain and its contradiction is a muscular contraction, a fleshdance without Biblical ontologism."

Hodge sighs and looks disgusted, though he doesn't open his eyes, part of him is alaunch in the twilight.

"I don't know, man, fifteen, twenty; I don't know," Pops mutters. He is half crouched in front of Ellie, ready because she is beginning another contraction, knowing if she permits it to happen instead of happening it, it will hurt.

The mechanical force of unfelt (unfelt because accepted) anguish is transmitted as foot-pounds of energy to the bed which shimmers and the legs vibrate and the casters rumble a little on the floor, pushing the whole tableau with repulsive force in the direction opposite to the equal expected muzzle velocity of her vagina: and a match could set the exhalation of her expectancy or the beam of her I-Believe smile, either one, on fire.

Pops's feet dance, moving around, anticipating. Instead of holding a Simpson OB forceps with those sharp knurl-grip handles and cruel-shaped gripper on his right hand (traditionally he is a lefty), Pops wears a Roy Hobbs fielder's mitt which he pats with his free hand from time to time pattering encouragement. *"Well, I random into Ellie this night and we get to palavering and to slavering a cup of this Ginzo Johnny-V at this espresso joint—you know, underground cinema, freedom songs, French cats in strapbeards—and we talk and talk and finally I say this is like a drag, let's cut out. She comes with me and I say, now look, I have no more bread for the Johnny-V or Johnny-W, but at my cave . . ."* Between contractions he keeps turning to three music racks ranged close on which books on natural childbirth are propped open. He keeps looking from the books to the nexus of her leg muscles, where the child will come. *". . . I have a stick or two I've been saving for a festivities and if it favors good, why we'll hold it for a century or two and she says to me why not,"* Pops sings.

Starkie shifts his chair and strikes a strong chord, hard, but not jangly, just for the way things are. "Hear the word of a singing bird," he sings to help Ellie press down to the beat. Ellie moans, half singing, half pained.

"Because," Hodge says out of his contemplation of some endlessing essence, perhaps generated out of the bright bubble pinned to his chick's breast, "a Swiss study tells us that the average number of contractions are one hundred and thirty-five with a point or two margin for error." How square he has become indeed. Perhaps that is why he seeks metaphysical consolations.

Laurie passes around the room holding a plank of wood on which are Dixie cups full of wine, home-grown, pre-rolled marijuana cigarettes, peyote buttons, morning glory seeds, oregano powder, LSD cubes, Kaopectate for the big kick. She wears black tights, but a loose Mexican sarape, yet her blonde hair is middle-parted and pasted down to her skull. She passes under decorations; Tibetan horned masks, Mardi-Gras masks, Tlingit deadman masks (wearing the traditional look of surprise), a papier-mâché model of the Goddess Rati, her breasts misled upward like two Italian breads over a bronze basketball belly, nudie calendars, college pennons, collages, and the trembling walls. She stops and goes, giving out, picking up the empties, threading her way through bolts and pillars and cones of light, brushing past the crimp-edged leaves of the great mobile-make, past the hanging and potentially noisy tom-toms and tamburas, avoiding butt-pattings and pinches and lecherous intellectuality.

The girls meet again. Wasileska clangs her arm-bangles, Aviva admires and borrows five or six, she cuts off her braid to give to Wasileska who hangs it from a big hoop earring. Wasileska says, "But why this way?"

Pops says, *"So we cut out and come down and light up and waver that stick like shuttle it and I palaver myself and she palavers herself and she looks around and she digs my Make, see, and I tell her about the way it* Happens *and she digs that because that is the only way to do it. And like we stay a long time and I say, you want to cut out I'll take you home and I am so surprised at what I say because I haven't made that scene since I was all cadavered up with* Their Way, *dig? She says no, if I don't mind, she'll stay with me. Are you making it with anyone? I ask. She says yes and no, like wherever it is. And I think that is* the *Way, not, 'Oh, one of those.' But she says— before we fuse—you ought to know I'm three months hungup and sober gone, so if we fuse it you'll know I'm no enslaver. All right, I say. And we make it. Well, it was the wildest."*

"Man," sneers Hodge, interrupting, "but what about destiny?"

"Destiny? Fuck their destiny. I don't believe it. W⸱ ⸱make it. We cut around it."

"Genetic programming . . ."

"Shit on their programming. That's *possession,* man, slavery. Love's my program. That's *unwanting,* man, pure and un-fucked primeval . . . Unplanned parenthood, man . . ."

"So it's a happening," Wasileska says.

Aviva says, "He means *they* don't let the father into the delivery room. Who has a better right? If *they* had *their* way, *they'd* keep the mother out too."

Wasileska comes close and whispers in Aviva's ear, "He's not the father. You heard him."

"He loves her. He wants the baby. He's the father."

"But . . ."

"Honestly, how square can you get?"

They press cheeks together and part, but not before Wasi-leska winks slyly at Aviva. Wicked Wasileska.

The door opens: big Nat Kupferman with the thick lenses hefting the washtub bass fiddle comes in. He waddles over to Ellie and greets her and contributes to the layette fund, takes up a spot at one foot of the bed and strums his string. His beat is not in time to Starkie's, but it vibrates through the room. The mobile begins to swing a little. Ellie's buttocks peak high, lifting her body: the bed rolls: Robert, an engineer, shifts an always carried slipstick and tries to compute whether the hydro-dynamics of a piston throb on a resistant irisic f1.4 orifice is enough to dilate the tensility of skin the necessary and tradi-tional no more than four inches without the scalpel's slice and finds, oddly enough, that all birth is impossible, has never happened. Have they all gone mad and should he or shouldn't he call in a doctor? The grand Iris winks roguishly at him and Ellie's behind reflattens: the grand tsunami is over: her thighs are smooth, looking unflayed again, as if she were a little girl.

"Untimed gestation . . ."

"And so, of so many here tonight, who is the father to the child?"

"Don't be spiteful."

"We all are."

"I mean," Aviva's voice explains, " *they* persist in treating it like it was something quick and shameful to get over at the doctor's convenience, pay so much and next please . . ."

"But what if something should go wrong?" Wasileska is heard to ask.

"They indoctrinate you with bourgeois hangups and corrupt a beautiful moment with economics."

"Economics?"

"Yeah, the prices they charge."

"So Pops will have to sell out a sculpture." They laugh.

"What could go wrong? She's healthy. He's healthy. We're healthy. What could go wrong?"

"Something."

"All over the world, since the dawn of time . . ."

". . . are making themselves high priests, fostering *accoucheur* slavery."

". . . blue babies . . . deformities . . . cord strangulation . . . breech birth . . . hernia . . . pain, pain, pain . . . I mean something . . ."

"No sirree . . . no barbiturates to rob us of that big moment. Twilight sleep is the opiate of the pregnant masses."

"I dig it."

"And no trauma for the babe which will no longer carry the shame of its birth, feeling ejected like a turd in secret. A loving oneness, father, mother, child, friends."

And while they are talking, the baby has moved down to the countdown position.

Meyer, a disyarmulked Yeshivanik, a *pilpul*ician from way back, has made an error. He is limped in one of those sling chairs, his knees close to his face, and cannot get up. He is near a coupling, Bon-Bon and Lillie on the floor. Meyer is analyzing Dostoevski, making points devastatingly while Bon-Bon's lips are all over Lillie's ecstatic face. Laurie comes by and gives Meyer a cup. She steps on Bon-Bon's ankle because she was once loved by him, and goes on. Meyer peers wistfully at her behind flickering under the sarape as she passes. She comes to old and fatherly Finkel sitting deep in the mohair easy chair, but Finkel has his own bottle and refuses with gracious hostility: he is Godfather and they must treat him well.

Finkel is old; Finkel is very old now and quite degenerated, even though his clothes are expensive, for Finkel is rich too. Finkel is a lover of Art and Youth and has a great eye for a businessman, and he is permitted to look at Pops's Make so long as he doesn't mention price. One hand trembles, the other hand holds the bottle. The trembling hand rests on a nameless blond boy's head; the strong and liver-spotted fingers among the soft strands. But then Finkel always had an intentional tremor. The boy stares, from time to time, with troubled intensity at what Pops fields; looks away and is drawn back to look against his will. "Life and death," Finkel burbles. "Me, on the Edge, an old *gepeygerte* invited to the birth, an old fag, don't deny it, a *course* you wouldn't believe it, but I started out like that," he points to Ellie, "just like that, to become first a cutter, then a Socialist, a big man in women's wear and now . . . now . . . I have seven children who spit at me every day." A tear trembles at the marge of his thick lid but he manages to flash, for Marty's simpering camera, one gold tooth, a triumphant canine spike from which his other teeth are cantilevered. He sips from the bottle and though everything is trembling with love, nothing is spilled. He offers the bottle to the boy who slugs a quick one and tries not to look. Finkel's fingers tighten and loosen rhythmically: his cutter's fingers have not lost their skill. "Who knows what will come out, ask yourself? A me. A you. A Christ. A Hitler. A Mr. Zero."

"I'll drink to that," Hodge says and inhales grass and with a pneuma full of dreamsmoke, gasps, not letting any out, "Go man, go Finkel." Starkie sings "That Midnight Special."

The bed has come to a stop against a threshold bar on the floor. It runs up the sides and across the ceiling, a pine sphincter. But now the muscles in Ellie's stomach tense and knot and a shudder passes down her body. "It's coming," someone shouts and Ellie, helping Nature's Way, her very pure eyes innocent with their athletic effort, her cheeks fluttering as she sucks in little bubbles of air, bears down and the orifice dilated softly and the baby began to emerge through the doors of deception. They all shouted and began to come closer, to crowd around. Starkie began a long roll and Fat Nat thrumthrummed hard, and Ellie's full breasts seemed suddenly to deflate. The opening widened. Pops tensed, his knees flexed. The shiny baby behind emerged toward Pops's glove. Everyone was packed close in the narrow space; even Meyer makes an effort to get up out of the sling chair and Bon-Bon and Lillie turn toward the crowd, trying to look through the legs screening the event, even though their bodies do not stop pressing nor their hands caressing.

But, seeing it coming out all wrong, they all begin to shout in horror, "No. No! NO! Go back. Go back." Cheeks are sucked in. Eyes pop. Mouths hang open. The buttocks pause just free of the extended vaginal edges. And after a second full of warning shouts and screams, the behind pops back in with a whoosh. The bed lurches again and clatters over the threshold into the kitchen area where the cauldrons are steaming. The crisis over, they all sigh, mop their brows, smile and disperse around the huge studio, leaving three children standing there, still staring. One sucks a cherry lollipop. Wasileska tries to shoo them away, but Pops says not to; after all, they should learn . . . is it shameful? Here the studio is narrower and Starkie sits on the bed by Ellie's foot, crosslegged and gravefaced; Nat stands on the other foot-corner of the bed.

Laurie passes around to where Aviva sits by Ellie's head, stroking Ellie's brow steadily, encouraging her, slipping into English, Israeli, Arabic, Yiddish, Russian, and back to English again. She shakes her head, refusing wine, but dips a finger into a cup and rubs it against Ellie's dry lips. Ellie's eyes stare slightly and she listens to all the words of love and encouragement and remembering, always, Acceptance; she smiles. Wasileska, sitting on Ellie's other side, worries a now-useless wedding ring and fights to keep from saying how stupid and childish the whole thing is. Ellie's nakedness is shameful not to say dangerous. "What if a chill . . ."

Starkie starts to sing an old Negro saint's song. Ellie's Pops, he stands and waits for his fielder's choice, hitching up his pants, popping gum into and out of his mouth, circling in a tight space and, ready, stares from Ellie's blinding homeplate to the how-to books, saying, ". . . *ball I ever happened and she won't let it stop and what with that old achronic roll of M-Johnny, we go on for like till it is dawn at the end's edge and she kind of closes her eyes and then opens and she looks up and she first thing digs the thing Making out of me and says I see the* Happen *there big son of a bitch it was. Like left*

242

it there. Fellow, he slavered over it and said like 8 *an I told him I'm no engraver and I left it there. Still there for all I know—well, I knew that we favor each other the most and the* wander jahre, *they were like gone. I say let's make it. She says but, and points to her* Make *inside of her. I say so? it's mine. And then I got to penalize the self for saying 'mine' and like 'mine' is property and you're like giving, but to say mine is to* thing *it and . . ."* Marty comes, passes, leaving a trail of sudden light blazes.

The blond boy, whose head is under Finkel's hand, looks away, and back to Ellie's terror-stricken face . . . no, not that, because she is relaxed and Accepting that emergent turmoil, so he accepts Finkel's big hand like it was a rakish workman's cap.

Meyer asks, "No, who can see the Dostoevski in Mozart or Dostoevski's *bel canto?*" Bon-Bon burbles his lips from side to side in the cleft between Lillie's breasts and Meyer, thinking Bon-Bon disagrees, continues the argument.

"Look, boychik, look," Finkel says. "Life's mystery. One day, a few weeks ago, Mrs. Piltdown was dropping a child and what was it, I ask you, what was it?"

The boy cannot shake his head because Finkel's hand holds it.

"Lo, it was a Neanderthal. Believe me, a star burned in the sky and they came around with treasures, bone, stone, Art. Me, I never had a single Cro-Magnon, only businessmen. So this is why I am the way I am. Look sonny, look. Tonight might be the night."

The blondheaded boy tries to look again at the space which lies between Ellie's crotch and Pops's encouraging hands. Marty photographs. Ellie smiles at someone's joke. Hodge breathes it in, in, deeper and deeper; soft dreams permeate his being and each blood vessel is filled with a divine gray buoyance. Starkie sings. Lillie feels that she will any minute orgasm but Meyer won't stop talking. Fat Nat strums the washtub fiddle. The boy doesn't want to watch. What is he terrified of . . . is it coming? It came shiny pout lips tremble. How would it come? It would have to come with blood and piss and maybe even a little shit, wetness and shininess in general and it was the *shininess* that was the worst . . . so he looks away from Ellie's shiny, radiant, big-eyed face, away from the rolling-past bed, high to where steampipes traverse the receding ceiling to where the walls narrow, to the steamclouds climbing and the mobile circle-swings.

But did a spark bound free and go from womb to glove without passing the distance between? Or was it the hysterical flow of ruby (blood, wine, or jewel), or the cherry flash of Marty's floodlight on the slowly sucked lollipop? Did a little hand reach out and wave? The blond boy giggled: it was, after all, becoming a *Camp,* and he was thankful for Ellie's cleanliness. Ellie hears Finkel's voice, more bass than words, and smiles as the last of the squeeze stops. The baby came back a little lower; the dilation began again.

"Sometime I feel the night is long.

"Sometime I feel the night won't end," sings Starkie.

A trumpet-man has come in: instead of giving bread, he blew two crisp notes into the collection box. He is playing cool dissonances, antiphonies to Starkie's soft song, muted, but far-out. Laurie walks around holding out, now, a scraped-down palette piled high with Oreo cookies. Marty moves back for a shot of the shiny top of the baby's head from behind Pops's shoulder; he shoots Pops's ready Roy Hobbs mitt from over the

244

baby's head, propping his camera on Ellie's belly. "Relax, honey," Aviva says. "In Israel they drop them in the field while shooting the bastard Arabs two minutes before and after. It is all in how you feel about it." Ellie smiles and relaxes again and the sweat dries on her face. More people come in, shouting hello, patting Pops " . . . *I say that three months without anyone's, not really, which makes it a holy child and she laughs. Well, we decide that we'll cut*" on the back, kissing Ellie, giving money to the layette fund. Marty stands high on two men's shoulders to shoot down and get Ellie in with the crowd from above. Tata-lal has come and is saying things in Bengali; he unlimbers his N³ stringed instrument and begins to play now, sitting on the side of Ellie's bed which has moved out of the narrow space. The four of them, Starkie, the trumpeter, Fat Nat the washtub bass player, and Tata-lal can't seem to hit it right. Meyer's hand hesitates three inches from behind Laurie's behind, but, instead, he chooses to watch the writhing figures of Bon-Bon and Lillie and says, "Did you know that it was Dostoevski's original plan to make Grushenka a cheap whore, to have Alyosha hump her, and the bastard was to be the new Christ-Child?" Bon-Bon agrees by bumping his hips hard against Lillie's two or three times. Two men bear the ladder with Widmer closer and decide that the best place for it is on the bed, its legs straddling Ellie: half-minute sketches flutter down, flutter down.

Suddenly there is a banging on the door as the child's head came a little free. All turn that way, even Ellie, and the baby took advantage of the diversion to slip out as far as its eyes. It is the Fuzz. They bust in and it is "All right, all right," and "What's coming off here?" When they see, they have to be shocked, bull-like N'Malley and bumbling D'lancy. They are ready to can the whole scene and someone begins to shout "Freedom now," and Starkie begins to sing "We Shall Overcome." The baby's head is almost out and someone bends over, puts his finger on the baby's lips, telling the infant to clam it, tell nothing to the Finest, not even the time: resist passively. But even the cops are not devoid of a certain humanity and what can they do, the mother being the way she is? And anyway, their hearts melt at the sight of mother and child and N'Malley says, "Well, my mother had all hers at home."

"No harm in that, is there?" D'lancy moves to shoulder Pops out of the way, who tells him " . . . *out to dig a new cave and we do. I leave it all there, that whole scene, because that is the old life and the old skin and she digs that and I take the bowls and the robes and that is the scene . . . too much as it is, if you ask me, but you favor women because they don't cut the mine away without a quaver, and we come on this cave and I say I have to* Make *the* Make, *like can't cave it without a* Make." There is another banging on the door.

Hodge, though bed-bound, rushes into the vaster reaches of an endless and pink twilight. His chick is not with him anymore but is over talking to a writer (black turtleneck sweater and a corduroy jacket, bleached dungarees, desert boots, and smokes a pipe . . . though it is true that there are some shreds of hash wound in there). He talks to the chick but turns, now and then, to say, "Police brutality," "Nazi suppression of freedom of expression," and "Cossacks." While he protests he cups the chick's slender buttock, feeling slyly for her garterbelt while he wreathes Rum and Maple No. 5 into her bouffant hair. "Isn't this the wildest?" "It is." "You know, I think I'll have mine this way too." "Oh!" stiffening, fingers stop kneading, shoulders and head staring to lean away a little, looking

246

down at her, his chin pressed against his neck, eyes up high "are you . . ." he dares not say it. "Oh no, not yet," and relieved, they giggle. She doesn't even bother to look at Hodge's betraying but lifeless shape.

Starkie is about to try another song but this time it is the firemen who bust in to dig the scene. Some passing square has misinterpreted the tea-fire and the steam from the boiling water and the photo flashing-lights against the monk's cloth window drapes and alarmed it. And, of course, there *is,* now, occupancy by more than the legal number of people and the "No Smoking" signs have been changed to nonsymbolic schema (though still hard-edge as a concession to reality). But a diversion saves the hour: a good-natured argument breaks out between the Finest and the Smoke-Eaters as to who will deliver because it is a traditional operation for both of them. Cups of Scotch are given to them and they stand, arguing, while the bed rolls away through Pops's monumental arch-sculpture, Invocations of Treblinka No. 6 where beads of brass-braze writhe against a perpetual cold-roll flame-shape which is activated by an inner clock mechanism. The firemen and the police follow. One of the firemen is so startled by the gate (the acrid smell of the brazer's torch seems still to cling there) that he dashes the fizz from a fire-extinguisher against it. The rolling drops shimmied by the perpetual shaker-mechanism (fed by an ion-stream gatherer on the roof and thus will not only prevail but endure as long as the universe itself) tremble like quicksilver figures.

The head came out a little more. Pops reaches forward to touch, to guide the head out. The opening is almost four inches wide. The head was squeezed into a bullet shape, shiny and conoid, surrounded by a retaining ruff of Ellie's flesh, like a turtleneck sweater, coming coming into the waiting glove of its father. Ellie rests for a second. There is a strong smell of alcohol in the air. Aviva wipes Ellie's face and smiles a worried smile. Ellie says, "It doesn't hurt a bit. Like those peasant women . . ." she gasps, "you read about who drop them in the field, isn't it?" "Just like," Aviva tells her in French.

"I just can't bear to look," the nameless blond boy tells drunken Finkel. "Why not? Look. Look, be a *mensch*," Finkel bellows. "A porter is coming out. A messiah." "It's disgusting," the blond boy says and Finkel, after patting his head, reaches down and kisses the blond strands trailing from his fingers; the boy leans his head against Finkel's stout knee and blond threads weave in with pinstripe ordinates.

A shudder seems to pass down Ellie's body and once again a descending constriction seems to start from her eyes themselves, and a great ridge of catatonicked muscles crest, a frozen wave down the abscissa of her body. She grunts mightily, a monumental sound for such a little girl but which, fortunately, covers little fart-sounds threaded like beads on a string of wind: and the baby's head was clear now. It stretched its hands up and clasped them above its shining head and, fingers pointed and joined, began to projectile into the waiting Popsglove. "Sticks for the six who look to get fixed," sings Starkie. The bed is almost against the far wall of the studio. A red bulb burns over the exit as required by law. Here, the studio is almost narrowed to a corridor band. Thrumcord bouncing out chords against the resonant belly of Fat Nat. *Bodoolpredowk* sings the now unmute trumpet. And Marty, higher still, seeking the perfect shot, photographs through the leaves of the mobile, high, high against the ceiling now, clambering among hoist chains and steampipes, looking always for the fascinating frame, sees the mother, a faint white splayed figure, the baby almost free of the opening and flying now, both down and as far away as a fetish, the crowd almost like pebbles, the swaying forest of the mobile obscuring, yet interposing fascinating colored floats and twigs as it moves, while the surge of the noise through the whole immense room ripples, for an instant, the forest in front of Marty. And Tata-lal's syncopation tries to seek unity (for he comes from the oldest culture) among the trumpeter, Starkie, and Nat, almost has it, but cannot make it because a longhair girl with an alto recorder stands by their side and blows sweet baroque notes down to cool Ellie's impassioned and trans-figured face.

Hodge, almost out of it, feels that he hovers above it all and mutters, but is that one hundred and thirty-five? and dreams he meets Marty flashing who tells him, I don't know; where's everybody gone?

The baby floated out farther, farther and up, up and high, high. Its face was all covered with primeval slime, but at least there were no forceps marks on it. There was a strong turps smell, for the paintings are almost finished.

Hodge wanders in perfect darkness now. A face swims up, lighting and darkening as it comes. And past. Hodge was in empty streets, untouched by life for many years now and even Marty is an event never to be repeated. Words blur at him, but Hodge turns away and contemplates paint shredding off a brick wall and patchy binding cement, all the edges hard and clear and capable of only *one* interpretation because streetlights make this reality immutable. Something trailing glorious clouds of exhaust whizzed past him, past and up, and hovered for a second, frozen for a lamplight moment in the apogee, and began to descend, on its face a hot reentry smile. But

249

Hodge cannot be bothered to do more than to lave his hands in its glorious track as it hurtles past.

People are yelling, "Catch it, catch it, put it away, pack it in, thataboy!" as Pops, his face up, his glove up, turns and turns, looking up, shielding his eyes with his free hand, saying, "*And she says yes. So this mobile* Happens *and it is the best yet ever because it swings to a prayer's wind, cools to a paradox's still and there are parts of it* Made *under LSD and they are tesseracty, organic, and growing all the time and we're balling it and I'm the most creative I ever was now. And I know that it is the child in her belly, the Best Make of all, that bless-favors this cave and my work and I wake up one morning and I dig that I am father and from my creation I am fed back the creative urge longest in one cave ever. I got it I got it give me room it's mine I got it I got it.*"

But now, the long-neglected figure of Hodge on the bed-couch stirs, gets up, begins to stagger. An old bum, he wanders through. He wears a stained-brim fedora and his clothes are large, clown-checked, rorschached by symbol-accreting stains. And his face, rather than being sensitive, emaciated, is now full and the skin stained red, as liquor is stored in the tissue interstices. Possibly he has pissed and shit without bothering to go to the bathroom; certainly he seems not to have bathed for centuries. He grabs a Dixie cup full of wine from passing Laurie, makes a grab for her tit, but gets his hand tangled among the fringes of her sarape and reels through the studio after her, unable to disentangle himself, while everyone makes way for them. They no longer seem to hear the noise or see the people, she fleeing, he following, but float erratically in a bubble of avoid-space, a place of hate. People murmur, wondering whose too-much friend he is, not recognizing Hodge.

250

The baby is having trouble coming now; its feet seem tangled in the umbilical cord which arcs from Ellie, high, high in a frozen parabola whose top cannot be seen. Pops is bobbling it. Everyone is yelling to hold it, to field it, to grab it. Laurie and the bum come close. Pops, who is busy, doesn't see them. His feet dance. He circles. His head is thrown back. "Got it gotit gotit ga tit." His neck muscles stretch, pulling the skin of his upturned face tight. People try to shoo the bum away. A little fight breaks out as the police try to push him away and he screams in anger, trying to shoulder them away while he is trying to grab Laurie or a cup of wine and Laurie is bounced back and forth and her wine cups are scattered and the fixes flung among the scrabbling people and no one notices that Ellie is shouting now, in pain. Someone has the presence of mind to cut the cord. And then the baby came down and into the glove. The cord floats up, light as a paper streamer, up and up till it is lost, twined, part of the mobile which, overloaded, cants and begins to fall apart and pieces rain one by one among the people who try to dodge. The bum is shooed out; Laurie is thrown out with him. Ellie closes her eyes. The baby's face is wiped off, but it makes no sound. It doesn't breathe. Pieces keep raining down. The child's blind eyes stare up at the father's face. Everyone is still, except for the eddy of cursing mutter that will not go away.

Starkie tries: "Oh little buddy," he sings, "if you had shoulders, we'd throw our arms around them." Everyone laughs. Pops peers at the last book on the music rack while he holds the baby by the feet and slaps its behind.

"Can't wait to start that Oedipus bit."

"It's not really his: what does he care?"

"It is his. Look at his face. Look how he loves."

"That's not love, that's jealousy."

"Jealousy?"

"Sure. Ask yourself, how does he *really* feel inside?"

The baby makes no sound.

"You see? Call that love?"

They stand there, fearful, afraid to ask if it is all right. The angry mutter meanders through the people, even though the bum is gone, past Ellie, past the music players, weaving around and through the falling mobile shards, around the father holding his silent infant.

But then, just in the nick of time, a great canvas on the wall swings out. Cool, fluorescent, comforting lights streamed in from a room behind it. A figure, all in white, came in, walked through the people, didn't even bother to look at the clanging down pieces (for parts of the roof itself were now beginning to come down), and took the baby from Pops. Everyone broke their silence and applauded, though unwillingly. The doctor (for it was indeed a doctor, with even a small toothbrush moustache visible through his surgical mask) looked around, shook his head, perhaps a trifle contemptuously, and his black surgical glove touched the baby's lip and it began to breathe, he turned and went back through the little passage they made for him, through the muttering that the bum had left behind, not seeming to notice it, or the lingering stink, through the rain of pipe and skylight, through the doorway and into the delivery room where the noble gaslights multiplied themselves in each shiny white tile and long reception lines of masked, cool nurses waited among the edges of the OB machinery. The canvas doors of conception shut close again and from behind came now the triumphant and joyful wail of a newborn child.

They were all silent for a second: even the bum's mutter was still. Everyone looked toward the great canvas which was spattered with nothing more, after all, than abstract shapes of innermost passion; genetic forms, blood, cosmic smudges, come, shit, spit, electronic detritus of the soul. Ellie, looking tired, closed her eyes and now looked quite young, almost a child. Aviva covered her up. Wasileska shook her skinny arm; bangles cacophonied. The dancers had stopped. Pops said, "This place drags me, man. I think I'll move to a new cave. Wait till you see the mobile it Happens then." But nevertheless he is charged with an error and made the goat. From somewhere, among the crowd, came the sound of a sob deep, obviously a male's, and it was, surprisingly, a sentimental N'Malley weeping.

"He got the whole world in his hand," Starkie begins to sing.

72 73 74 75 10 9 8 7 6 5 4 3 2 1